"_____ _____ _____ _____ ___ered right back to your door, and well before midnight, too," Seth drawled.

Adrienne slid her helmet off, shaking out her hair. It fell like a silken blanket over her bare, sun-kissed shoulders. She raised an eyebrow. "Are you suggesting your motorcycle will turn into a pumpkin at the stroke of midnight?"

"You never know, princess. Depends on whether today was real or only a fairy tale."

His insides twisted as he hung his helmet on the handlebars. He'd meant his comment lightheartedly, but the truth of his words echoed in his head. If it was real, then he hadn't yet accomplished his objective, which was to pry information from the Widow DeBlanc using any means necessary. If it was a fairy tale, then— Seth stopped. It wasn't a fairy tale. There would be no happily-ever-after, not if what Conrad Burke and the others thought about her was true. He didn't want to believe that she was involved in any of the drug dealing or corruption. But whether he wanted to believe it or not didn't matter.

He had a job to do.

Dear Harlequin Intrigue Reader,

August marks a special month at Harlequin Intrigue as we commemorate our twentieth anniversary! Over the past two decades we've satisfied our devoted readers' diverse appetites with a vast smorgasbord of romantic suspense page-turners. Now, as we look forward to the future, we continue to stand by our promise to deliver thrilling mysteries penned by stellar authors.

As part of our celebration, our much-anticipated new promotion, ECLIPSE, takes flight. With one book planned per month, these stirring Gothic-inspired stories will sweep you into an entrancing landscape of danger, deceit…and desire. Leona Karr sets the stage for mind-bending mystery with debut title, *A Dangerous Inheritance*.

A high-risk undercover assignment turns treacherous when smoldering seduction turns to forbidden love, in *Bulletproof Billionaire* by Mallory Kane, the second installment of NEW ORLEANS CONFIDENTIAL. Then, peril closes in on two torn-apart lovers, in *Midnight Disclosures*— Rita Herron's latest book in her spine-tingling medical research series, NIGHTHAWK ISLAND.

Patricia Rosemoor proves that the fear of the unknown can be a real aphrodisiac in *On the List*—the fourth installment of CLUB UNDERCOVER. Code blue! Patients are mysteriously dropping like flies in Boston General Hospital, and it's a race against time to prevent the killer from striking again, in *Intensive Care* by Jessica Andersen.

To round off an unforgettable month, Jackie Manning returns to the lineup with *Sudden Alliance*—a woman-in-jeopardy tale fraught with nonstop action…and a lethal attraction!

Join in on the festivities by checking out all our selections this month!

Sincerely,

Denise O'Sullivan
Harlequin Intrigue Senior Editor

BULLETPROOF BILLIONAIRE

MALLORY KANE

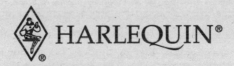

TORONTO • NEW YORK • LONDON
AMSTERDAM • PARIS • SYDNEY • HAMBURG
STOCKHOLM • ATHENS • TOKYO • MILAN • MADRID
PRAGUE • WARSAW • BUDAPEST • AUCKLAND

Special thanks and acknowledgment are given
to Mallory Kane for her contribution
to the NEW ORLEANS CONFIDENTIAL series.

ISBN 0-373-22789-2

BULLETPROOF BILLIONAIRE

ABOUT THE AUTHOR

Mallory Kane took early retirement from her position as assistant chief of pharmacy at a large metropolitan medical center to pursue her other loves: writing and art. She has published and won awards for science fiction and fantasy as well as romance. Mallory credits her love of books to her mother, who taught her that books are a precious resource and should be treated with loving respect. Her grandfather and her father were both steeped in the Southern tradition of oral history, and could hold an audience spellbound with their storytelling skills. Mallory aspires to be as good a storyteller as her father. She loves romantic suspense with dangerous heroes and dauntless heroines. She is also fascinated by story ideas that explore the infinite capacity of the brain to adapt and develop higher skills.

Mallory lives in Mississippi with her husband and their cat. She would be delighted to hear from readers. You can write to her c/o Harlequin Books, 233 Broadway, Suite 1001, New York, NY 10279.

Books by Mallory Kane

HARLEQUIN INTRIGUE

*Ultimate Agents

THE CONFIDENTIAL AGENT'S PLEDGE

I hereby swear to uphold the law
to the best of my ability; to maintain the level of
integrity of this agency by my compassion for victims,
loyalty to my brothers and courage under fire.

And above all, to hold all information and identities
in the strictest confidence...

CAST OF CHARACTERS

Adrienne DeBlanc—The lovely mob widow is an unwilling pawn of the Cajun Mob because of their threats to harm her mother.

Seth Lewis—This street-smart weapons expert is recruited by the Confidential Agency to seduce a wealthy mob widow for information. To his surprise, he's captivated by the aching vulnerability he glimpses in Adrienne's sapphire eyes.

Jerome Senegal—The notorious but elusive Cajun Mob boss ruthlessly exploits young prostitutes and distributes a deadly drug to wealthy businessmen for money. He'll stop at nothing to retain his power—not even murder.

Sebastian Primeaux—The district attorney has a fatal flaw, a predilection for young prostitutes.

Tony "the Knife" Arsenault—Senegal's sadistic enforcer, Tony derives particular enjoyment from threatening Adrienne and her ailing mother.

Conrad Burke—Steely determination and a knack for putting together an excellent team make him the perfect leader for New Orleans Confidential.

Philip Jones—Seth's newly married partner, Jones is a fun-loving former private investigator who doesn't believe for an instant that Adrienne DeBlanc is innocent.

Tanner Harrison—A hardened ex-CIA operative, he is the undisputed expert on covert operations, despite the fact that his daughter is missing.

Lily Harrison—Seventeen-year-old estranged daughter of Tanner Harrison, she ran after witnessing a double murder. If only her father would rescue her....

To Tina, for your unwavering belief in me
and all your patience and help.

And to Kim, thanks—
from Seth and Adrienne, and from me.

Chapter One

Thank God for sisters.

Seth Lewis sent a silent prayer heavenward as he pulled up in front of the fancy wrought-iron gate of the three-story house in the Garden District of New Orleans. The hot mid-July evening and the recent rain lent a freshly painted look to everything, even the manicured lawn. Damn, he hated this part of the city and the people who lived here. He'd promised himself a long time ago that he'd never set foot in this part of town again. But this wasn't his party. He was on assignment.

He glanced at his reflection in the rearview mirror of the new Mercedes Cabriolet convertible that was part of his cover. He still wasn't used to the face that stared back at him. Clean-shaven. Expensive haircut. Designer suit. He lifted his chin and cocked a brow.

Seth Lewis, billionaire businessman. His lip curled in a wry grin. More like Seth Lewis, master of disguise.

It was only because of his three younger sisters that he had any chance of pulling off this assignment. When he'd told them he needed to impersonate a suave continental financier, no questions asked, they'd rallied around him. Just like they had seven months ago when he'd been shipped back to the States by the army with both his kneecap and his dreams shattered.

Mignon had forced him into her upscale Warehouse District salon and given him a complete makeover. It had been humiliating but necessary, he supposed. After all, he couldn't enter the chic multimillion-dollar mansion of one of the wealthiest widows in New Orleans with shaggy hair, a ratty beard and rough, broken nails. He'd drawn the line at a full body wax and a spa treatment though. A man had to hold on to some pride.

Mignon had worked miracles, just like her ad campaign promised. He'd walked in looking like a homeless man and walked out looking as if he'd stepped out of *GQ*. No one would have known he was the same person.

Serena, the elder of the twins, had taken him shopping for a designer wardrobe that probably cost more than his VA disability pension for a year, using an untraceable credit card issued by Conrad Burke, the head of New Orleans Confidential. Teresa, the younger twin who planned to marry a millionaire as soon as she found one who fit her high standards, had decided what kind of car he should drive and had rented and furnished him a trendy apartment in the renovated Warehouse District. The lavish apartment would be his home for the duration of his "visit" to the States.

He'd almost choked at the amount of money the elite Confidential agency had spent on his cover story. It backed up Burke's emphasis on the importance of Seth's part in the investigation.

A limousine pulled up behind him and Seth recognized New Orleans District Attorney Sebastion Primeaux arriving with the mayor. He'd known he'd be in exalted company at this shindig. But the D.A. and the mayor? His target, the woman who was hosting this charity auction, sure traveled in important circles.

As Seth stepped onto the sidewalk, he assessed the

other vehicles parked along First Street. Teresa had been right. Nobody drove economy iron. Every vehicle here cost at least six figures.

Seth closed his eyes for an instant, getting into character for the part he was about to play.

He was no longer a Special Forces Weapons Sergeant. His career had ended when his knee had been in the right position to save two young Iraqi kids from a bloody death. Nor was he the bored, pissed-off-at-the-world drifter who'd moped around the French Quarter for several months. Not since he'd accidentally happened upon a bank robbery and neatly disarmed the idiot waving a semiautomatic weapon. His fast action and his faster field-stripping of the weapon on the spot had ended up on the evening news and had caught the attention of a Southern gentleman with a whiskey-smooth drawl and the unyielding strength of steel.

Conrad Burke had contacted Seth and invited him into an abandoned warehouse that turned out to be a high-tech operations center the like of which Seth had never seen, even in the army.

There Burke had introduced Seth to the Confidential agency. At first, Seth had laughed at the idea of a secret agency operating above the law under the auspices of the Department of Public Safety. It sounded like something out of a spy movie, but he soon discovered that Burke was deadly serious. He'd given Seth a brief rundown of the history of the agency and the reason this branch had been established in New Orleans.

Seth had listened, fascinated and bewildered. The idea that Conrad Burke had chosen him to join New Orleans Confidential because he'd been in the right place at the right time and foiled a bank robbery was daunting.

For the first time since he'd come home, Seth found

himself interested in something besides his own rotten luck. Listening to Burke, he began to believe he might be able to do some good. Be somebody. Make a difference.

So he'd stepped into the persona Burke had outlined for him. He told himself it would be a like a special operation and he treated it that way—studying, preparing himself mentally and physically. He forgot about Seth Lewis, street kid. He was continental, suave and filthy rich.

This assignment was nothing like a desert campaign. Even so, he felt as if he were on foreign soil. He'd grown up in the Ninth Ward, a poor, beaten-down section of the city. Now he was in the exclusive section of New Orleans that ran along St. Charles Street. His assignment—to win the confidence of the lovely widow of rumored Cajun mob mouthpiece Marc DeBlanc, then seduce her for any information she might have.

Refusing to imagine what this Garden District rich bitch who casually threw hundred-thousand-dollar parties without blinking an eye might look like, Seth squared his Gaultier-clad shoulders and prepared to beard the lioness in her den.

He hesitated with his hand on the ornate knocker, his confidence challenged by a twinge of doubt. It worried him that he was so anxious to live up to Burke's expectations. What if he failed? All he knew was that he was tired of waking up every day wondering what the hell he was going to do with his life. Burke's offer was a second chance. He was not going to blow it.

He affected a polite, bored expression as the door swung wide, releasing muted conversations, an undertone of New Orleans jazz, and soft lighting, along with a whoosh of air-conditioning.

When his eyes lit on the vision who'd opened the

door, he had to clamp his jaw to keep his mouth from dropping open.

Framed in the doorway was an angel. He blinked. Working hard to maintain his cool, he remembered what Mignon had told him about the patrons of her exclusive spa salon. *The very rich are never in a hurry. They don't have to be.* So he stood there as if he had all the time in the world and let his gaze roam over the woman.

She was golden-white all over. From her sleek, pale hair pulled back from her face into some kind of intricate knot to her simple floor-length dress, which looked white but shimmered with gold, she glowed. She looked like a fairy princess sprinkled with gold dust.

Seth took the hand she proffered and could have sworn he saw a spark as his fingers touched her silky smooth skin. He knew he felt it.

When he met her gaze, his heart thudded to somewhere south of his stomach. Her eyes were a deep sapphire blue. But it was the look in them that hit him like a blow. She looked sad and surprised and fearful all at once. He had an unfamiliar urge to gather her close and protect her from everything bad in the world.

"Hi," she said, her mouth turning up in a smile that stole a bit of the sadness from her eyes and lit them with delightful flickers of lighter blue. "Do come in. I'm Adrienne DeBlanc. I don't believe we've met."

Calling on his military control to keep his gaze bland and bored, Seth swallowed his surprise. This was the mob widow, answering her own door? She didn't look at all as he'd imagined. She was young, beautiful, elegant. Her neck, bare of jewelry, curved enticingly above the plain neckline of her dress. Her nape invited a kiss, while the delicacy of her diamond-studded earlobes made his mouth water.

"Seth Lewis," he said, affecting the vague continental accent he'd been rehearsing for days. "Brechtman Forbes. We just opened Crescent City Transports here." Now came the tricky part. He gestured vaguely. "A new business acquaintance mentioned the charity auction. Hope you don't mind me dropping by. I have a soft spot for literacy causes."

Adrienne DeBlanc's smile drooped almost imperceptibly and her fingers went rigid in his. "A business acquaintance. Of course."

She sounded disappointed.

"Please come in. Now who did you say—?"

She paused as a young man in a crisply starched white coat apologetically whispered in her ear.

She inclined her head briefly. "Please pardon me. I have a small hors d'oeuvres crisis to avert. Make yourself at home."

Seth nodded. He'd dodged the first bullet. His breath whooshed out in relief as he snagged a flute of champagne from the tray of a passing waiter.

The large front room with its hardwood floors and gauzy flowing curtains was sparsely furnished, giving it a cool open feeling. The furniture was all white, with varicolored pillows and accent pieces. She didn't have children, he surmised, or all that gleaming upholstery would be gray and stained.

Scattered around the dark wood-accented room were a dozen slender easels that held pencil sketches. Seth worked his way through the crowd, affecting a bored nonchalance he didn't feel. The room was filled with familiar faces. Burke had shown him photographs of the suspected members of the Cajun mob, quite a few of whom were here tonight.

Seth's palms itched. His collar was too tight. Out in the desert, he could break down and reassemble an

M-16 in seconds. Field-dressing a wound was routine. But navigating a party crawling with New Orleans big shots and members of the Cajun mob made him sweat. He was way out of his league here.

A woman rumored to be eyeing the governor's seat in the next election looked him up and down as he passed. Others he'd seen on the news—politicians and socialites—assessed him. He put on a half smile and let his gaze slide over them as if he could not possibly care less who they were.

He read the note attached to one of the easels. *Starting bid $5,000. All proceeds to go to the Garden District Literacy Foundation.*

He shook his head in wonder. The drawing looked like something Serena or Teresa might have scribbled at age seven. But then he wasn't here to judge the value of the art or the legitimacy of the charity. He was here to seduce the hostess.

He sipped his champagne, wishing it was a frosty cold beer, and let his gaze roam around the crowded room. Where had Adrienne DeBlanc gone?

"So what you think of this one, eh?" a voice said next to his ear as a strong hand clapped his shoulder.

Seth turned. The speaker was taller than Seth, powerfully built with a thin puckered scar running down the right side of his deeply tanned face. Seth recognized him immediately.

It was Tony Arsenault, a tall drink of swamp water rumored to be Jerome Senegal's most trusted lieutenant. Only a few days before, Alexander McMullin, one of Burke's agents, had confirmed from a dying drug dealer that Senegal was the leader of the mob.

Seth took a swallow of champagne and shrugged off Arsenault's hand. "No accounting for taste, I suppose." Damn. He sounded like a freakin' pansy!

The tall Cajun laughed. It wasn't a pleasant sound. "That is a polite way of putting it. *C'est rabais,*" he said and leaned closer. "It is…" He shrugged eloquently. "I come because it is expected. So where you from?"

Here goes. "I'm here to assist with the opening of Crescent City Transports. Perhaps you've heard of it?"

Arsenault's expression became guarded. His dark eyes glittered. "Crescent City Transports. That is the new trucking company on Tchoupitolous?"

"Right. We're quite proud of the location."

"So. What's your *connexion?*" he asked, putting a French inflection on the word.

Seth held out his hand. "Seth Lewis. I work for Brechtman Forbes, the company that is expanding its transport business to New Orleans."

"Never heard of 'em."

"Based in Germany. Multinational corporation," he tossed out. Was he overdoing the bored continental rap?

"Yeah?" Arsenault ignored Seth's hand. "*Qu'est-ce que vous faites ici?* What brings you to this place tonight?"

Seth grinned, then inclined his head toward the killer who was known for his inventive use of his machete. He could almost smell the blood on Arsenault's hands. There was a reason Arsenault was known as "The Knife."

"Business, *mon ami,*" he said quietly. "I overheard someone at a coffeehouse talking about the auction, and thought this might be a good place to meet some of the bigger players in New Orleans."

Arsenault's eyebrows rose. "You heard about this event at a coffeehouse, eh?"

"Yep. I like to keep my eyes and ears open."

"And so now you want to meet the big players?" Arsenault laughed again. The scar on his face gave him a demonic look.

Seth shrugged. "It is a waste of time to deal with those who have no authority to—shall we say—deal."

Arsenault appraised him. "You are a bright boy." He clapped him on the shoulder again. "Be sure and buy one of those pieces of junk." He nodded toward the easel. "We like to see everybody help out."

"And I like to help out, however I can."

The scar-faced man grabbed a flute of champagne from a tray and saluted Seth. "I will remember that. Keep in touch." He walked away.

Seth released the breath he'd been unconsciously holding. Shaking off his tension, using breathing techniques he'd learned in the army to keep his mind clear and his body prepared, he looked for Adrienne De-Blanc. He didn't see her, but he saw a lot of money.

Serious money. The kind of cash that had caused his father to abandon him and his sisters and his mother when he was just a kid. The thought stoked his anger.

God, he hated money.

A soft touch on his arm got his attention.

"Mr. Lewis?"

It was Adrienne. "I noticed you talking with Tony Arsenault. Was he the business acquaintance you mentioned?"

Seth sensed her agitation and it grated on his already sensitive nerves. Didn't she like the idea of him talking business in her home with a sadistic hit man? According to his briefing, she knew everyone in the Cajun mob. After all, her deceased husband had been Jerome Senegal's lawyer, which made him the mob's lawyer.

He nodded and quirked his mouth. "I don't think he shares my enthusiasm for the works up for auction. Tell me about the artists. Are they local? Did you pick these pieces yourself?"

"You like the sketches?" she asked, her voice polite but carefully devoid of expression.

He studied her. Her back was stiff, her smile looked fake. Judging by her body language, she was hiding something, just as he was.

"They have a certain primitive charm," he murmured, raising a brow.

She blinked, then sent him an impish glance. "Primitive charm? You mean as if they'd been done by a six-year-old?"

He smiled. She'd known exactly what he meant. She had a good sense of humor in addition to her ethereal beauty. He leaned closer. "At six, my sister Theresa could draw better than that."

Her blue eyes widened, intent on his face. "You have a sister?"

"Three, actually." Seth checked the urge to tell Adrienne about his sisters. He had to be careful. No one could know that he or his family lived here in New Orleans.

He changed the subject. "So Mrs. DeBlanc, how do you manage such an interesting mix of people at a party this large? Didn't I see the mayor a moment ago?"

Adrienne DeBlanc tried to tamp down her disappointment. She should have known better than to think Seth Lewis was different from the other people here. *He was either connected or he wanted to be.*

From the moment she'd opened her door and seen him standing there, his broad shoulders and lean hips perfectly clad in that ultra high-fashion Gaultier suit, her breath had stuck in her lungs. She'd almost forgotten she was a virtual prisoner in this house. She'd let herself get carried away by a pair of amused hazel eyes.

Tony Arsenault had supplied Adrienne with the guest list, written in Jerome Senegal's own hand, and had instructed her to set up the auction. Every person here was connected to the Cajun mob in one way or another. Even most of the politicians were suspect.

Seth's name wasn't on the list, but that didn't mean he was different. He'd said he was new in town. But he was wealthy, and the politicians were always looking for another source of campaign funds.

Besides, Tony had not only spoken to him, he'd laughed and clapped him on the shoulder, a gesture reserved for the few people Tony liked. That erased any doubt in Adrienne's mind. Seth Lewis was involved with Jerome and his goons, or he soon would be.

It was a shame. He was so attractive. He was much taller than she, probably almost six feet, and younger than most of the people here. Everything about his appearance screamed money and power, and there was an aura of watchfulness about him. She had the feeling that no matter what happened, he would be prepared.

But his hazel eyes shone with honesty and intelligence, and when he focused his attention on her she felt as if she were safe, really safe, for the first time in her life.

"Mrs. DeBlanc?"

She blinked. His eyes threatened to delve beyond the surface down to the heart of her. She smiled quickly—too quickly, and ran a hand down the side of her neck, where muscles were tensing. She didn't miss the drifting of his gaze as he followed her gesture.

"I apologize. I must be tired. I'm not usually so rude to my guests. Please, have some more champagne." She motioned to a waiter, who hurried over with a tray and exchanged Seth's empty glass for a full one.

She thought she caught a brief flicker of contempt in the curve of his lips. The unguarded expression was like a slap to her face. But he smiled as his gaze traced the slim line of her gold-flecked, floor-length gown, then turned to the glass he held up to the light.

"Krug?" he drawled, indicating the delicate crystal flute.

"Ninety-one," Adrienne agreed. He certainly knew his wines. She met his gaze. She didn't like the way he was looking at her. The contempt remained, along with a touch of amusement and discomfort. His attitude didn't fit his clothes. But there was something else—something sexual that passed between them in that look. A hunger grew in her, an awareness she'd never expected to feel again.

Seth Lewis wanted her.

The thought sent ripples of sensation over her, like the ruffling of a bird's feathers when it awakened.

Seth took a sip of wine without taking his eyes off her. He rolled it around on his tongue as he held the glass up to the light.

"This is nice. A lovely representation of the class," he drawled, his gaze flickering to her face, her mouth. "Not so young as to be undeveloped, but not too old to have fun with."

Adrienne had the uncomfortable sensation he wasn't talking about the champagne. Her face flushed. Suddenly, his carefully controlled body exuded sexuality. Was he trying to titillate her with double entendres?

His gaze drifted over her body like fingers of fire licking at her heated skin, as if she were his for the taking. He held up his glass. Watching him, Adrienne knew just how the bubbles floating lazily to the surface would feel fizzing against their entwined tongues.

"I like mine golden, sophisticated, with a subtle fragrance that's difficult to describe." He passed the flute briefly under his nose. "Mmm, seductive."

As his wide, firm mouth curved upward, a deep thrill

pooled in her loins, causing a reflexive tightening of her thighs.

Immediately, apprehension constricted her throat. The fact that she was responding with such abandon to this stranger frightened her. She quelled the urge to glance around, to see if Tony was watching her reaction. Was this some kind of test of her loyalty to the mob?

"The flavor," he paused for an agonizing few seconds as his gaze dropped to her mouth and then farther, to her satin-draped breasts, which ached at his blatant stare.

"The flavor should be full, rich. A mouthful to be savored, to delight the tongue."

Adrienne gasped softly as she anticipated the touch of his tongue over their distended tips, the slow, gentle suction as he pulled them into his mouth. Heat flushed her cheeks and spread through her. She shivered.

She should slap him. He was describing how she would taste when he kissed her, when he made love to her. Yet strangely, she wanted to smile. He was intriguing, charming and brash, and he was coming on to her.

She tried to swallow but her throat was dry. She should stop this conversation. Shouldn't she?

He looked her in the eye and Adrienne noticed that his eyes were an interesting mix of green and gold and brown. At this moment, the green glinted like dark jade. She had to hear what he planned to say next.

"Of course, no truly excellent experience is complete without a satisfying finish. Don't you agree?" He drained his glass, then grinned at her.

She bit her lip, but she couldn't stop herself from smiling back at him. "Mr. Lewis, you are a rogue," she said, hardly believing she was actually flirting with him.

"And you, madame—"

His eyes flickered and his attention was gone. His gaze bypassed her and settled across the room. She turned her head and saw Jerome Senegal headed into her dead husband's study with Sebastion Primeaux entering behind him. So that was why Senegal had wanted her to host this charity event—so he could talk to the D.A. without drawing attention. A shudder of revulsion quivered through her.

The playful mood Seth had evoked was gone. How long was her nightmarish existence going to last? She'd thought that after her husband's death, she could escape from these crooks and their underhanded schemes. Instead, because of her mother's illness, she was more deeply entrenched than ever.

When she looked back at Seth, his jaw was tense and his expression hard. But as soon as he realized her eyes were on him, his face relaxed into a charming smile. He met her curious gaze. "Let's have some more of this fine champagne and you tell me how you came to be so involved with—charity work."

DISTRICT ATTORNEY Sebastion Primeaux loosened his tie as he stepped into Marc DeBlanc's study behind Jerome Senegal. "I told you, Jerome, I do not appreciate you dragging me into these dramatic little meetings. Especially now. Do you have any idea how close I came to being caught in that raid on the McDonough Club the other night?" He smoothed his hair back, then took a handkerchief out of his pocket and wiped his hands and face. It was too close to election time. After the raid, he'd vowed to keep his hands clean for the next few months.

Then, he'd received the invitation to this charity event from Adrienne DeBlanc and almost panicked. An invitation from Mrs. DeBlanc was an invitation from Senegal. What did the mob boss want from him?

Senegal sat down behind DeBlanc's desk and leaned back, resting his interlaced fingers on his barrel chest. His leathery face was bland, but Primeaux knew the man, once known as "The Bat" for his weapon of choice back in the days before he'd attained his current position, was fully capable of beating a man to death without so much as a grimace. Senegal's black eyes pinned Primeaux like a butterfly to a display board.

Primeaux swallowed hard, trying to stay calm. He patted his inside jacket pocket for reassurance. The cardboard coffee sleeve was there. One of his favorite girls had given it to him in return for the promise of a Get Out Of Jail Free card.

Primeaux reminded himself that he was the district attorney, one of the most powerful men in the city.

The thought was too quickly followed by the next logical one. He was in the same room as one of the few men in New Orleans more powerful than him.

He wondered if Senegal knew how much he hated him.

"Sit down, Bas. Take a load off. You worry too much. You gonna have a heart attack."

Primeaux paced, loosening his tie a bit more. "Is there any whiskey in here?" He licked his dry lips.

Senegal pulled a carafe and two glasses out of a desk drawer. "Sure thing, Bas. Marc always kept some sippin' whiskey for his friends."

"What do you want, Jerome?" Primeaux took the glass and downed the whiskey in one swallow. It burned going down. It felt good in his stomach.

Senegal sipped his. "I just need a little insurance."

"Insurance?" The whiskey in Primeaux's stomach began to churn.

"Yeah. Maybe I should say I have insurance. What I need is assurance." He laughed. "Insurance, assurance." Reaching into his jacket pocket, he tossed a small stack of photographs onto the mahogany desktop.

"What are—" Primeaux's throat closed up when he realized what he was looking at. "Why you—" he croaked. He picked up one of the pictures. Terror streaked through him at the sight of his own pale naked body splayed on an opulent bed. A teenaged girl knelt beside him.

He picked up another picture, and another. They were all damning. He recognized the room and the girl. The pictures had been taken at the bordello a few nights before the raid.

He sank into a leather chair. "How did you get these?"

Senegal sipped his whiskey calmly, no emotion in his sharp black eyes. "Those are video stills. And there's plenty more. You're a pig, Bas."

Primeaux set the photos down on the desk and gripped the chair's armrest. Senegal had actually chosen some of the milder shots.

"What do you want?" he rasped.

"I can see you understand the gravity of these photos," Senegal said. "Obviously, if these, or others, were to be released to the press…" His voice trailed off.

Primeaux knew what would happen. Not only would his career as district attorney be over, he'd be indicted for statutory rape and a half-dozen other charges. "You can't do this to me."

Senegal sipped his whiskey. "Oh, I guarantee I can," he drawled, as if he were discussing the price of peas. "These aren't the only copies either. Anything happens, and they go to the media."

Primeaux's chest tightened and his left arm started to tingle. "Tell me. Tell me what you want."

"I need your help with Customs. Since the bordello raid I've had to decentralize some of my activities."

Primeaux realized Senegal was talking about his drug dealings. "Yeah?" he said, resisting the urge to pat his breast pocket. He poured more whiskey into his glass with trembling hands, then gulped it.

"There will be some special coffee bags coming in. I trust there won't be any trouble passing them through?"

"Special, how?"

"You don't worry your head about that. Can I count on you?" Senegal picked up the pictures and shuffled them, then laid them out on the leather surface of the desk like a game of solitaire.

Primeaux wondered how far he could push the Cajun mob kingpin. "I'm running a little short on campaign funds."

Senegal sent him a glance rife with distaste. The first emotion Primeaux had seen. Then he sighed. "Bas, you never change, do you? You take care of me and I'll take care of you." He rose and held out his hand. "Ain't that the way it's always been?"

Primeaux looked at the man's hand for a second, considering what would happen if he tried to take down Jerome Senegal. The idea was daunting. He finally gripped the mob boss's fingers, knowing he was shaking hands with the devil. "What about the pictures?" he asked.

Senegal scooped up the photographs and slipped them into his jacket pocket. "As long as my supply of coffee is not interrupted, the pictures stay here with me. Safe and sound." He stepped around the desk and walked toward the door. "Coming?"

Primeaux leaned heavily against the desk. "I think I'll have one more shot of whiskey first."

The other man shrugged before disappearing through the door.

Sebastion Primeaux sank down into a leather armchair and fumbled in his pocket for his little bottle of nitroglycerin.

"*Maudit,*" he muttered. His angina attacks were getting worse, happening more often. Now this. He ought to just give up the D.A.'s job and retire. Go back home to the bayous of south central Louisiana. He snorted. Easier said than done.

He craved the attentions of the young *putains,* he loved the money and he liked the idea of bucking the very system he had sworn to uphold.

After downing the last gulp of whiskey, he locked the study door, then surveyed the room.

DeBlanc's office. DeBlanc had been a good attorney. If these walls could talk, Primeaux could probably bring down the mob single-handedly. Then he'd be a hero.

But walls didn't talk and Primeaux needed some insurance of his own. So, using his handkerchief, he took the protective cardboard sleeve, printed with the words *Cajun Perk,* out of his pocket. It was thicker than a normal sleeve.

He glanced around, trying to decide on the perfect place. He hadn't thought far enough ahead to consider when or in what circumstances the sleeve should be found, or exactly how he could use the discovery to his advantage. He had good instincts though, and those instincts had been nagging at him for days to plant incriminating evidence somewhere.

Adrienne DeBlanc's house was the closest Primeaux would ever get to Senegal. He had more sense than to go to Senegal's house, and Senegal had more sense than to invite him.

But he needed a place where she wouldn't be likely to come across it.

A reflection from the bookcase behind DeBlanc's desk caught his eye. Retrieving the silver box, he realized it was a sterling silver photo album. Marc and Adrienne's wedding album, to be precise.

Primeaux smiled as he ran his finger along the book's surface and picked up a fine sheen of dust. It wasn't likely that the Widow DeBlanc would open the album, not if even half the things Marc had told him were true.

He quickly inserted the cardboard sleeve with its damning evidence between two photos, then closed the album and carefully set it back on the shelf. His fingers shook as he repocketed his handkerchief.

With the nitroglycerin kicking in and the pain in his chest and arm fading, he straightened his coat and unlocked the study door. A half smile curved his lips. It was amazing how much better he felt, now that he had an ace in the hole.

BY THE TIME the crowd had thinned out, Seth had drunk a lot of champagne, and he was beginning to feel it. So far, the high point of the evening had been the meeting between Senegal and Primeaux. Most of the others, the mayor included, appeared to actually be here in support of literacy. Surprising.

The champagne had given Seth a headache, so he slipped into the Widow DeBlanc's massive gourmet kitchen and asked one of the caterers for some coffee. He sat there for a while, talking with the hired help, drinking java and munching on huge peeled shrimp. If he timed it right, he could wander out of the kitchen just as the last guest left. That would give him some time alone with the lovely young widow.

Adrienne. He smiled. All golden light, with delicate hands and a perfect, shapely body. Not to mention the graceful neck that made his mouth water as he imagined the soft warmth of it beneath his lips.

She was a study in contradiction. Obviously spoiled, used to servants, used to compliments, used to money. But there was a vulnerability about her that called up a protective urge in him. He didn't like feeling that way, especially not for a rich socialite from the Garden District.

He remembered as if it were yesterday the last time he'd helped his father on a job. Seth had been twelve, and puberty and hormones were kicking in.

Robert Lewis had made a fairly good living as a gardener in the Garden District. He'd taken care of lawns for successful businessmen and rich socialites like Adrienne DeBlanc. On that last day, Seth had walked in on his father kissing the skinny-hipped wealthy homeowner, his hands hiking her designer skirt up above her thighs. His dad had looked guilty and chagrined, but the woman's look had been hard as flint.

The mere thought of that day sent fury coursing through Seth's veins. That moment, frozen in time, had defined his relationships with women throughout his life. He enjoyed them, but he didn't trust them.

He'd expected Adrienne DeBlanc to be like that woman. But she'd surprised him. There was nothing hard about her. She might be spoiled, but she wasn't cold. Not by a long shot. He'd seen the fire and longing in her eyes as he'd described the champagne.

Popping one last shrimp into his mouth, he strained to hear what was going on in the living room. The conversation had waned. The front door opened and closed a few times. Except for the undertone of quiet music, there were no other sounds. He pushed through the swinging door that separated the kitchen from the dining room just in time to see Senegal grab Adrienne's arm and whisper something in her ear. Her face drained of color and her back went stiff as a board. She pulled against Senegal's grip, but he held on tight.

He was hurting her.

Every muscle in Seth's body screamed for immediate and deadly action: He clenched his fists. He had the expertise to kill Senegal in seconds with his bare hands if he so desired. What he wasn't sure he had was restraint.

Chapter Two

Seth controlled himself with an effort, drawing on the stony control of his military training. He wanted to flip Senegal and smash his face against the wall, but rushing to Adrienne DeBlanc's aid would blow not only Confidential's case, but also his own cover. There was too much at stake.

So he forced himself to remain still, clamping his jaw so tightly that pain reverberated through his head.

Adrienne nodded jerkily at whatever Senegal had said, and he let her go. The mob boss left without even noticing Seth, and then it was only Seth and Adrienne, and about a dozen servants.

Seth watched her curiously. When the front door closed behind Senegal, Adrienne's back curved in relief. She rubbed her wrist and let out a weary sigh.

Approaching her quietly, Seth worked to keep his voice soft as he spoke. "Rough evening?" he asked.

She jerked, then quickly recovered. Up came the stiff back and the pleasant expression. She stopped massaging her wrist, but Seth could see the red marks left by Senegal's cruel grip. The bastard.

Controlling his anger with an effort, he touched her wrist gently. "Any man who lays his hand on a lady doesn't deserve to be called a man."

He watched closely for her reaction. It wasn't impossible that the interaction was a lovers' quarrel. Sadness clouded her eyes for an instant, then she blinked and looked down. "I didn't see you as the guests were leaving. I assumed you'd already gone."

So she'd looked for him. The thought gave him a deep satisfaction that had nothing to do with Confidential's case. He let his fingertips slide softly over the satiny skin of her inner wrist. "I couldn't leave until I had a chance to speak to you. I have an important question."

She glanced up at him, her expression guarded.

He held her gaze. "Is there a Mr. DeBlanc?"

Her eyes widened, the only sign that he'd surprised her. "You could have asked anyone that question."

"I wanted to ask you."

She shook her head. "My husband died over a year ago. I'm a widow."

"I'm sorry for your loss," Seth murmured, stepping closer. She smelled like gardenias. The scent was fitting. She had all the attributes of those delicate pale flowers, beautiful but fragile, the petals bruising from the slightest touch.

"However, I can't help hoping that means you're free for lunch tomorrow."

She stared at him for a couple of beats. "Lunch?"

"What's the matter, princess? Is your social calendar full?"

She swallowed. "My social calendar," she repeated, a mocking tone in her voice.

Seth touched her cheek, sliding his fingertips down over her jaw and along the side of her neck, finally proving to himself that the skin he'd craved to touch ever since she'd opened her door to him was as soft and velvety as it looked.

In a way, the betrayed child inside him had looked forward to this part of his assignment, the satisfaction of performing a calculated seduction of the wealthy widow. A bit of revenge on the type of woman who had seduced his father.

But he was having trouble equating Adrienne De-Blanc with that woman.

Still, the softness of her lips, the drifting down of her long-lashed eyelids, told him she hungered for the touch of a man. And given Senegal's treatment of her, Seth figured if he showed her a bit of gentle respect, she would be putty in his hands.

Every protective instinct in him had risen at Senegal's treatment of her, but he couldn't deny the question that remained.

Was she a willing participant in the mob? Was she an excellent actress who underneath her delicate mask was cut from the same hard calculating mold as the woman who had lured his father into her web of seduction? He pushed aside the doubts as he wrapped his fingers around her nape and bent his head to kiss her.

When his lips touched hers, she gasped and pushed at him. "No."

Startled, he withdrew.

Her perfectly manicured hand flew to her mouth, and for an instant sheer panic shone in her eyes.

Adrienne took a long breath, trying to calm her racing heart. Seth studied her and she could almost hear his thoughts. They echoed through her, too. What was the big deal? They'd flirted, and he'd tried to kiss her. There was no reason to panic.

But he didn't know that it had been years since a man had kissed her. A few had tried, but after Marc, Adrienne had thought she'd never again be tempted by a man's kiss. She'd panicked not because Seth had tried to kiss her, but because she'd wanted him to. The idea that she was vulnerable to a man's attentions frightened her.

"You should be going, Mr. Lewis." She pulled herself to her full five feet three inches and lifted her chin, pasting on her best serene, perfect-hostess smile.

He cocked a brow. "I'm free for dinner if you're busy for lunch. Or lunch the next day, or dinner, or—"

She smiled reluctantly and shook her head at his tenacity. Why not? From what he'd said he would only be in New Orleans a few weeks at the most. She longed to be in the company of a young handsome man, even if just for lunch. The last time a man had looked at her with such open admiration in his eyes had been her senior year at Loyola University. He was the brother of one of her sorority sisters, and she'd come very close to falling in love with him. But her dreams of happily ever after had been harshly cut short when her father had announced that she would marry Marc DeBlanc.

Now, older and wiser, she knew she'd been naive. She'd watched her sorority sisters planning their own weddings and had fallen in love with the idea of love.

Still, the way her pulse sped up at Seth's charming flirtation reminded her of those carefree days, and she actually found herself thinking about what she should wear. "Lunch tomorrow will be nice, Mr. Lewis," she said, edging away from him.

"Good. Say noon?"

She blushed. "Make it one. I have a commitment in the morning. We could meet—"

"I'll pick you up. Wear something a little more casual than that."

Adrienne was still smiling as she closed the door. She leaned her forehead against it for a second. Had she really agreed to have lunch with Seth Lewis, a man she didn't even know?

"Adrienne? Is everything all right?"

Adrienne turned and nodded at the owner of the pleasant New Orleans accent. Jolie Sheffield was one of Adrienne's few trusted friends. The daughter of the sous chef at The Caldwell, her father's flagship hotel, Jolie had been Adrienne's childhood companion, playing with her in the kitchens and hiding in the laundry chutes of the hotel when they were children.

Now, thanks to Adrienne, Jolie owned her own catering business.

"The food was perfect, as usual," Adrienne said, giving Jolie a hug. "Thank you."

Jolie smiled and sketched a mock bow. "Pleased to be of service, ma'am."

"Stop it," Adrienne laughed. "Is there a cup of coffee left in the kitchen?"

"Probably, but I can't stay. I have a brunch in the morning, and I haven't even started on the brioche." Jolie hugged Adrienne again, and slipped an envelope into her hands.

Adrienne's fingers curved around the bulky package. "Jolie, this is too much! I told you, there's no rush in paying back the loan."

"Oh, please." Jolie's straight black hair slid over her forehead and she tossed it back with a shake of her head. "Let's not go through this every time. It's only fair I pay you back a percentage of Cater Caper's profits— especially since you're not charging me interest. I'm more successful than I ever dreamed I'd be, and I have you to thank for it. You were the one who told me there was nothing I couldn't do." Jolie's dark eyes crinkled as she smiled. "Good words for you to remember, too. There's nothing you can't do."

Adrienne swallowed against the tightness in her throat. Nothing she couldn't do. Did Jolie suspect why Adrienne needed cash?

Jolie's dark eyes sparkled as she gave Adrienne a quick kiss on the cheek. "Now I've got to go," she said, and looked Adrienne in the eye. "Be careful."

"I will, I promise. I always am."

"Call me."

Alone in her multimillion-dollar mansion, Adrienne clutched the thick envelope to her breast. On paper, Adrienne was one of the wealthiest women in New Orleans. But in truth, the only money that was really hers was the cash that she secreted away, mostly on her own, but occasionally with the help of friends like Jolie.

Tonight she was twenty-five hundred dollars closer to freedom.

SETH DROVE TOWARD his apartment, enjoying the feel of the powerful Mercedes engine through the steering wheel. He drew in a huge breath. He just might have done it. In the privacy of his car, he slipped a finger beneath the starched collar of his shirt. He couldn't wait to get home to his fancy Warehouse District apartment, where he could change into a worn, comfortable pair of jeans and relax.

Pulling out his Confidential-issue phone as he maneuvered toward Magazine Street, he speed-dialed Conrad Burke's cell.

"Burke? Yeah. Interesting evening. Apparently Jerome Senegal set up this highly promoted and advertised charity auction for the sole purpose of having a private meeting with District Attorney Sebastion Primeaux. The D.A. spent a half hour closeted in the dead husband's study with Senegal."

Seth heard babies crying in the background. He'd

caught the head of New Orleans Confidential at home with his six-month-old twins.

"The D.A. Interesting. We've suspected Primeaux, but nobody has ever put the two together in private before. Good work. How did it go with Adrienne DeBlanc?"

"Smashingly," Seth said wryly. "I'm not clear on her relationship to Senegal and the others, but we have a date tomorrow." His body reacted in anticipation of seeing the beautiful widow again. "Don't worry. If she knows anything, I'll get it."

JEROME SENEGAL WAITED impatiently in his limousine while Remy "Swamp Rat" Brun and Jacques Vermillon made contact with Gonzalez and his guards. Senegal chuckled at the memory of the frightened look on Bas Primeaux's face. Then his mouth twisted.

"Hah. Primeaux ought to be scared, the pervert," he said as the flicker of a match lit the darkness, filling the car with the smell of sulfur. He puffed at his cigar as Tony Arsenault held the match.

"No problem with Customs?"

Senegal settled back in the glove-leather seat. "No problem. If Gonzalez has everything ready on his end, we can move forward. Whoever engineered the raid on the McDonough Club will be back where he started."

"Here they come," Arsenault said. "Want me to pat Gonzalez down?"

"No, he's fine. Even if he has a weapon he will not use it. He may be ruthless and cruel, but he's not stupid. He kills me—number one, he's dead, right?"

Arsenault laughed.

"And number two, his supply of guns is cut off."

The limousine door opened and a lean dark man with a pockmarked, ravaged face and a well-groomed goatee slid in, bringing with him the smell of the wharf.

"Señor Senegal. It is a pleasure, as always." Ricardo Gonzalez smiled, revealing gleaming white teeth. They reminded Senegal of an alligator.

"You've worked out a method to provide me with additional inventory, I hope." Senegal rolled his cigar between his fingers.

"*Si.* I was gratified to learn that you were expanding. We have much coffee in Nilia, and we are only too happy to share. For an appropriate price, of course."

Senegal waved away both the cigar smoke and the South American rebel leader's words. "Cut the bull and get to the point. I've made arrangements to get the bags past Customs, but what if there's a screwup?"

Gonzalez splayed his long dark fingers on his knees. "Not to worry. The way we have manufactured the coffee bags, it would take a genius to suspect that the dark brown fiber is actually the bark that contains the raw material for your drug."

"Woven into the bags. Clever. Will my people know what to do?"

"*Si.* It is the same procedure as always. They only have to separate the darkest fibers from the lighter material."

Senegal raised an eyebrow to Arsenault, who nodded.

"Got it," he muttered.

"Now, Señor Senegal, what about my equipment?"

Senegal jerked his head at Arsenault. "Tell Jacques to show the gentlemen the guns." He looked back at Gonzalez. "They're ready to be loaded."

"All five hundred, plus ammunition?" Gonzalez's eyes glinted with undisguised greed.

"Two-hundred-fifty. You'll get the rest once the first shipment of coffee arrives safely."

Gonzalez laughed. "Fair enough. It is a pleasure doing business with you, señor."

He held out his hand but Senegal raised his cigar to his mouth and took a deliberate puff.

Gonzalez laughed again. "If the circumstances were different, Señor Senegal, I would take great pleasure in flaying every inch of skin from your body."

Senegal blew a smoke circle into the air. "If circumstances were different, I'd let my second-in-command loose on you with his machete. He's quite talented, you know." Senegal rolled down the automatic window and tossed his cigar out onto the damp pavement. "Have a pleasant trip back to Nilia, Señor Gonzalez."

Arsenault opened the car door and Gonzalez got out. Senegal tapped on the privacy window of the limo as a signal to the driver to pull away.

Arsenault grinned. "That should show the bastards who tried to shut us down, eh?"

Senegal tented his fingers thoughtfully. "Is the new location ready?"

Arsenault grunted. "*Oui.* We're using the house on Jackson Street, right off Annunciation. Looks fine from the outside. The lab is on the first floor. We have heavy curtains on the windows."

"Security?"

"Iron gates—locked. Oleanders hide the entire front from the street and our friend Deandra Jameson has listed the house as an exclusive, at a price no one will even consider. The real estate sign will explain the comings and goings of people, and supplies will be delivered and the refined drug removed by a renovations company truck."

"Good. And the last matter? Adrienne DeBlanc's investment portfolio?"

"No problem. If anything goes wrong, she'll take the fall, I guarantee it."

LILY HARRISON HUDDLED in a dark alleyway on the edge of the Warehouse District. The summer heat lingered in the asphalt and burned her feet through her thin-soled, high-heeled sandals. Every noise, from a laughing couple passing on their way to their car, to a rustle in the garbage bags that lined the alley, grated on her raw nerves.

She was scared and tired and hungry. She had no idea how long she'd been hiding, but she knew she couldn't last much longer. She'd spent the last of her folding money on a burger and fries a couple of hours ago.

Her mouth was dry. Her throat hurt. She was so thirsty. The guy who owned the seedy hotel across the street was getting tired of her using his bathroom.

She twisted her hair up off her hot neck and tried not to cry.

She could call Mum.

No. She couldn't. Not with three quarters and a dime, not all the way to England. And Mum's disgusting boyfriend had warned her weeks ago when she'd threatened to run away not to come crawling back. As if she would, after he'd put his filthy hands on her. He'd refuse to reverse the charges on her call anyway.

Lily's eyes burned. She couldn't call her dad, either. She didn't know where he was.

That was nothing new. Special Agent Tanner Harrison was probably off on some top secret CIA assignment, just as he'd been on her sixteenth birthday, and when she'd graduated, and when she'd arrived in New Orleans. He was never around when she needed him. His job had always come first.

Carefully inspecting a section of wall, she leaned against it, tears filling her eyes.

She was in such big trouble.

She never should have listened to that tart, never should have followed her into that fancy club. What a stupid twit she'd been to believe the girl was actually offering her a free meal.

Once Lily had walked into the opulent establishment, she'd been denied the freedom to leave. Someone was always watching her. Horrified, she'd quickly discovered the gentleman's club was a front for a drug and prostitution ring. Most of the girls were her age or a little older. If it hadn't been for Pam—an older hooker who'd tried to help the underage prostitutes escape—taking her under her wing, there's not telling what would have happened to Lily.

The tears spilled over and dribbled down her cheeks. Pam wasn't the only one who'd tried to protect her. Undercover government liaison Gillian Seymour had promised to get Lily to her father, but Gillian was nowhere to be found when pimp Maurice Gaspard drew a gun on Lily when she was in the wrong place at the wrong time. So she'd run.

In the alley behind the McDonough Club when she'd fled, she had come upon a grisly sight.

She'd watched in horrified disbelief as a man had shot Jack, the bartender, and Madame Dupre in cold blood. The images of their shocked faces and the splatter of blood would never leave her. But even that hadn't been the worst of it.

The shooter had removed his mask and stared right at her. Lily shivered as she recalled his creepy scarred face and the deadly look in his eyes. Those few seconds had seemed like a slow-motion video. Then he'd swung his gun around and aimed it right at her.

Without thinking, Lily had turned and sprinted away, her high heels clacking on the streets, not caring where she ended up, just running to get away from that awful man and his deadly gun.

She knew he was looking for her. And when he found her, he would kill her.

Footsteps sounded on the sidewalk beyond the darkness of the alley. Lily shrank back into the shadows as a couple walked by arm in arm.

She'd been so sure she could take care of herself. So sure she could find a job and make her own way alone. Well, she didn't feel grown up and independent now. She wanted her mum, or her daddy.

Clutching the last four coins she possessed in one grimy fist, Lily crouched down in the alley, so tired she didn't even check around her for rats.

SETH WOUND HIS way through the main offices of Crescent City Transports and unlocked his office door, stepping inside and locking it behind him. On the opposite wall, behind his desk, was another locked door with a security camera mounted over it. The camera was similar to the ones located throughout the offices of Crescent City Transports, but this one was much more high-tech. Seth looked directly into the lens, staring intently until he heard a faint click that indicated that the specialized security system had scanned his retina and found him authorized to enter the secret headquarters of New Orleans Confidential.

He pushed on the door and stepped into a silver metal corridor. At the other end, another door swung open, revealing the main briefing room.

Conrad Burke stood in front of a bank of plasma-screen monitors. Alexander McMullin, the undercover operative who had engineered the raid on the bordello, stood next to him. Phillip Jones, Seth's contact and partner for the operation, lounged with his hip propped on the edge of a table.

Without turning around, Burke spoke. "Lewis, I want you to see this." His Southern drawl was at odds with confident stance and commanding presence. There was no doubt that he was the leader of this elite, secret organization.

Seth nodded at the other two men.

"How's it hanging, Mr. Billionaire?" Jones said, grinning. "Was the lovely widow everything you expected?"

Seth shot Jones a quelling look, but the young former private investigator was undaunted.

"I hear you've got a date with her today. Way to move right in."

"Jones. Lewis." Burke's voice commanded attention as the door behind Seth opened. Burke nodded at the tall, imposing man who entered.

It was Tanner Harrison, an ex-CIA operative in his early forties. Seth had met him during his interview. Today, Harrison seemed distracted and tired, as if he hadn't slept.

"All of you have met Tanner Harrison."

Seth shook Harrison's hand and met his strange, silvery gray eyes.

He gave Seth a quick assessment. "I didn't get a chance to tell you. Nice work with that bank robber."

Seth shrugged. "He ran into me. I had to do something."

The corner of Harrison's mouth lifted. "I understand you were with Special Forces. Last time we met, you had a lot more hair. You cleaned up pretty well. Wouldn't have recognized you."

"My sisters have been after me for months to get a haircut and ditch the beard."

Harrison nodded as Burke turned back to the monitors.

"We caught a break," Burke said. "One of the prostitutes picked up in the raid the other night has pleaded. She seems to have a lot of good information." Burke indicated the monitors.

Each monitor showed a similar establishment. Seth looked closer. "Those are Cajun Perk coffeehouses."

Burke nodded. "The prostitute, whose name is Darlene Green, told the police that Cajun Perks are the distribution points for *Category Five.*"

Jones stepped closer. "*Category Five.* Supposed to be the greatest thing since Ecstasy and the little blue pill," Jones said. "Doesn't even give you a headache."

McMullin grunted. "No headache. Just a stroke or a heart attack."

"Cajun Perk?" Seth said. "That explains something Tony Arsenault said last night at Mrs. DeBlanc's house. He was checking out the crowd. I mentioned hearing about the charity auction at a coffeehouse, and he got real interested real fast."

"How so?" Burke turned around.

"He seemed suspicious of me at first, but then I said something about wanting to meet the major players in town and introduced myself. He'll remember me."

"Good. Be careful with these guys though, Lewis. Arsenault isn't known as 'The Knife' because he can chop onions."

Jones laughed.

Burke turned back to the monitors. "Now, here's what Darlene told us about how it works. The girls get their supply by requesting a specific blend of coffee. Apparently the drug is hidden inside special cardboard sleeves that are only given to the customers who know about the special blend."

As Burke talked, two girls dressed in revealing tops and low-rise miniskirts walked into view of the monitor trained on the Warehouse District Cajun Perk. Even with all their thick, overdone makeup, it was obvious they weren't more than sixteen or seventeen years old.

Harrison cursed under his breath. "That's the disgusting part of all this. They're using teenagers. These girls aren't even old enough to vote, yet they're being turned out onto the streets." His voice was rough with emotion.

"Right. That's part of what we're going to stop." Burke's jaw twitched. "Jones will be working surveillance. Lewis, keep in touch with him. Let him know everything you get from DeBlanc's widow, soon as you get it. If you can use her to get close to Senegal, we may be able to find the missing piece linking the Cajun mob with Ricardo Gonzalez and his Scorpions."

"I thought the South American rebels had disappeared."

"For the moment," McMullin said.

Then he continued. "Odds are that there's a connection between the mob and the rebels. If Senegal is supplying the drug to the prostitutes, he's got to be getting it from somewhere. That's our primary goal—to find out where it's coming from and stop it."

Conrad Burke glanced at his watch. "Okay. That's it. Keep your cell phones with you and report anything unusual."

Alexander McMullin nodded, then headed toward the rear of the building where the trucks were serviced. Seth and Philip Jones exited through Seth's office. As they parted in the parking lot, Jones grinned at Seth.

"You decide you can't handle the widow alone, give me a call, you hear?"

"Yeah right. Like your bride would let you do that. Don't worry," Seth tossed back. "I can handle her." He kissed his fingertips in a continental gesture and put on his accent. "She is like a fine wine, and I intend to sample that wine today."

Jones laughed and saluted Seth, then got into his car and drove away.

BACK INSIDE the secret offices of New Orleans Confidential, Conrad Burke sat down and nodded at his friend to take a chair.

"No luck?"

Harrison dropped into the chair and wearily scrubbed his hands over his face. His gray eyes were dull as gunmetal, his granite-jawed face haggard. "Nothing. I showed some pictures of Lily to the prostitute who pleaded, but she can't—or won't—confirm whether she'd seen her."

"But the undercover cop Seymour confirmed it was your daughter?"

Harrison nodded. "I talked to Gillian Seymour myself. She's positive. That means Lily was at the club. She was—" Harrison stopped and rubbed his eyes.

Conrad studied the former CIA agent. He'd been a legend in the company, dependable, ruthless and devoted to his job. Maybe too devoted at times, but right now he looked like any worried father. His seventeen-year-old daughter was missing, and Detective Gillian Seymour, an undercover cop planted in the bordello, had identified Lily as one of the young prostitutes involved with the use of Category Five. Thinking about his own precious children, Conrad understood Harrison's desperation. If one of his children were missing or into drugs, he'd be frantic.

Conrad was torn. He needed Harrison's experience

and his ruthless determination, but he couldn't take the chance that Harrison's worry over his daughter's safety might compromise Confidential's investigation.

"Look Tan, if you need to spend your time looking for Lily, I'll understand."

The gunmetal eyes flashed with silver glints. "No way, Conrad. My child is out there. Alone, possibly hurt, and these scumbags are responsible. I have too big a stake in the outcome of this investigation. You don't have to worry about me. I'm going to bring these bastards down, and find my daughter in the process."

ADRIENNE LOOKED PAST Seth in horror, her gaze riveted on the enormous shiny motorcycle parked in front of her home. She'd expected the red convertible he'd driven last night. "What is that?"

Seth grinned, his hazel eyes twinkling and his hair picking up golden highlights from the sun. "It's a genuine American-made motorcycle. A Harley-Davidson."

"I know what it is. I mean, what are you doing with it? Where's your convertible?"

"I bought this beauty this morning. Impulse purchase. It's an antique, a collector's item." He patted the helmet he had tucked under his arm. "It came with two helmets, too."

Speechless, Adrienne stared at the man who had fascinated her last night with his odd accent and designer clothes, and frightened her by coming on too strong, too fast.

Today he looked even more dangerous. Dressed in snug black jeans, a black T-shirt that hinted at excellent abs, and motorcycle boots that probably cost as much as a bottom-of-the-line compact car, he resembled the ultimate bad boy from a cult TV series.

Biting her lip nervously, Adrienne tore her gaze away from the tight, revealing front of his jeans.

Earlier this morning, as Adrienne was dressing to go to St. Cecilia's Nursing Home to visit her mother and spend some time helping with recreational activities for some of the residents, Tony had called and grilled her about Seth Lewis. Trying to be noncommittal, Adrienne had given Tony an abridged version of her opinion. Seth was probably *nouveau riche,* not shy about wearing or driving his money.

Last night, the red Mercedes sports convertible had gone perfectly with his sharp designer suit. This morning, as much as she hated to admit it, the motorcycle fit his wild appearance.

When Tony had pressed her, asking why Seth had stayed after everyone else had gone, Adrienne had told him about their date.

Tony warned her to be careful today. "You know how to keep your mouth shut," he'd said. "I'm not so sure I trust that guy. So listen, don't talk."

Returning to the present, she realized Seth's gaze was roaming over her body. He took his time, starting at her pink-painted toes peeking out of her multicolored espadrilles, up her bare calves to the pale-pink capri pants and on to the sleeveless top that barely covered her midriff.

She felt her body respond. The thrill that coiled through her and settled in her deepest core was shocking. She couldn't stop the tightening of her breasts. Her nipples ached and her knees grew weak. Had she ever felt like this in the presence of a man before? She didn't think so.

Like last night, she had the heady, reckless urge to flirt with him. "I supposed you think I'm overdressed."

He smiled. "I do, but it's more a matter of quantity than style."

Her face flamed with heat as his meaning sunk in. "Let's go."

"I can't ride that thing." Adrienne eyed the narrow leather seat and the powerful engine with apprehension.

For an instant Seth's features hardened, but he quickly covered with a grin. "Sure you can, princess. There's nothing like the freedom of a bike. All that power vibrating between your thighs, the speed, the feeling that nothing can hold you back."

An unfamiliar yearning fluttered through her at his suggestive words. She had never ridden a motorcycle in her life. But she'd watched movies and seen kids on the streets and wondered. The idea of sitting with her body pressed against Seth Lewis's back and her arms around his muscled abdomen while the wind whipped around them was seductive. Very seductive.

It wouldn't be as much fun as it seemed—she knew that. Nothing ever was. But she wanted to try it.

She ran a hand down the side of her neck where a muscle twitched. "Okay. What do I do?"

Before she knew it she was wearing a helmet and sitting behind Seth, closer to him than she'd been to a man in a long, long time.

As he revved the Harley and maneuvered through the streets to the Interstate, Adrienne held on with all her might, the rumble of the engines echoing through her, Seth's deep steady breaths reassuring her and his strong body shielding her from the wind.

She felt a new sensation. Her mind tentatively explored it just like her eyes explored the long, sinewy muscles of Seth's arms as they controlled the powerful beast beneath her.

The sensation was vaguely familiar, like a long-forgotten memory. She felt alive. She'd been numb for so long that her mind and her body felt like limbs that had been asleep. Prickly, aching, but alive. When had she last felt alive? Not in years. Certainly not since she'd realized how her father had betrayed her by forcing her to marry Marc DeBlanc.

Adrian Caldwell hadn't held a gun to his daughter's head, but he might as well have. Adrienne had always done her father's bidding, just as her mother had. So when he'd told her that Marc DeBlanc would make a fine husband, she hadn't questioned him.

After only a few months of marriage, Adrienne had fully realized what her father had done to her. She hadn't married a young, successful lawyer; she'd married the infamous and legendary Cajun mob. DeBlanc was mob boss Jerome Senegal's lawyer.

The first time DeBlanc slapped her was the last time he had touched her. Adrienne had agreed to play the perfect wife and hostess in public, but she'd moved out of his bedroom. Thankfully, he hadn't seemed to mind. Eventually, she'd found out why.

Lost in bad memories, Adrienne was surprised when the motorcycle's roar died. She looked around. They were beside Lake Pontchartrain, in the shell-covered parking lot of what appeared to be an old Cajun house on sticks.

Seth pulled off his helmet and chuckled.

She felt the ripple of his abdomen and her insides thrilled.

"You're going to have to let go, princess," he said over his shoulder.

She looked down. She was still holding on to him with all her might. "Sorry."

He climbed off the Harley and held out his hand to her. She let him help her off. Then she took off her helmet and looked up to find him staring at her.

"My hair is a mess, I know." She reached up to smooth it back into its bun, but he stopped her.

"You look gorgeous."

"Thank you, I think." She gave him a wry smile and pushed a strand of hair out of her eyes. "What is this place?"

"It's called T-Jean's. They have the best crawfish on the Pontchartrain, or so I've heard."

They walked across the crunchy parking lot and over the rickety bridge to the house. The place's only concession to commercialism was a big metal crawfish with dozens of Mardis Gras beads hung around its neck and dangling from its claws.

With a finger, Seth hooked a bracelet made of purple and green and gold beads. "Here. Hold out your hand."

When she did he slid the bauble onto her wrist, right beside her Lady Rolex. She laughed and fingered the beads. "Thank you, kind sir."

"It's not a diamond tennis bracelet, but it goes with the decor."

"It's beautiful," Adrienne said, an odd sadness swelling in the back of her throat. The worthless string of beads was probably the only gift she'd ever received that hadn't been picked out by a secretary or a hired buyer. For that reason alone, it was worth more to her than Seth would ever know. She would treasure it beyond diamonds or pearls.

The raucous sound of a Zydeco band swelled as Seth pushed open the creaking door.

Adrienne stopped, disoriented, waiting for her eyes to adapt to the dark. The place was lit only with lanterns that bravely shone through the smoky interior. The band's noise filled the room, but nobody seemed to be listening to them. People dressed in everything from ragbag throwaways to cocktail dresses sat around, talking loudly over the music, drinking and eating. The smell of spice and fish pervaded the air.

Seth put his arm around her waist and urged her forward. Bending, he whispered against her ear. "We'll go out on the deck, where it's quieter."

Adrienne leaned a little closer to him. Everything he did, from a casual touch on her wrist to a breath of air against her ear, to a laugh that rippled the muscles of his belly, streaked through her the same way, stirring desires she had forgotten she could feel. Other people touched her hand, whispered to her, but Seth's touch was different. He made her feel safe and cherished.

She was afraid to examine her feelings too closely. A dose of reality would come soon enough, she knew. Nobody was ever what he seemed.

Folks glanced up as they passed, but paid little attention to them. Out on the deck, with the door closed, the music was muffled.

"*Allô, cher,* what you be having?" a frizzy-haired waitress asked.

Adrienne looked around for a menu, but Seth spoke right up.

"Crawfish and beer."

"I don't drink beer," Adrienne said, but Seth just laughed.

"You do today," he said, leaning back in his chair and looking out over the dark, calm waters of the lake.

Adrienne looked, too. The shack was tucked into a corner of the lake lined with mangrove trees. A warm breeze lifted her hair and carried the smell of rain, although the sky was clear and blue. She heard some sort of animal grunt, then the flapping of wings caught her attention as a flock of white birds took to the sky.

She reached up automatically to rub her neck and re-alized it wasn't aching. She arched it and shrugged her shoulders. She'd lost at least some of the tension that had become a part of her. She glanced at Seth's strong profile. How had a motorcycle ride done what thou-sands of dollars in massage therapy had failed to do? She smiled and shook her head.

"Tuppence for your thoughts, princess."

She laughed shyly. "I was just noticing that the knot in my neck is gone. I should hire you to be my masseur."

His hazel eyes glinted amber in the sunlight. "I think we could come to terms."

Chapter Three

Adrienne's mouth grew dry. Her careless remark about Seth massaging her neck had backfired on her. After Seth's response, she couldn't stop thinking about his hands and how they would feel massaging other parts of her body. They were big and graceful, with long blunt fingers that looked so incredibly strong but could touch so gently.

Desperate to wipe away the erotic image of him caressing every inch of her body, she searched for something to say. "How do you know this place?"

His mouth curved into a slow grin. She wasn't fooling him a bit. He knew exactly what she was thinking. It surprised her how little that bothered her right at this moment. She had already dared more in the last twenty-four hours than she ever had in her life. She liked this carefree feeling. She could get used to it.

"I like to sample the local cuisine wherever I go. You know, conch in the Caribbean, eel in the Loire Valley, beef in Kansas City. Someone told me T-Jean's had the best crawfish in the world. I wanted to find out for myself."

"You're an interesting man, Seth Lewis."

Seth looked at Adrienne. She'd given up trying to smooth her hair and he was glad. It had fallen out of its constraining knot and now framed her face with sun-struck gold, making her look more like an angel than ever.

"Not so interesting, actually," he said, distracted by her loveliness. Her body had been anything but angelic during the torturous motorcycle ride, with her breasts pressed against his back and her hands and arms squeezing his middle. He'd had a devil of a time controlling his reaction to her closeness. If she was an angel, she was a damned sexy one.

As innocent as she appeared, she was as aware of him as he was of her. He'd known it last night and he knew it today. He knew that whenever he wanted to, he could—he stopped his wayward thoughts. Plenty of time for that later. Right now, he needed to get her to talk about herself.

"Now you. You are interesting. May I ask how long ago your husband died?"

Her eyes darkened. "A year and a half."

"I'm sorry. Was it unexpected?"

She pressed her lips together tightly as the waitress came slamming through the door and dumped a huge pile of steaming crawfish right onto the table. The air filled with the sharp scent of the peculiar mixture of spices that made boiled crawfish one of the wonders of the South.

Tumbled in with the crawfish were tiny golden new potatoes and half ears of corn. The waitress set down a pitcher of beer, and a basket of French bread. "Y'all holler if you need anything, *cher.*"

Seth's mouth was watering, but Adrienne eyed the table full of crawfish as if they were about to rise up and attack her.

He smiled inwardly. She really was a princess. "So how do you peel these?" he asked, holding one up close to her nose, tamping down on his hungry urge to just dig into the fragrant pile of mudbugs. He couldn't blow his cover, though. A wealthy continental type who'd never been to New Orleans before wouldn't have the first idea how to peel crawfish and eat them.

"I don't know."

"You've never peeled a crawfish? You must not have lived in New Orleans very long."

"But I have. I grew up here. My father owned a chain of hotels. Our flagship hotel was on Canal Street. We actually lived there when I was a child."

"You lived in a hotel? What hotel?"

"The Caldwell."

Seth pretended to be surprised. He had been apprised before he took the assignment that her father was Adrian Caldwell, the internationally renowned hotelier. Although he knew she'd been rich all her life, he felt his contempt returning hearing her confirm how she'd lived the stereotypical life of a pampered socialite. He chided himself. He'd known from the beginning she couldn't possibly be the angel she seemed to be. In fact, he'd counted on it. He concentrated on his real reason for being here.

Feigning fascination with the hot boiled crawfish, he took one and pulled off its tail, deliberately fumbling a bit. "They're similar to the tiger prawns I've had in Sydney, but smaller," he improvised.

Adrienne finally picked one up with her pink-tipped fingers. "I've watched the servants. Apparently you split them like this, then dig out the meat, then—" she stopped.

Seth knew what came next. He hid a smile. "Then what?"

Her cheeks flamed. "Then you're supposed to, um, suck the head and pinch the tips."

"Show me," he rasped, unable to take his eyes off her, controlling his growing desire with a ferocious will. He knew exactly how to eat crawfish. He'd even teased girls with the words Adrienne had just spoken, using them as a double entendre. But until this moment, he'd never completely understood just how sexy eating crawfish could be.

His body reacted like a teenager's as she put the head of the crawfish to her luscious lips. He shifted in his chair, his jeans suddenly way too tight, his heart pounding, his gaze riveted on her mouth.

She pinched the tail and pulled the last bit of meat from the shell with her teeth. A tiny drop of juice ran down her chin.

Seth reached over and stopped the droplet with his thumb, then slid it up to her parted lips. Her tongue touched his thumb and he groaned. Lust raged through him.

No, it wasn't going to be hard to seduce her. It was going to be hard to avoid being seduced by her. *Very hard,* he thought wryly as sensitized flesh rubbed against rough denim.

Seth set his jaw against the urge to lean over and kiss her. *Job, man. Remember the job.* His assignment was to seduce her for information. And he would complete his assignment as planned. In Special Forces, there was no room for distractions.

Adrienne hadn't meant to touch Seth's thumb with her tongue. She was shocked, both by her action and by her reaction. Her insides quivered, her thighs tightened. She felt heat spread through her like a fire fed by pure oxygen.

She glanced at Seth, who looked away and took a long drink of beer. He'd felt it, too. She was sure. She'd heard his barely suppressed groan.

What was happening to her? She'd never been all that interested in sex. But every move Seth made, every word he spoke, acted on her like an aphrodisiac.

"Did you say your husband's death was unexpected?"

Her heart took a nosedive, landing in her stomach. She grabbed another crawfish and picked at its shell with her fingernails, just for something to do.

She'd half expected Seth to try to kiss her, as he had last night. She'd been waiting for it, wondering what she would do if he tried. So his abrupt switch back to the topic of her husband had shocked her. His question was a blow. As if he'd forced himself back to business.

"Yes, it was unexpected, in a way."

Seth watched her.

She met his gaze, feeling the numbness threaten to creep back inside her. "He died of a heart attack. He was in bed with a prostitute at the time."

Seth's eyes went wide.

She'd surprised him. A tiny sense of satisfaction swept through her. She popped a morsel of crawfish into her mouth and took a sip of beer. "Anything else you want to know?"

"I'm sorry, Adrienne. You must have been crushed."

She almost choked on the beer, coughing and laughing at the same time. "Could we talk about something besides my boring life?"

What would he do if she told him the truth? The whole truth? This wealthy young executive who'd been so confident she'd go out with him would probably be shocked if he knew what her life was really like. But she couldn't tell him. For all she knew, he was just like Jerome. Just like Tony. She couldn't trust him.

She remembered Tony's warning to not talk, just listen. Ever since Marc had died, Adrienne had been watched over by Tony Arsenault.

Tony had been Marc's best friend, but she knew the reason he had taken her under his wing. It was not out of affection or friendship. The Cajun mob liked her social position. They liked her influence. And they liked her money.

She'd tried to get away from them, but she'd quickly found out there was no getting away. Only a few months after Marc's death, her mother had suffered a debilitating stroke. St. Cecilia's was the safest place Adrienne knew. But it wasn't safe enough.

Tony never failed to ask about her mother. And every time he did, a knife blade of terror cut through Adrienne's heart. The message was clear. *Your mother's continued survival depends upon your cooperation.*

"What are you thinking about, princess? You've mutilated that poor crawfish."

Seth's deep voice penetrated her thoughts and pulled her back to the present. She looked at his plate, which was had mysteriously become piled high with crawfish carcasses.

The sight made her forget her troubles for the moment. A chuckle escaped her throat as she shook juice off her fingers and reached for the roll of paper towels sitting on the table. It was an odd feeling—a welcome feeling. "You certainly didn't waste any time learning how to peel crawfish."

"Hunger is a good teacher. Besides, I read that guy's T-shirt." He inclined his head to their right.

A bald man with a big spare tire around his middle drained a beer as he peered out over the lake. The back of his red T-shirt had a diagram of how to extract the meat from a crawfish with the words *Suck Dem Heads, Pinch Dem Tips* plastered across his shoulder blades.

"You read a T-shirt?" Seth's simple solution struck her as funny. Covering her mouth, she laughed. He reached over and pulled her hand away.

"Don't do that." He held on to her fingers, running the pad of his thumb across her knuckles.

Her laughter died in her throat and a sensual awareness took over. She could have sworn a sparked flared when their hands touched. Her senses were becoming hyperaware of the warmth of his closeness, of the indulgent smile that played about his lips, of the silky rough feel of his hand over hers.

"Don't what?" she asked.

"Cover up your laugh. I like it." He let go of her hand and brushed the backs of his fingers across the corner of her mouth. "You need to laugh more, princess."

She thought about the irony of that thought. She did need to laugh more often. She'd forgotten how good it felt. But when would she ever feel free enough to? When would she ever feel safe enough to just laugh for the sake of laughing?

Seth leaned in closer to her. "Laughter becomes you," he whispered, bending his head to take her mouth in a swift, hard kiss.

She didn't stop him. By the time she felt the fullness of his warm mouth on hers he was done. He sat back, his hazel eyes pensive.

Her mouth tingled. She'd like to think it was the spice from the crawfish, but she knew it was the effect of his lips on hers.

"Here." He picked up a crawfish and peeled it like an expert, then held the succulent meat to her mouth. She parted her lips and he fed it to her, letting his fingers linger.

Then he went back to peeling and eating his own.

Adrienne licked her lips, her gaze returning again and again to Seth's mouth.

"I may have another tuppence in my pocket," he commented, raising his beer.

"What?"

He smiled. "What are you thinking now?"

"I was thinking I'm glad you brought me here. This is fun." As she said the words, she realized they were true. Seth Lewis was funny, he was unpredictable and he seemed to genuinely care about her feelings.

"You say that as if you're not quite sure what fun is."

If he knew how right he was, he'd probably think she was pathetic.

"Well, now I know it's riding on a motorcycle and eating crawfish with my fingers."

He grinned. "It's a lot more than that, Adrienne. Today you've done two things you've never done before."

Three, Adrienne thought. *I've been kissed by a man who takes my breath away.*

"What else haven't you done? My mission in life will be to introduce you to all the fun you've missed. Now let's finish eating. I want to explore. I want to see an alligator."

"Okay." She laughed. "But the only ones I've seen are in the Audubon Park zoo."

He popped open another crawfish. "No. No zoo. I want to see one in its natural habitat."

Adrienne studied him. He seemed to be everything her husband hadn't been. Open, kind, loving. What if she could trust him? Her heart leapt. Had she finally met someone who was exactly who he seemed to be? Or was he using her to try and get in with the mob?

BY THE TIME they got back to Adrienne's house, the sun was hidden by tall buildings and shadows were creeping in.

Seth killed the engine of the Harley. Adrienne slid her helmet off, shaking out her hair. It fell like a silken blanket over her bare, sun-kissed shoulders.

"Here you are. Delivered right back to your door, and well before midnight, too."

She shook her hair back and raised one light brown eyebrow. "Are you suggesting your motorcycle will turn into a pumpkin at the stroke of midnight?"

"You never know, princess. Depends on whether today was real or only a fairy tale." His insides twisted as he hung his helmet on the handlebars. He'd meant his comment lightheartedly, but the truth of his words echoed in his head. If it was real, then he hadn't yet accomplished his objective, which was to pry information from the Widow DeBlanc using any means necessary. If it was a fairy tale, then—Seth stopped. It wasn't a fairy tale. There would be no happily-ever-after ending, not if what Burke and the others thought about her was true. He didn't want to believe that she was involved in any of the drug dealing or prostitution or corruption. But whether he wanted to believe it or not didn't matter. He had a job to do.

"Would you—"

His head snapped up.

She stopped.

He took the helmet from her fingers and buckled it onto the back of the Harley.

"Would I what? Like to come in?"

She inclined her head slightly.

"That depends." He nodded toward her house. "How many servants are hanging around in there?"

She lifted her nose almost imperceptibly, but he noticed it. "None. I don't have servants. I have a house-keeper who comes twice a week. There's a man who does the lawn and maintains the house and the cars. But

I like privacy. There's no army of servants lurking in every corner of the house. That was my husband's style, not mine."

He heard the bitter tinge in her voice. She was such an enigma. He longed to strip her Southern politesse away and get down to the real person beneath.

"Yes, I'd like to come in. Would you rather I parked the Harley down the street?"

She laughed and shook her head, her hair floating around her shoulders. "No. I don't care if there's a motorcycle parked in front of my house."

But he saw her glance around furtively as they headed inside. If she really didn't care, what was she worried about?

After he'd scrubbed the crawfish smell off his hands, Seth walked into the massive white-and-chrome kitchen. Adrienne, who had changed into a long flowing dress and put her hair up again like a princess, was pouring iced tea.

"Thanks." He picked up the glass and drank, then grimaced.

"Oh, don't you like sweet tea?" She shot him a teasing glance. "It's a staple of the South."

He hated it. Had ever since he was a kid growing up in the rough, poor neighborhoods of the Ninth Ward. He thought about his cover story. "Sorry. Didn't mean to be rude. One develops a taste for it I suppose."

She frowned at him. "Where did you grow up?" she asked, surprising him.

It was as if she'd read his mind.

"You are American aren't you?"

He set down the glass. "I've lived in a lot of places," he parried. "Could I have water instead?" Then, before she could continue to question him, he turned the tables on her.

"This is a great house. How long have you lived here?"

"My husband bought the house when we married."

"So that would be—"

"Eight years ago." She handed him a bottle of water without meeting his searching gaze. As he drank she played with her glass, tracing her finger along the rim, her back stiff.

Seth didn't miss the change in her body language when she spoke about her husband. "You married young."

She shrugged. "I was twenty-two. Just out of college. My husband was older. He was an attorney, a very successful one." Her fingers wrapped around the glass until her knuckles whitened. Seth covered her hand with his.

"What's the matter, princess? You still miss him?"

She looked at him then, a flicker of pain crossing her face. "That doesn't even come close to describing how I feel."

He stepped closer. Was the pain because she missed her husband, or because she didn't? He filed away the question to consider later. "I don't mean to bring up bad memories. I just want to know more about you. A lot more about you."

She slid her hand from under his and took a sip of her tea. Her hand was trembling slightly, and a drop of condensation fell from the glass. The dress's neckline revealed just enough skin so Seth could watch the droplet trickle down between her breasts. She stopped the drop with her fingertip.

"Adrienne," he whispered in a strangled voice, his body throbbing with reaction.

She lifted her gaze to his and her lips parted. "Seth, I don't—do this kind of thing—"

He rounded the granite-topped island to stand in

front of her. "Shh," he whispered. "I don't either, usually."

Then he leaned down and took her mouth in a soft, questioning kiss. She didn't recoil this time, but she didn't react, either. She stood there, stiff and unyielding, her lips parted but passive.

She tasted like sweet tea and salt and lipstick, and he hungered for more. Lifting his head briefly, he looked into her eyes, afraid he'd see the hard look he'd seen all those years ago on the face of the woman his father had kissed.

But her long thick eyelashes rose, revealing her dewy, questioning gaze.

"Adrienne, it's up to you," he murmured, his heart pounding. Was the look in her eyes passion or fear?

"I'm not very experienced—" Her teeth scraped her lower lip.

"I don't care," he growled and bent his head again.

Adrienne felt as though she were losing control of her mind and her body. Both were betraying her. Seth's mouth moved over hers, kissing her in a way she'd never been kissed before. His lips were firm and warm, yet gentle as the brush of a spring leaf. He pulled at the knot of her hair, and the single clasp that held it popped open. He ran his fingers through the golden strands, then entwined it around one hand as he circled her waist with the other. She felt the strength of his thighs and the obvious swell of his desire against her.

Her knees went weak, but Seth held her, steadied her. His tongue touched her lips and she responded, dizzy with the suddenness of her reaction.

His gentleness turned to fierce need as he tore his mouth from hers and grazed her jawline, then her neck, planting kisses along the muscles that had been so tight for so long. The knots relaxed beneath his questing lips. Without thinking about what she was doing, she put her arms around his neck.

He picked her up and set her on the countertop, urging her legs apart and stepping between them without ever stopping his kisses. When he slid his hand under the silky material of her dress and up her calf to her thigh, she tensed.

"Seth, I can't," she gasped against his mouth. "Not like this."

His hand slid higher.

Adrienne was close to panicking. Her body throbbed with need, her breath was short, her head spinning. But she couldn't do this. Not in the kitchen, with the lights on, in full view of any passerby who might glance in the windows. She'd never done anything so brazen in her life.

"Please stop!"

Seth pulled away, cursing silently. What the hell was wrong with him? This was supposed to be a calculated seduction, designed to get Adrienne to confide in him. Instead, he was acting like a randy kid. And he'd probably blown it by not taking it slow and sweet. But damn, he'd never felt this hot for anyone. *Ever.*

He tried to ignore his aching arousal. "Sorry, princess. I got carried away."

He pushed his hands through his hair and wiped his face, then looked around for his bottle of water.

"Seth?"

"Look, um, Adrienne. I apologize."

She caught his arm. When he turned, her eyes were bright and her face was a becoming pink.

"We could go upstairs." Her cheeks flamed and she avoided his gaze. "Although, perhaps you don't—"

Seth stared at her for a beat. Was she actually inviting him to make love to her? His body heated at the thought. "Believe me, princess," he said, reaching out and sweeping her into his arms. "I do."

She was light as a feather. He mounted the stairs like Rhett Butler, only his armful of loveliness wasn't struggling. At the top, he hesitated.

"There," Adrienne whispered into his neck, nodding toward his left.

He entered a bright, feminine room that looked like it belonged in a different house from the sparsely furnished, dark-paneled living room with its modern white furniture. This room was painted a creamy yellow, with white accents. He laid her on the bed amidst a pile of pink and green pillows, then knelt beside her and pushed her hair back from her face. "Are you sure about this, Adrienne? Really sure? I don't want any morning-after regrets."

She nodded and reached out to touch his cheek. He turned his head and kissed her palm, then stood and shed his clothes.

She gasped. "Oh Seth, what happened to your knee?"

He cursed silently and fluently. He'd forgotten about the network of bright scars that crisscrossed his knee like a road map. *I stopped a piece of shrapnel in a desert where kids and innocent people die every week, princess. What do you think of your international billionaire now?*

But he didn't tell her the truth. The truth was not part of this job. Thinking about his assignment almost dampened his desire. Almost, but not quite.

Back in character, he shrugged as he climbed into bed beside her and ran a hand beneath her filmy dress, amazed that not even thinking about his ruined knee or the fact that what he was doing was under orders from Confidential dimmed his desire for her. "Motorcycle accident," he said in what he hoped was a bored tone. "I was careless."

Then he slid her dress up and over her head and took in her slender loveliness. She was small, with perfect breasts and a tiny waist. When he slid her panties off he was awed at the perfection of her body.

He touched her breasts, palmed her flat abdomen, slid his fingers down her slender thighs and back up to caress her intimately. She gasped. Once or twice, she reached out to catch his hand and he slowed his pace, waiting for her to catch up, but finally, shyly, she touched him.

Seth didn't think he could last another second. He was on fire, his body screaming for release. He didn't care what he was supposed to be doing. He existed only for the here and with the sexiest, sweetest, most beautiful woman he had ever met.

She moaned and grasped him tightly.

"Ah, careful," he growled, barely holding on to control.

"Seth? Please?"

At the last possible second, he slipped on the condom he'd pulled from his jeans. Then he plunged into her, finding her tight, hot, ready. She cried out and he stopped, afraid he'd hurt her, but she pulled his head down and kissed him, and urged him on. Just before he lost it, he felt her find her own release.

Then there was nothing but the shadows and her supple golden body curved into his side, her floral-scented hair tickling his nose.

ADRIENNE AWOKE in a panic, pushing at the strong arm that trapped her.

"Whoa, princess," a sleepy voice said. "It's me, Seth."

She sat up and pulled the sheet with her, her heart pounding, her brain whirling with confusing images. She'd been dreaming about Marc. A bad dream.

The pale glow of the streetlights gave her a tantalizing vision of Seth leaning up on one elbow, the hard planes of his chest like a moonlit desert landscape. That silk-over-steel skin had slid against hers; she'd been lifted and held by those strong arms.

He caressed her wrist. "Are you okay?"

She nodded.

"You sure? You look like you just found a spider in your bed."

His words made her smile. "No. I'm fine. It's just—" She stopped for a second. "I can't believe I did this."

She'd thought she would never again feel desire for any man. Yesterday, she'd have sworn no man on earth could get her into bed on their first date. She was shocked by her behavior.

"Didn't you enjoy it?"

She nodded, blushing. "But I'm not the kind of woman who falls into bed with just any man."

Seth sat up, the sheet sliding down his body to rest tantalizingly low on his lean hips. Her insides quivered with an echo of the incredible desire he'd coaxed from her. She'd never felt this alive before.

He held out his arm and she slid over, still covering herself with the sheet.

"I know you're not like that."

With her head against his shoulder she couldn't see his face, but his voice sounded odd. "Was it obvious? I guess you're used to more sophisticated women." She closed her eyes, feeling gauche and awkward.

"Hey," he said softly. "That was a compliment, not a slam. You are an incredibly sexy woman."

"Really? My husband used to say—" She stopped. She'd spoken without thinking.

"What?"

"Never mind."

"If your husband ever said anything except what a beautiful, sexy woman you were, then he was an idiot."

Adrienne wanted to laugh. If Seth only knew. Almost from the beginning of their ill-fated marriage, Marc had heaped insults on her, words like *frigid, ugly, stupid.* A shudder ran through her.

Seth kissed the top of her head. "Haven't you dated since your husband's death?"

She tensed. She didn't want to think about Marc, much less answer questions about him. It reminded her that she wasn't free. That it could be dangerous to indulge her newfound feelings. She had to be careful. She had to protect her mother.

Yet despite the risk, all she wanted to do was forget about the world. She wanted to savor the afterglow of the most satisfying moment of her entire life. She wanted to stay within the cradle of Seth's arms and never have to go back to her real existence.

"Does it upset you to talk about your husband?"

Yes, but not for the reason you think. "A little."

"I'm sorry. I just wanted to get to know you better."

The tense muscle in her neck began to ache. "You won't get to know me by learning about my husband." She heard the bitterness that scratched her throat.

"Let's talk about something else. Like how beautiful you are." He put his fingers beneath her chin and lifted her face to his. His lips grazed her eyebrows, the corners of her eyes, her cheek, her jaw. Then he covered her mouth with his and urged her lips apart with his tongue. Adrienne moaned softly and kissed him back.

He nuzzled her ear. "What do you do when you're not giving charity auctions and riding on motorcycles?"

Adrienne ducked her head. It was a perfectly reasonable question from a man who had spent the night in her bed. She'd have a hard time refusing to answer.

She ran her fingers over the hard bulge of his bicep, and realized she did want to tell him. "I do yoga and Pilates at a health club, I read a lot and I spend two days a week at a nursing home."

Laid out like that, in one sentence, her life sounded so lame.

"A nursing home? Doing what?"

"I volunteer. I help out in various ways. I have a reading group on Tuesday afternoons. I help out with lunches, feeding the residents who can't feed themselves, and I'm starting a chair aerobics class for some of the ladies."

"Wow. You do all that for strangers?"

Adrienne looked up at Seth, worried that he was making fun of her, but his face reflected admiration. "Don't give me too much credit. My own mother is a resident at the home."

"I'm sorry. What's wrong with your mother?"

Adrienne sat up. She didn't want to go any deeper into the specifics about her life. She'd spent too long under the shadow of her husband and the Cajun mob. Her first instinct was to keep her mouth shut. She remembered Tony's words.

But Seth's questions were ordinary, just as her answers should be. And he seemed genuinely interested. She shifted nervously, aware that she was taking far too long to answer.

The silence was shattered by the shrill jangling of the phone.

Adrienne jumped.

"Don't answer it." Seth kissed her temple.

But she pulled away to look at the caller ID. It was Tony. "I have to take this call." She picked up the portable handset. "Yes?"

"Adrienne. *Chère.* I have interrupted something with your new boyfriend, eh?"

She held the phone tightly against her ear and moved to the edge of the bed, reaching for a lavender silk robe draped over a chair. She slid it on, transferring the phone from one hand to another.

"I wouldn't put it that way," she said quietly, her hand cramping on the receiver. "Was there something you needed?"

Tony's voice plummeted her down from her fantasy, back onto the tightrope she'd had to walk all these years. Once again she was trying so hard not to allow the mob to suck away her identity, while at the same time struggling to keep them placated for her mother's sake.

"Do not forget Aimée's engagement party next Thursday."

Helpless anger burned inside her. She knew Tony hadn't called her about Jerome Senegal's daughter's party. They had just talked about it the other day. He'd called to remind her that the mob knew every move she made.

"I haven't forgotten. I'm looking forward to it." She choked on the lie. Her free hand massaged her neck.

A large, strong hand brushed hers away, then squeezed her shoulder. *Seth.* His touch felt reassuring, protective. She wanted to rest her cheek against his wrist, to lean on him for support. But she didn't.

"You will bring your boyfriend. Jerome wants to meet him."

"Why?" Jerome wanted to meet Seth? The idea set off alarm bells in Adrienne's brain.

"Now, *chère,* you know you don't ask why. You just do."

"All right."

"That's good, then. Your mama still doing okay?"

Adrienne bit her lip, fighting the fear that rose up into her throat like a scream. "Yes. Fine."

"So we will see you and your boyfriend next Thursday." Tony hung up.

She didn't even realize she hadn't turned off the phone until Seth took it from her nerveless fingers.

Seth clicked the Off button. He'd heard the last few words of the conversation. He'd have thought it was normal, except for Adrienne's body language.

"What's happening next Thursday?" he asked, watching Adrienne closely in the darkness. Her face was pale, her eyes wide and staring at nothing. She looked terrified.

She blinked when he spoke. "What?"

"I heard 'see you and your boyfriend Thursday.' Or maybe he was referring to someone else, not me."

She pulled her robe tighter and knotted the sash. "He was referring to you. There's an engagement party I have to attend. You'd be bored."

"Whose engagement?" Seth was pretty sure the voice on the phone had belonged to Tony Arsenault.

"Jerome Senegal's daughter."

His heart sped up. An invitation to Senegal's house. This could be the break he'd been looking for. He'd have to watch his step. Senegal hadn't gotten where he was by being careless. There were only two reasons Jerome Senegal would want Adrienne to bring "her boyfriend" to a mob gathering. Either Senegal was interested in him because of his money and his connection to Crescent City Transports, or he was suspicious of him. Either way, it was an opportunity Seth couldn't miss. He'd talk to Conrad. Maybe he could find a way to plant a bug in Senegal's office.

Adrienne turned on the lights. She was lovely, a vision in the lavender satin robe. Her cheeks were pink where his beard had rubbed them, and her lips were swollen from their kisses.

Seth finished buttoning his jeans, wincing at the discomfort caused by his rekindled desire. He grabbed his T-shirt. "Senegal. Doesn't he have a lot of business interests in New Orleans?"

"Yes."

"Then your boyfriend would like to meet him."

She nodded. "I thought you might." Her voice was flat.

"Hey, princess." He crossed to her and took her in his arms. "What's the matter?"

She strained against his arms. "I'm a little tired."

"Yeah?" He grinned at her. "I know a guaranteed way to make you feel better."

She shook her head, rubbing her neck.

He caressed her cheek. "I heard him say something about your mother. You never told me. Is she all right?"

Adrienne went rigid. "She had a stroke. That's why I put her in the nursing home."

"I'm sorry, Adrienne. That must be hard on you."

"You have no idea." The bitter tinge was back in her voice. "Seth, if you don't mind—"

He stopped her words with his mouth. She stood impassively for a few seconds, but as his hands roamed over her body and his mouth coaxed and teased hers, she yielded. He felt it in the subtle relaxation of her tense muscles, in the response of her kiss. Seth forgot about Confidential and his assignment as she moaned and clutched at his shoulders. He scooped her up and carried her back to the bed. The only truth he wanted at this moment was the feel of her in his arms.

Chapter Four

A week later, when Adrienne directed Seth to turn onto Sixth Street and pointed out Jerome Senegal's spacious home, Seth gaped in disbelief at the familiar mansion. Bile churned in his gut. That rock garden in the front yard had been built by his father seventeen years before. Seth himself had carried some of the stones.

This house, grander and more ostentatious than Adrienne's, had a vine-covered walkway between the veranda and the garage. The vines were lush and tangled, their trunks as thick as his wrist. When he'd last been here, they had been saplings, newly planted by his dad.

"Seth? Is something wrong?" Adrienne touched his fist clenched on the steering wheel.

Unwrapping his fingers from the leather, he took a deep breath. He drew upon the relaxation techniques that had helped keep him alert during field operations in the desert. "This is Senegal's house?"

"Yes. Why? What's the matter?"

In the past few days, many hours of which had been spent in her bed, his princess had learned to read him very well. Too well. He had to be more careful.

But he also had to know.

"Has he lived here long?" He tried to make the question sound casual as they got out of the car.

"I believe so. They've lived here since the mid-Eighties at least."

Seth clenched his jaw. "They?"

She looked at him, confusion wrinkling her brow. "Jerome Senegal and his wife live here with their two boys."

Seth spotted two youngsters playing in the yard. "The boys must be a lot younger than his daughter, if she's engaged."

"Aimée is from his first marriage."

Seth put his hand on the small of Adrienne's back as they started up the sidewalk. His gut clenched. He couldn't ask any more questions.

Adrienne tugged on his arm. He leaned down so she could whisper. "They say his first wife ran off with the gardener, like something out of *Lady Chatterley's Lover.* Promise me you won't say anything."

Feeling sick and disgusted, Seth nodded. "I promise," he grated. Senegal's wife had run off with the gardener. *His father.*

Inside, the house resembled a bordello. Red velvet curtains and flocked wallpaper gave the place a decadent, old-fashioned feeling. Seth felt claustrophobic.

He knew he had a job to do, and he knew he couldn't let his old hurt and anger get in the way. But how many times was his father's abandonment going to rise up and slap him in the face? He'd already faced the irony that his latest assignment was to seduce a woman just like the one who'd stolen his father's love. Now the irony was doubled. Seth had a personal connection to the man he was supposed to prove was behind drug dealing in New Orleans.

The evening was a whirl of activity, centered around Senegal's daughter and her bland fiancé. Obviously, Senegal was keeping it in the "family." The fiancé was the son of wealthy New Orleans entrepreneur Antoine Gerraux, another name that Seth had heard in connection with the Cajun mob.

After a famous magician entertained the guests by making a brand new Jaguar—Senegal's wedding gift to his daughter—appear in his backyard, the moment Seth had been anticipating and dreading all evening long came. Senegal invited the men into his study for cigars and brandy, playing the rich, indulgent father to the max. Seth casually stuck his hand in his pocket and palmed the bug. The tiny, high-powered listening device was activated, and Conrad had arranged for a team to listen in. All Seth had to do was make sure that when he left Senegal's office, the bug stayed behind. Tony Arsenault sat next to Seth in the dark leather-and-mahogany room. Senegal himself offered cigars and a man Seth didn't know poured brandy as Senegal leaned back in the huge leather chair behind his massive desk.

"A toast to the proud father," Arsenault said, standing and holding up his glass. The men stood and toasted Senegal. Another man called out a toast for the son-in-law and they drank again, then sat down.

Seth played with his cigar, not interested in lighting it. He hoped he could sit quietly and unnoticed. All he needed was a few seconds to attach the bug under his club chair. He sipped his brandy politely as conversations swirled around him. He heard tantalizing snippets of information—about coffee, about money, about business—but nothing concrete.

When the man came around pouring more brandy, conversation waned. Keeping his expression bland as he swirled the brandy snifter, Seth prepared to casually drop his right arm and attach the bug beneath the chair.

Senegal swirled his snifter. "So, Mr. Lewis. Is it true you've not visited our fair city before?"

Seth tensed, closing his right fist. Damn. He was so close.

"Right." *Don't forget the continental persona.* "Fascinating city. I hope to stay for a while."

"Seth here is a big shot with Crescent City Transports," Tony said. "He likes the coffee at Cajun Perk and he has an interest in the 'major players.'"

Seth heard the emphasis Tony put on his words. For an instant there was silence, then Senegal laughed. At his cue, the other men laughed, too.

Rolling his cigar between his fingers, Senegal turned his attention to Seth. "Major players, eh? I hear you already got into one of the major players."

Laughter surrounded Seth again.

"I'm sorry?" he said, pretending he didn't understand. The mob boss's remark was crude and insulting, and Seth wanted nothing more than to knock out the man's teeth, but his life and the lives of innocent people depended on him keeping his cool.

"Our lovely Mrs. DeBlanc."

Seething inside, Seth allowed a satisfied smile to play around his lips. "She is certainly lovely. But is she a major player?"

"Ah, now, Mr. Lewis, that would be telling." Senegal swirled his brandy and sent a look toward Tony. "Let's just say that Mrs. DeBlanc makes good investments."

The sick dread churned again in Seth's gut. "Such as?"

Arsenault clapped Seth on the shoulder. "He asks a lot of questions, eh, Jerome?"

Senegal nodded, inspecting the tip of his cigar. "Questions can be good. Or bad. Mrs. DeBlanc is a very wealthy woman, Mr. Lewis, with a large and varied portfolio. For instance, she owns Cajun Perk."

"Cajun Perk? The whole chain?" Seth almost choked on his brandy. His stomach churned. His princess owned the coffee houses that were the distribution centers for Category Five?

"That's right, *cher.*" Arsenault chuckled. "She's the sole owner. You could say she has invested everything in the coffeehouses."

Seth didn't miss the warning glance Senegal shot at Arsenault.

"But that should not impress you, eh?" Arsenault continued quickly. "I understand you're rolling in the dough."

Seth inclined his head while his brain whirled. As the other men talked and smoked, Seth absorbed the information Arsenault had given him.

The brandy burned in his stomach as he fought the urge to hurl his glass across the room in angry denial. He breathed deeply and slowly, forcing himself to think logically, not emotionally.

Maybe Burke's instinct was correct. Maybe Adrienne DeBlanc was involved in dealing drugs. What they were saying matched Seth's first impression of her. Rich and spoiled and up to her neck in the corrupt activities of the Cajun mob. The cold glare of the skinny-hipped socialite—Senegal's wife—rose in his mind.

No. The woman he knew was nothing like that. His princess could not be a willing participant in their drug scheme. He unclenched his fist from around the brandy snifter as Senegal stood.

Every fiber of his being wanted to grab Arsenault and strong-arm him into admitting he was lying about Adrienne's involvement with Cajun Perk. But in his gut, Seth knew it was the truth. Business ownership was too easy to check. One call to Jones and he could have the answer in minutes. If Adrienne was the sole owner of

Cajun Perk, it would be public knowledge. The realization, coupled with the cloying smell of cigars and brandy, made him nauseous.

Forcing himself to breathe normally, and realizing he was about to have to shake Senegal's hand, he stretched his right arm as he took a last sip of brandy. As the other men rose, he stuck the bug between the cushion and the frame of Arsenault's chair.

Seth turned away, feeling apprehension like drops of sweat on the back of his neck. All the other men had left, but Tony stood at the door. When Seth exited, Tony closed the door behind him. Seth ducked into the bathroom and threw the lock. He pulled out his cell phone and speed-dialed Jones.

"The bug's planted."

"Good. The guys are in place."

"I need you to do something for me. Check out a connection between Adrienne DeBlanc and Cajun Perk."

"Your sweetie and Cajun Perk? So she is involved. Burke'll be glad to hear that."

Seth ignored Jones's dig. "Just check it out. I'll call you later."

Someone knocked on the door. "Just a minute," Seth called, then he quickly flushed the toilet and washed his hands.

He exited the bathroom and went looking for Adrienne, a new determination soaking through to his bones like the damp chill of a New Orleans winter. He had to separate his emotions from his job. As attracted as he was to Adrienne, he couldn't get involved. She could very well be the enemy.

TONY "THE KNIFE" ARSENAULT looked at the little blond icicle who'd been his friend Marc's wife. She was a frigid bitch, and he would be happy to see her take the fall for the drugs. Nothing would please Marc more than to look down from Heaven, or up from Hell, and see his wife in prison.

As Adrienne's eyes searched the room, Tony smiled. She was looking for her boyfriend. Well, Tony had a surprise for her. He savored the anticipation of telling her what he knew, just like he always savored the anticipation of a hit. It was like foreplay, leading up to the climax and the resulting afterglow of adrenaline when it was over. Tony's right hand twitched and he flexed his fingers. The absence of his machete ached like an amputated limb. He was not whole without it.

Still, the blow he was about to give the lovely widow would be almost as satisfying as the slick, meaty feel of a body under his blade.

"Adrienne," Tony said sweetly. "How is your mother?"

God, he loved doing that. He loved seeing the fear darken those blue eyes, loved to see the color leave her cheeks and the tension bunch her shoulders.

"Why do you do this to me?" she asked in a whisper. "I'm cooperating. I do everything you tell me to. Leave my mother alone."

"I just ask after her health. That is all. I have to say I'm worried about you, too. You're pale. You should be more careful. Your mother depends on you."

Adrienne's haunted eyes pleaded with him. "What do you want this time?" she asked flatly.

"Jerome wants you to do *un petit* favor for him."

She stood stiffly, like a queen awaiting execution. She'd always been so damned haughty. He shook his head. She acted like a thousand-dollar-a-night hooker. As if she thought she was too good for the likes of him.

"Jerome would like for you to find out about Seth Lewis."

Her eyes went wide with surprise. "Seth? What about him?"

"Jerome does not trust him. He is too interested in you, and in Jerome. He wants to know what Lewis's angle is."

She lifted her nose. "I don't think Seth is interested in Jerome."

Tony took her arm, as if in an affectionate gesture, but he squeezed until he saw the shadow of pain cross her face. "Jerome thinks he is. And Jerome has a personal interest in him."

"Let go of me."

"When I am sure you understand. Jerome wants to know where Lewis came from. Who his family is."

"His family? Why?"

"You don't need to know why." He squeezed her arm. "Find out why he showed up now."

"You know why. He's involved with Crescent City Transports."

"Just do it."

Adrienne's face drained of color. "What do you want me to do?"

"Whatever it takes." He leered at her and licked his lips at the look of disgust she sent him.

"You expect me to—"

"*Chère,* you already are. You think I'm stupid, eh? All you got to do is find out what he wants."

"Let go of my arm or I'll scream."

Tony squeezed one more time, then let go.

Adrienne massaged her upper arm. "I don't know what you think I can find out."

"There is something fishy going on. And Jerome thinks your boyfriend is a part of it. Someone is fooling with the business. Things happen which should not."

"I don't follow," Adrienne insisted.

"Things are known which should not be known. Now, suddenly you got a boyfriend who's a big shot with Crescent City Transports. Jerome don't like his name, and he don't like him. Find out who he really is. Screw it out of him." Tony laughed. "Of course, you better thaw out or you'll give him frostbite."

SETH NOTICED THAT Adrienne was quieter than usual on the way home from the engagement party. He felt the tension radiating from her like heat from sunburned skin.

He was feeling his own tension. Jones's words wouldn't let go of him. *So she is involved.* Seth shook his head. He couldn't believe it. His princess, knowingly participating in drug dealing? In the deaths of wealthy older businessmen? He'd only known her a few days, but his instincts told him it didn't add up. Was he so naive that his attraction to her was clouding his judgment?

The fact that she was the sole owner of the Cajun Perk coffeehouses bothered him. For all he knew, it was a business investment she knew nothing about. Maybe it had been her husband's investment, or she was being set up to take the fall if anyone ever connected the coffeehouses to the drug dealing. Seth had to find out how much Adrienne really knew about the day-to-day operations of Cajun Perk.

He glanced over at her as he parked in front of her house. She met his gaze and forced a smile. "Would you—?" Her voice sounded choked. "Would you like to come in?" she said stiffly.

"How can I resist such an enthusiastic invitation?"

She closed her eyes for an instant, then took a deep breath. "I'm sorry, Seth. I'm kind of tired, and I need to be up early tomorrow. I need to check on my mother."

There was that guarded, cautious tone she used when talking about her mother. He frowned. "Is she worse?"

She rubbed her neck. Seth was beginning to recognize the gesture. Her neck muscles tightened up whenever she was tense, whenever she lied, whenever his questions probed too deeply. He reached across and slipped his hand under her hair, massaging her nape gently and firmly.

"No" she said, sighing. She arched against the tender pressure of his hand. "I just like to visit every few days. To make sure she's all right."

"You've said that before. But you also said she's getting the finest care." Seth pushed a strand of hair away from her face. "You worry too much."

"You don't understand."

He touched her cheek. "I understand more than you realize. It's starting to rain. Let's go inside."

Inclining her head toward his palm, she nodded.

In the kitchen, Adrienne handed Seth a bottle of water and took one for herself.

"You're tense, princess. Let's go upstairs and I'll relax you." He kept his voice light, but he didn't like how she looked. She appeared defeated, beaten down. The sleek royal blue dress with its pencil-thin skirt and the fine embroidery across the bodice made her look elegant but frail, and highlighted the paleness of her skin.

He took her in his arms. "Is all this about your mother?" he whispered in her ear.

She sighed and yielded, relaxing against him, lifting her head so he could kiss her neck and jaw. "I'm very worried about her. She's so—vulnerable."

Seth's desire stirred as he felt the supple yielding of Adrienne's body. Drowning in her delicate scent of gardenias, he struggled to hold on to rational thought. Vulnerable was an odd word to use.

"Vulnerable? What do you mean?" he asked as he trailed kisses along the curve of her neck.

Adrienne stiffened. "She's partially paralyzed and unable to speak from a stroke. She can barely feed herself. She depends on me."

Her words echoed the anxiety Seth had seen etched in her face. He straightened and cupped her face. "You're doing everything you can, right? St. Cecilia's is the best."

"Oh sure. St. Cecilia's is the best. I'm spending piles of money on the best home, private duty nurses, the best of everything. But she's alone and helpless. And I can't—" She stopped.

"Can't what? Why don't you bring her home? Hire nurses around the clock to care for her? You can afford it."

Adrienne laughed shortly and flung off his touch. Anger flared in her eyes. "Money. Why does everyone think money will solve any problem? Money is nothing but a cage."

Her reaction surprised him. If she was telling the truth, she hated money as much as he did.

In his opinion, it was a curse, an addiction. People who had money seemed to never have enough of it. His jaw tightened.

"There are things that money can't buy," Adrienne continued. "Things like safety, like freedom."

Safety? Freedom? Were they still talking about her mother? Were Adrienne and her mother being threatened by the mob?

"Is there some reason you don't think your mother is safe at St. Cecilia's?"

Adrienne clamped her mouth shut. She was saying too much. It was obvious from the concern in Seth's face. Concern about her.

She longed to confide in him, to bask in his warm protective embrace and forget the life she was forced to lead. She'd give up every last penny if it meant being able to live a normal life with someone who truly loved her.

But she had an assignment, and she could never forget that Seth could be the enemy. Leave it to the mob to defile even her love life, she thought bitterly.

He took her hand and kissed the palm. "Princess? Are you afraid of something?"

Adrienne shook her head and touched his lips with her fingers. "I don't want to talk about this any more."

Seth opened his mouth and sucked lightly on her fingers. "Then we won't talk." He licked her fingertips.

His suggestive action sent a thrill of awareness through her, weakening her knees and turning her insides soft and liquid.

She couldn't make herself believe he was using her. She knew he desired her, knew he liked her. Maybe if he cared enough, he could help her and her mother escape from the mob's vicious clutches.

She would do what Tony asked—she'd find out what Seth's angle was. But she wouldn't be doing it for Tony or for Jerome. She'd be doing it for herself. She had to know if Seth was worthy of her trust. Not even orders from the mob could cool her attraction for this handsome, enigmatic man who seemed to really care about her. She craved his touch, missed him every minute he was gone, yearned to confide in him and have him confide in her. But she couldn't tell him everything yet.

He trailed kisses along her wrist, up her forearm to her shoulder, and now he was nuzzling her neck and sliding his fingers through her hair.

She turned her head. Their mouths met. Flaming desire flowed through her, and his quiet groan told her he was affected in the same way.

"Are you still too tired?" he whispered, his evening stubble scratching her cheek.

"I'm feeling better," she responded, realizing that she really was. His lovemaking revitalized her, and the weariness she felt afterward was a good, relaxing weariness, not the tense aching exhaustion that usually cloaked her like a fog.

She ran her hands up the front of his shirt and pushed his suit jacket off his shoulders.

"We can turn off the lights," she murmured, unbuttoning his shirt and kissing his bare chest.

Adrienne's lips and tongue trailed across Seth's chest and stopped at his nipple. A streak of fire burned through him as she gently grazed it with her teeth. His erection throbbed against the confines of his pants. Damn, she was sexy.

Still, even half-crazed with lust, he couldn't shake his concern about her. She'd sidestepped his question about her mother. He made himself a silent promise. He would do everything in his power to protect her and her mother from the mob.

He let his jacket drop to the floor and reached for the zipper on the back of her dress. "Or we could leave the lights on this time," he panted, pulling on her tight skirt, sliding his hands underneath and up her thighs.

Suddenly, the memory of his father doing the same thing in Jerome Senegal's kitchen slammed him, as shocking and sharp as a bucket of cold water in the face.

"No." He stopped. He was *not* like his father. And Adrienne was not like Senegal's skinny, adulterous wife. His princess was worth more than a quick bang in the kitchen. He framed her face with his palms and kissed her forehead gently.

She was worth so much more.

Adrienne stared up at him, her blue eyes dark with stirred passion. "Seth? What's the matter?"

He shook his head. "Let's go upstairs."

"Whatever you say," she said.

Leaving his jacket on the floor, he took her hand and brought it to his lips, and led her up the stairs to her bedroom. He lifted her in his arms and kissed her, cherishing her like the precious treasure she was, then laid her tenderly on the bed.

He shed his clothes and stretched out beside her, pulling her on top of him. Under her dress were tiny delicate royal blue panties and bra, but he hardly noticed them. His gaze fastened on a different shade of blue. Dark blue fingerprint-shaped bruises marring the pale perfection of her upper arm.

He sat up, cradling her on his lap, anger momentarily quenching his desire. "What the hell is this?" he growled, touching her fragile damaged skin.

Her hand moved to cover the bruises but he stopped it. Gently, slowly, he wrapped his hand around her arm, fitting his fingers over the blue marks, remembering the grimace that had crossed her face when Tony took her arm at the engagement party.

"Arsenault did this, didn't he?"

Adrienne wouldn't meet his gaze.

He put a finger under her chin and urged her head up until he could see into her eyes. "Didn't he?"

"He was telling me something. He probably didn't know—"

"That's bull. He knew. What did he say to you?"

She shook her head. "He—it was just something about the party. I know he didn't mean to squeeze so hard."

Fury burned through Seth like a brushfire. She was

lying, obviously too afraid to tell him the truth. Arsenault, that bastard, had hurt her, and no matter what the outcome of Confidential's investigation, there was one thing Seth would personally handle. Arsenault would pay for hurting Adrienne.

"Seth?"

He realized he was staring at her arm. "I will make sure nothing like this ever happens to you again. You can trust me on that."

Her eyes sparkled with tears. "I do." She reached out and ran her hand across his muscled wrist, up his forearm, over his bicep to his neck, where she slid her fingers into his hair and pulled his head down.

"Now didn't you promise to help me relax?" she whispered, kissing him slowly and thoroughly.

Shaking off his anger, he smiled at her and lay back, lifting her on top of him again. He disposed of her little blue bra and panties quickly and cupped his hands around her perfect breasts.

"I don't know how to do it this way," she whispered, her legs tight around him. Her hands grasped his wrists as her hair angelically fanned out over her shoulders.

Seth groaned as his arousal hardened and throbbed against her inner thighs. "You just follow me," he growled. "I'll take care of everything."

And he did.

Adrienne had never thought she could be so abandoned, so willing. The gentleness and care with which Seth made love to her made her want to cry with joy.

They'd made love a dozen times in the past few days, and it had been more erotic each time. She hadn't known sex could be like this. She wanted to stop time, to capture that moment right after he drove her to completion, that moment when her body, still throbbing with release, lay cradled in his arms. Capture it and stay in it forever.

"Tuppence for your thoughts," Seth said.

She stretched luxuriously, like a cat rubbing against its beloved human. "I was thinking how perfect this is."

Seth pulled her close and kissed her forehead. "It is."

The rain outside intensified, insulating them with a blanket of sound. Adrienne snuggled into his side and closed her eyes. But she couldn't relax completely. A sliver of guilt slipped as neatly and painfully as a splinter into her mind.

She'd been indulging herself, pretending her relationship with Seth was normal and innocent. She'd been pretending *she* was normal.

She should be working on her plan for getting out from under the thumb of the mob. Thanks to her dead husband and friends like Jolie, she already had over a hundred and fifty thousand in cash stashed in the house. After Marc had died and she was collecting his clothes to give to charity, she'd found cash hidden in various places. A lot of cash. Marc had been hiding money from the mob. That meant that Jerome probably had people monitoring all their accounts and investments. But if Marc could keep the mob from knowing he had a private stash, then so could she.

She systematically skimmed money from the household account and she had an arrangement with a small boutique where she bought clothes on her credit card, then returned them for cash. Soon she would have enough to move her mother to a facility in another state, take back her maiden name and get a job in the hotel business. She lay still, listening to Seth's even breathing and the soft rhythm of rain on the roof. Somehow, lying cradled in his arms, anything seemed possible, even freedom.

Chapter Five

"Princess." Seth's voice whispered in Adrienne's ear.

She didn't want to wake up. "Hmm?"

"You hungry?"

She shook her head against his warm skin. "Not really. Didn't you eat at Jerome's?"

He caressed her arm that lay across his chest. "Nope. Just a few boiled shrimp. You didn't eat either."

He threw back the covers. "Come on. I could use some breakfast."

Adrienne groaned. "It's midnight."

Seth chuckled, his chest rumbling against her ear. "Actually, it's morning."

She squinted at the clock. "No, it's not. It's only six a.m. Nothing's open."

"It's six-thirty. Anyway, I thought everything stayed open all night in New Orleans."

She yawned. "That doesn't mean you're required to be there before dawn."

"Come on. It'll be fun."

There was that magic word. *Fun.*

She groaned as she climbed out of bed, pulled her hair back with a barrette and slipped on a linen sundress and backless sandals.

Seth drove down St. Charles to the heart of the Arts

District. He turned onto Julia Street and parked in front of Cajun Perk. A couple of buildings farther down was Adrienne's favorite spa, Mignon's Spa Salon.

"Oh, this reminds me," Adrienne said, seeing the blue neon sign that spelled out Mignon's. "I need to pick up some lotion at Mignon's. I wonder if she's in this early?"

"No," Seth barked, his fingers tightening reflexively on the steering wheel. Seth knew his sister Mignon was there. She arrived at her salon at six o'clock every morning to greet the before-work crowd and to make sure the salon was ready for the day. He swore silently. He should have guessed that Adrienne would be one of Mignon's customers.

Adrienne glanced at him in surprise. "She might be. It'll only take a minute to check."

Seth tried to look unconcerned. He couldn't risk the possibility that his sister or one of her employees might blow his cover. "It's too early. Let's eat. I'm starving."

As Seth got out of the car he glanced at the delivery truck parked across the street. It was one of Confidential's surveillance vehicles, with its cameras trained on the entrance to the original Cajun Perk. He opened the car door for Adrienne.

When she stepped out of the car, she gave him a beaming smile that hit him solidly right under his diaphragm. "I'm glad you brought me here. It's actually one of my investments. This is the original Cajun Perk, the first store to open in the New Orleans metropolitan area. It's funny. I've never been inside one, even though I own them."

"You're kidding."

She shrugged her slender shoulders and tucked her hand into the crook of Seth's arm. "I'm no business-woman. I understand they're doing well." Her gaze drifted toward the other end of the street, where newly painted signs on old buildings announced galleries, antique stores and stained glass factories. "They're doing wonders with the renovation here. It's so great for the city to have an Arts District. And I love the retro look on this block, with the neon and curved corners." She looked up at him. "Didn't you say you were staying around here?"

"Yep." Seth was relieved and a bit confused. She'd admitted she owned the coffeehouses that were suspected of being the distribution points for the Cajun mob's drug trade. Yet she claimed she'd never been inside one. She was either the world's best actress, or she knew nothing about the drugs. Seth knew she was not a good liar.

He held the door for her and thought wryly of how good a liar he'd become in the past few days. "I'm leasing a sublet, on Camp."

She smiled at him. "Am I going to get to see it?"

He didn't answer. He sat her in one of the booths and fetched a latte and a plate of hot, fresh beignets for each of them.

Sitting next to her, he bit into one. "Don't you think these are as good as the ones in the French Market?" he asked.

Adrienne bit delicately into one of the fragrant doughnuts, sending tiny puffs of powdered sugar everywhere. She giggled and shook sugar off her fingers. "I've never eaten beignets in the French Market."

"Never? But everybody—" He stopped. He was straying into areas he shouldn't know anything about if he were what he claimed to be, a first-time visitor to the city.

During the short time he'd known Adrienne, he'd discovered how sheltered her life had been, but to find that she hadn't done so many normal things that people who grew up in New Orleans did was truly sad. She was beginning to seem like the bird in the golden cage. Given everything that money could buy—everything but freedom.

Someday he'd make a list of things he wanted to show her, and they would check off each item as they experienced them together. The idea of being with her as she discovered all the wonderful things she'd missed caused a lump to grow in Seth's throat.

"These are delicious! No wonder my investment is doing so well." She took a sip of coffee and closed her eyes, savoring it. "The coffee is excellent, too." She delicately licked at the powdered sugar on her lips.

Seth couldn't take his eyes off her pink tongue. His desire stirred and strained against his pants until he winced. "Surely you've had beignets before?"

Adrienne's eyes sparkled like sapphires and there was a white smudge of sugar on her nose. "The Caldwell's chef could prepare a twelve-course meal that rivaled the Cordon Bleu, but his beignets could be used for hockey pucks."

Seth laughed out loud. She was so genuine, so open, when she was happy. If he had three wishes, he'd give two of them to her, so she could have all her dreams come true. He'd keep wish number three, though, and use it to wipe out her history with the Cajun mob.

"I think I prefer café au lait at the Café Du Monde," he said, watching her tongue dart out to catch a fleck of powdered sugar.

Adrienne opened her eyes and set her cup down. "You certainly seem to have taken to New Orleans quickly and easily."

Seth came back to reality with a jolt. He scrambled

for an explanation, reminding himself to use the fake continental accent.

"Everyone's heard of Café Du Monde. It was one of the first places I visited." Yeah, when he got back on his feet after knee surgery months before.

An odd look crossed Adrienne's face. "You know, listening to you talk, sometimes it almost sounds like—" She paused.

"Princess—" he said, but she interrupted him.

"You've been here before, haven't you?" she asked flatly.

He couldn't speak.

"In New Orleans. That's why you knew exactly where that crawfish place was, and why you knew how to peel them. And it explains how you get around the city so easily."

"It's been a long time. But I have a good sense of direction."

A shadow of hurt passed over Adrienne's face. "Why didn't you tell me?"

He ran a finger along the back of her hand, wishing with all his heart that he could explain, but Burke would have his hide if he gave away Confidential secrets to Adrienne, as closely connected as she was to the mob. Even if she was innocent, knowledge of Confidential's operation could endanger her life. "Hey, I wanted to enjoy New Orleans with you, not rehash old memories. It's been ten years since I've been here."

She nodded slowly, her eyes narrowed. She didn't completely believe him. He needed to get past this as smoothly as he could.

He sipped his latte. "Still, this is delicious. You're to be congratulated for your insight. Making such a solid investment without sampling the merchandise. Was it a whim, or did you follow the recommendation of an investment counselor?"

Adrienne set her cup down and looked at the man across the table, the only man who'd ever managed to get even a glimpse inside her heart. His question made her oddly uncomfortable. Was it just her upbringing, which had taught her never to discuss finances in social situations?

She knew very little about Seth, despite their physical intimacy. He'd shown up and swept her away with charm and an intense sincerity that appealed to her need to believe in someone. But she couldn't afford to trust him.

"Does it matter?"

"Sorry, didn't mean to get too personal." He reached over and touched her nose, then held up his finger to reveal the smudge of powdered sugar. Not taking his eyes off her he put his finger to his mouth. Adrienne's breasts tightened. He could turn her on with a look, a gesture, a smile.

"But I find myself wanting to know everything about you. You have to admit we haven't spent much time talking." He flashed her a quick, suggestive grin.

She wondered what he'd say if she told him she'd never talked to anyone, certainly not her husband, as much as she'd talked to Seth these past few days. His genuine interest in her had coaxed her into opening up to him in a way she never had before.

"What if we played a game?" His hazel eyes sparked with amusement, but behind them Adrienne saw him assessing her reaction to his suggestion.

"A game? What kind of game?" Adrienne's imagination fed her a picture of the type of games a man like him might invent in private. Her breath caught in her throat and desire swirled through her.

Seth grinned and bit into another beignet. "You answer a question for me, then I'll answer one for you. That way we can get to know each other."

Adrienne shook her head, but he kept talking.

"We both have to tell the truth, and they can only be yes or no questions."

His suggestion sent a brief soupçon of panic through her. "I'm not sure I want to do this."

"Hey, princess." He put his hand over hers and caressed her wrist with his thumb. "We're supposed to be having fun. I didn't mean to upset you. Are you afraid to tell me the truth? Is that it?"

"Yes—and no." She laughed nervously, and pulled her hand away from his distracting caress.

He smiled. "We'll start with easy questions, okay? Did you buy Cajun Perk on your own?"

She was mildly surprised. She'd expected something more personal. "No. Why? Are you thinking of investing?"

"No. Does someone handle your investments for you?"

"Wait! That wasn't my question. You're going too fast," she laughed.

"No cheating. Answer the question."

She took a deep breath. "Yes. Are you saying this is the game? Because if it is, so far it's pretty boring."

Seth grinned. "Yes, this is the game. Okay, Adrienne. Here's a question. Have you been with anyone else since your husband died?"

Adrienne's face burned. She opened her mouth, then closed it. She glanced around. People didn't talk about such things in public. To her dismay, his grin grew wider.

"You should have stuck with my questions about your investments. You want a do over?"

"Yes, I have someone who handles my investments." She smiled at him in triumph.

He raised his brows, his eyes full of mischief. "I see. You're too chicken to answer personal questions."

"I am not chicken. But what you asked goes beyond personal."

"So do we."

Adrienne stared at him for a moment, then looked down at her cup. *Beyond personal.* If only she could believe that his feelings for her were beyond personal.

He touched her chin and she reluctantly met his gaze.

"I made you blush," he said softly, brushing the backs of his fingers against her cheek. "Your turn for a question."

Adrienne realized she loved this. The silly games, the intimate banter. She wanted to know about Seth, about his background, about why he'd lied to her about New Orleans.

Maybe she could play this game to her advantage. Drawing in courage with a deep breath, she toyed with her cup, then glanced up at him through her lashes. "Have you been with anyone else since you've been here?"

His eyes widened and his cheeks turned faintly pink. His gaze burned into hers, sending heat coursing through her body. She'd gotten to him. She smiled as he cleared his throat and recovered his composure.

He grinned. "No. Are you having fun?"

"Right now?" She pressed her palms to her flaming cheeks. "Yes. I am."

He laughed. "You should be, sneaking up on me with that question. Why wouldn't you answer mine?"

"No fair. It's my turn. Are you going to break my heart?" She gasped and covered her mouth. She hadn't meant to say that.

"God, I hope not." He leaned across the small table and kissed her. He tasted like sugar and coffee. "I promise I won't, as long as you don't break mine." His voice was light but his green and gold eyes were serious. His hand gently curved around her nape. "My turn. Are you afraid of someone?"

Adrienne stiffened. Seth retreated but his gaze stayed on her.

She searched behind his eyes, looking for the truth inside him. Could she trust him? Was he a different kind of man? A man she could believe in?

"Yes." She wasn't even sure which question she was answering, his or her own.

Seth's eyes turned dark, and he seemed to loom protectively over her.

"Are you going to make a deal with Jerome Senegal?" Adrienne watched him closely.

He froze for an instant. He looked past her "No. Is the person you're afraid of threatening you?"

She had to stop this. He was getting too close too fast. Her instinctive trust of him was colliding midair with her fear for herself and her mother. "I don't want to do this anymore," she said, wiping her hands on her napkin. "Can we leave?"

Seth stilled her hands with one of his. "Not until you answer my question. Is he threatening you?"

His face was open and sincere. Everything he did and said told her he cared about her. She yearned to confide in him. But he'd lied to her. He'd deliberately led her to believe he'd never been to New Orleans before.

The conflicting things about him, like his obvious familiarity with New Orleans, and the sexy, fascinating way he slipped in and out of his odd accent, made her certain that he was not who he was pretending to be.

"Is your name really Seth Lewis?"

He stared at her for an instant, then took a swift breath and, right before her eyes he changed. His expression turned bland, his eyes lost their sparkle.

"Okay." He grimaced and sighed. "My real name is Sethan David Lewis. But look who's not playing fair now," he said, a sudden false lightness in his voice that didn't match his face or his abruptly tense body. "You didn't answer my question."

Adrienne felt like crying. She'd wager that Sethan David Lewis was not his real name. She was certain he'd told her more than one lie.

Who was he really? Her experience told her he couldn't possibly be as genuine as he seemed. Her first instinct was probably correct.

He was just using her to get in with the mob.

SETH KNEW HIS reluctance to open up to Adrienne had upset her. That's why she had cut their conversation short and insisted they leave immediately. He wanted to stop the car, take her in his arms and tell her the whole truth—about his father, about his shattered dreams, about his deception. He wanted to beg her to forgive him. But this wasn't just the two of them. It was much bigger.

The drug the mob was placing on the streets was deadly. Seth had signed on to stop the Cajun Mob from distributing the drugs and endangering lives. He had a responsibility that went beyond his personal feelings.

After he dropped Adrienne off at her home, he went by Crescent City Transports to see Conrad Burke, who was in conference with Tanner Harrison.

When Seth reported to them that Adrienne was growing suspicious of his cover story, Burke and Harrison exchanged a glance.

"That's not necessarily a bad thing," Burke said.

"What will be interesting is what she does with the information."

Seth bristled, but stood quiet and still.

"Will she keep it to herself or will she go to Arsenault or Senegal with it?"

Harrison looked at Seth. "How much did you tell her?"

"I thought it'd be better to keep my mouth shut."

"So you neither confirmed nor denied," Harrison said with a small smile.

Seth inclined his head. "But she's no fool."

Burke nodded. "We're counting on that."

AFTER A QUICK SHOWER Adrienne drove out to St. Cecilia's to see her mother. On the way, her mind kept replaying the way Seth had acted. Why had he refused to tell her about visiting New Orleans before? What was the big secret? As the security guard let her car through the gates of St. Cecilia's Nursing Home, Adrienne forced herself to stop asking questions for which she had no answers.

She concentrated on the beautiful grounds around her as she drove toward the turn-of-the-century building that had once housed a convent for Carmelite nuns. The grounds were impeccably kept, with graceful willow and oleander trees and beds of colorful annuals dotting the manicured lawn. Ancient live oaks guarded the circular drive to the main building that served as home to retired nuns, as well as an assisted living community and nursing home.

Residents paid according to their means, with many of the residents impoverished. She probably paid more for her mother's care than all the other residents combined. Adrienne had picked St. Cecilia's not only because it was Catholic, but because it was remote, gated and on the grounds of a convent, which she felt added an extra layer of protection.

Each time she saw her mother sitting slumped in the wheelchair with Velcro straps around her torso to hold her upright, it broke Adrienne's heart anew. Her mother's once vivacious energy was gone and her brilliant blue eyes were dull. Her hair, of which she'd always been so proud, was thin and straggly, faded from bright gold to dishwater blond.

Retrieving a comb from the bedside table, Adrienne ran it through her mother's hair, trying to give her some comfort.

"Hi, Mother," she said softly, neither expecting nor receiving a response. "You look pretty today."

Adrienne put down the comb and sank down into a chair near her mother and took her mother's limp, blue-veined hand in hers.

"Mama, I've met someone," she whispered. "He's so handsome, and fun. He makes me laugh. I forget everything except him when we're together. He's not like anybody I've ever known before." She patted her mother's hand.

"But he's also keeping something from me. He's lying about who he is. It's so confusing. I really like him but I don't trust him. He seems completely sincere even though I know he's not telling me the whole truth."

She laid her mother's hand back down into her lap. "You know you never talked to me about love and men. All the information I got, which was precious little by the way, came from Tante Louise and Jolie." She looked at the thin cheeks and pale blue eyes of the woman who had always been affectionate but distant. "I wish I'd known you better. I don't know if you were happy, or if Father was good to you. I hardly even remember you, except as my beautiful, elegant mother, who would come into my bedroom every night to say good night. You were always kind of unreachable. Father was the one who told me what to do and made sure I followed his instructions."

Adrienne's memories of her childhood were memories of servants, of hotel staff. Adrienne's personal maid had ensured she did her homework. The head of housekeeping for the flagship Caldwell Hotel, Tante Louise, had given her a snack after school each day. When Tante Louise died, Adrienne had felt as though she'd lost her closest friend.

Adrienne realized tears were running down her cheeks. She swiped at them and took a deep shaky breath. "I don't know anything about Seth. If I judged him by the other men in my life, I'd have to conclude that he's using me to get in with Jerome and his mob. I want to trust him. When he looks at me, when he holds me, I believe he won't let me down." Adrienne pushed a stray lock of hair back from her mother's forehead and peered into the vacant blue eyes. "And I feel safe when I'm with him. Do you know how long it's been since I've felt safe?"

The door opened behind her and Adrienne glanced up to see the petite, elderly director of St. Cecilia's in her starched white habit.

"Good morning, Sister," she said, quickly wiping her cheeks.

"Good morning to you, Adrienne. And how is Mrs. Caldwell today?"

"The nurse told me she had a good night." Adrienne smiled. "But, of course, there's no change."

Sister Ignatius's wrinkled face was grim. "Someone came by to see your mother yesterday."

"What?" Adrienne jumped to her feet. Her chair scraped across the wooden floor. "Who?"

"It was a youngish man, maybe in his thirties, rather rough-looking. He had a thin scar on the side of his face." Sister Ignatius looked up at Adrienne. "He was respectful, but he appeared dangerous."

Tony. Pure fear burned through her with the breathtaking fire of two-hundred proof alcohol. "Wh-what did he say?"

The nun folded her hands together. "He asked to see your mother, indicating that he was a friend of the family. Naturally, since you had requested that we allow no one to see her without your express permission, we declined his request." Her lined face set in a disapproving frown, and her lips pursed. "He was not happy. He left a message for you."

The fear churned in Adrienne's veins, whooshed in her ears, louder than Sister's voice.

The thought of what Tony could do to her mother with no more than a flick of his finger horrified Adrienne. Suddenly, her problems with Seth seemed trivial and her plan to escape the Cajun mob sounded ineffectual. A hundred-and-fifty thousand dollars was nothing. Not against people like Tony Arsenault and Jerome Senegal.

"Adrienne?" Sister Ignatius placed a hand on her arm.

"I'm sorry, Sister," Adrienne said. "What was the message?"

"He said to tell you how much you and your mother mean to him and that he wants to assure you he's always thinking of Kathryn."

Adrienne nodded carefully, afraid if she moved her head too quickly she might faint. The pleasant words coming from the saintly mouth of Sister Ignatius were terrifying. Tony had referred to her mother by name. It was the subtlest of threats, but his meaning was unmistakable.

"Is he a special friend, dear?"

"No." Time was running out. What could she do? She needed to move her mother soon. Every moment brought them both closer to danger.

"I didn't think so."

"I apologize if he bothered you, and thank you for not letting him in. I don't want Mother disturbed. By anyone."

"Adrienne, I'm sure you are aware that there have been rumors about your husband and his—business dealings."

Adrienne stared at Sister Ignatius. "Rumors?" Her heart pounded in dreadful anticipation.

"Yes, dear. I won't repeat them, but this has been a source of concern to me for quite some time. I understand that you are not responsible for what your husband may have done. Still, the sisters and the residents here are not accustomed to the sort of man who came here yesterday. His words were threatening."

Her throat constricted with uneasiness. She swallowed hard. "Sister, I don't want you to think—"

The tiny nun held up a gnarled hand. "This has not been an easy decision. I cannot deny that your generous contributions have been of great benefit to St. Cecilia's."

Adrienne shook her head. "Sister, please don't do this."

"My dear, you have your mother to care for, but I have over a hundred residents and my sisters in God to protect. I prayed all night for God's guidance."

Adrienne heard the nun's words, yet her brain still tried to deny it. Her worst nightmare had come true. She had counted so much on St. Cecilia's. She closed her eyes and waited to hear the words that would doom her mother and herself to a life in hiding.

"It would be best if you found other accommodations for your mother."

Chapter Six

As soon as he could, Seth went by his sister's salon. She spent several evenings a week, and sometimes the weekends, working in the office after the staff went home. He saw her car parked behind the building and used his key to let himself in through the delivery entrance.

Mignon was closest to him in age, being only two years younger. She had inherited all the best features of their parents—the lustrous dark brown hair, unsettlingly green eyes and perfect features. She was the perfect advertisement for her spa salon.

When she saw him standing in the doorway of her office, she jumped up and ran barefoot across the sisal carpet to give him a hug.

"Seth! Why haven't you called? We've been worried sick."

The tight hug and familiar voice warmed his heart. "Hey, Min. I can't stay but a minute. Tell the brats I'll see them soon," he said, referring to his twin baby sisters. "We'll go to Commander's Palace for lunch."

Mignon stood back and looked at him. "Wow. You've taken the role of big spender seriously. You even sound different. You've got that arrogant I-can-rule-the-world attitude you had in the army. I'm glad. It fits you much better than the beard and the self-pity. How's the big secret job?"

"It's big and secret. Listen, kid. What do you know about Adrienne DeBlanc?"

Mignon tilted her head. "Adrienne DeBlanc? She was one of my first customers. She's brought me a lot of business. I'm sure I've mentioned her before."

Seth knew he'd blown it even before Mignon finished her question. He should have called so Mignon couldn't see his face. She'd always been able to read him like a book.

She gasped and pressed a hand to her chest. "Seth! Are you dating Adrienne DeBlanc?"

He shook his head, but with sisterly instinct, Mignon knew the truth.

"You are!" She grabbed his arm. "You'd better be careful. She is a lovely woman, but her husband was connected with the Cajun mob."

"What do you know about her?"

Mignon sat down and drummed her perfect nails on her desk. "Okay, so you're not talking. This is part of the big secret job I guess."

"Don't even ask, Min. If you can't answer my question, that's fine. But I can't tell you anything."

"Well, promise me that as soon as all this is over you'll tell me everything."

"Mignon—"

"Okay. Adrienne DeBlanc. Most of this is gossip, you understand. She's one of the richest women in New Orleans. Horrible marriage. Her husband ran around on her. He died in flagrante delicto, as they say, with a prostitute. Adrienne has always been one of my best customers. I suggested a lotion for her mother, who's in a nursing home, I believe. She makes a point of thanking me personally every time she comes in."

"I know all that. Well, except for the lotion. Anything else? Did she ever talk about men, or the mob? Did anyone talk about her?"

"No." Mignon's gaze was relentless. "I've never heard a harsh word about her. The way she acts though, you'd think she was still married."

"What do you mean?"

"You've probably never noticed, but there's a way some women act when their husbands are control freaks who never let their wives out of their sight. She's always wary, always careful. Like she's afraid she'll make a wrong move and someone will punish her."

Seth nodded. Mignon was one of the most perceptive people he knew, and she'd just confirmed his suspicion about Adrienne. "That helps. I'll see you later."

"Wait. You can't just leave. Tell me about you and Adrienne. Are you dating?"

He shot her a warning look.

She sighed. "Well, at least tell me how long it will be until you're home? We miss you."

He leaned over and kissed his sister on the forehead. "I miss y'all, too. I don't know how much longer it will be. And I still can't talk about it." He tugged on her hair.

"Ow. Stop that." Mignon stood. "Seth? Please tell me this doesn't involve the Cajun mob."

He didn't look at her as he turned toward the back door.

"Oh, God. It does. How do you always end up in the middle of the most dangerous situation you can find? Please be careful."

"Hey, don't worry about me. But you can't talk about this to anyone, understand? Especially the brats."

"You know I always keep your secrets."

"I know. I'll talk to you soon."

"Seth?"

He frowned at the uncharacteristically serious note in her voice. She walked over and kissed his cheek, then rubbed off the lipstick.

"Stay away from Adrienne DeBlanc. Being too close to her could get you killed."

As MUCH AS she tried to hide it, Seth knew that Adrienne was upset with him. She obviously knew he was lying to her. When he'd called her after talking to Mignon, she'd sounded worse than he'd ever heard her. Her manner was subdued, her voice dull and lifeless.

He'd suggested going out, but when she hesitated before agreeing, there was such a polite distance in her tone that he felt rebuffed.

Mignon's words echoed in his ears. If Adrienne was an unwilling pawn of the Cajun mob, spending her life under the watchful eye of Tony Arsenault, she had every right to be suspicious of Seth. And it killed him that her suspicion was justified.

But as much as he wanted to hold her, to reassure her, to bury himself in her and forget for a while what his purpose was, he didn't try to persuade her to see him. He hoped that a few days apart from his princess might cool his desire to be with her every second of every day. He needed a clear head to do his job.

Right now, his emotions were in enough turmoil. He was stretched taut as a guy wire. Visiting Senegal's house, the very house where he had watched his father betray his mother and throw away his family, had been a shock.

Not only had it reminded Seth of that dark time when his father had left them, it also placed him at risk of being unmasked by Jerome Senegal. If Senegal happened to put two and two together and realize that Seth was Robert Lewis's son, Seth's life would be forfeit and Confidential's operation might be exposed.

He'd apparently done a first rate job of burying his resentment toward his dad because he was experiencing residual feelings he hadn't acknowledged in years. The shock of discovering that his father, whom he'd admired and loved, had feet of clay. The sense of betrayal and abandonment when he left them. Seth didn't like the idea that his emotions might overrule his logic and training.

Burke had advised him to spend more time at Crescent City Transports to keep up his pretense of being second in command, helping oversee the startup of the new trucking business.

For the last few days, he'd driven the Mercedes to the Crescent City Transports building on Tchoupitoulas Road and parked it there all day while he met with Burke, discussed strategies with McMullin and spent time listening in on Jones's surveillance of the Cajun Perk coffeehouses.

Today, he was going out in the altered delivery truck with Jones and his crew to watch the flagship coffeehouse he and Adrienne had visited only a few days before.

Riding in the truck with Philip Jones wasn't Seth's idea of a good time. Jones was newly married to a pretty young police dispatcher and had the good-natured arrogance of a man who had taken that brave step and therefore believed all men should be converted to marriage.

Seth could take Phil's constant praise of married life. What he found much harder to stomach was the ex-private investigator's ribbing about Adrienne.

They had been parked across Julia Street from the original Cajun Perk for three hours now, and Seth had made a pact with himself. If Jones came up with one more subtly insulting reference to Adrienne, he'd go to go home to his bride tonight with a cut lip and maybe even a black eye.

Seth might be the only one of the Confidential agents who believed that his princess was innocent, but he was also the one who knew her. The only one who'd seen the fear that marred her perfect features when she thought no one was looking. He was the one who had lain awake and held her when she'd cried in her sleep. He was the only one who really—

His cell phone rang. It was Burke.

"Your bug paid off. We taped a phone call in which Senegal alluded to 'the goods' and to 'special shipments' from his 'very southern friends.' He also said something about a Category Five hurricane on its way. Good work, Seth."

"Thank you, sir. That doesn't sound like much to go on."

"It's nothing we could use in court, but combined with other information, it's pretty solid proof that Senegal is involved with the drugs. We're putting a tail on Senegal. He won't make a move we don't know about."

Seth hung up just as Jones elbowed him. "Hey, take a look." He handed Seth the binoculars.

Seth trained them on the entrance to Cajun Perk. He saw a girl of about nineteen, dressed in short shorts and platform heels, taking the last couple of drags on the stub of a cigarette.

"That's the prostitute who gave us the intel that led to the raid on the bordello."

She was younger than his sisters. Where was her family? How had she gotten to this point?

Seth felt an echo of the panic that had grown inside him after his mother died and left him with the entire responsibility for his three sisters. Thank God he'd been able to take care of them. "She's already back out on the street?"

Taking the binoculars back, Jones shot Seth an odd look. "I keep forgetting your background is not in law enforcement. She's actually in less danger on the street. If she hadn't been arraigned and returned to her pimp along with the others, she'd have been made as an informer. She'd be dead now."

Seth studied the red neon sign, the innocuous front of the coffeehouse that looked like any of a dozen trendy franchises. His stomach turned over as a group of students jostled each other on the way through the arched doors. The idea that a lethal and dangerous drug was being distributed behind that art nouveau facade was a difficult one to believe. Seth needed to see for himself how the operation ran. He needed to prove to himself that Adrienne wasn't involved.

"What did the girl tell the police about how they move the stuff?"

"They hide packets in the cardboard coffee sleeves. Each specially made sleeve apparently holds three packets of Category Five."

Seth whistled softly. "Has anybody been inside?"

"Sure. But nobody's been able to see anything definitive."

"Adrienne and I had coffee here a few days ago, around six-thirty or so. Most of the customers were people dressed for work and the post-party breakfast crowd. I didn't notice any prostitutes."

Jones cackled. "The prostitutes come here to pick up the Category Five. At the hour of the morning that you were there you can bet they're still sleeping. Why do you think they call 'em ladies of the night?"

Seth acknowledged Jones's joke with a smile. He couldn't stay cooped up in the truck any longer. He was itchy, restless. He felt like he'd been crouching in a foxhole all night. "I'm going in. Maybe I can spot something."

"You better check with Burke."

Seth shook his head. "It'll be okay. All I'm going to do is order a coffee and drink it."

"Well, at least let us fix you up a camera. Maybe you can get a shot of one of the coffee sleeves. Here's one embedded in a Palm Pilot."

"I don't use a Palm Pilot. I'd be uncomfortable and look like an idiot."

"What about a cell phone?"

"Fine. Okay. How does it work?"

Jones showed Seth the tiny lens embedded in the top of the cell phone's belt clip. "It's wide angle. If you point it in the general direction of your subject, it will pick up about a six-foot radius."

"I assume the phone still works."

"Sure. It's a fully functioning cell phone. Just don't try to use the belt clip. It doesn't open. It's strictly there to house the camera. We'll be recording in here."

Seth exchanged his phone for Jones's. "What about sound?"

"The quality isn't the greatest, but as long as you're no more than five feet away, it should pick up conversations.

"Is your number coded in?"

Jones nodded and looked at his watch. "So are Burke's and McMullin's. Don't stay too long. Two more hours and I'm heading home to a hot feast—and pizza delivery." He laughed loudly at his own joke.

Seth smiled faintly. If Jones weren't so convinced that Adrienne was guilty, Seth might learn to like him.

He used the concealed exterior monitors to check the street before quickly exiting the truck and ducking into an office building. After studying the building's directory for a few seconds, he loosened his tie and stepped outside, crossed the street and entered the original Cajun Perk right behind the scantily dressed prostitute.

She stepped to one side, peering at the pastries in the glass case, obviously waiting for him to go first. He quickly ordered a latte and sat down at a mosaic-topped table near the counter. He retrieved the cell phone from his jacket pocket and set it on the table, aimed at the counter as the young prostitute gave her order.

"Hey, Leo. Let me have your special blend." Tapping her false French nails nervously on the counter, she glanced around, her heavily made-up eyes lingering on Seth for an moment. He didn't look away, just sipped his coffee as if he had all afternoon to sit and watch beautiful young whores.

"You know, the Hurricane Blend," she said quietly. As she waited, her gaze took in the rest of the patrons. When Leo returned to the counter with her coffee, she inspected the paper cup and the protective sleeve with a sharp eye, paid Leo and went over to the condiment counter, where she added several spoonfuls of sugar to the cup.

Seth casually turned the phone toward her as he studied the cup and the protective cardboard sleeve with interest. The sleeve on her cup was bulkier than the one on his, at least a quarter-inch thick.

His blood raced. He'd just watched the drug being passed right in front of his eyes, and he couldn't do a damned thing about it.

According to Jones, the prostitute had spilled to Courville that they used Category Five to drug wealthy older businessmen. The drug loosened inhibitions, stimulated arousal and was highly addictive. The prostitutes hauled in piles of money by bilking their johns, who kept coming back for another fix of both the drug and sex.

Just as the prostitute left the coffee shop, Jerome Senegal and a man Seth didn't know came in.

All senses on alert, Seth deliberately relaxed back in his seat and sipped his coffee. He aimed the phone camera at Senegal for a couple of seconds, then picked it up and keyed in Jones's number, keeping his attitude casual as Senegal swept the seating area with his sharp gaze.

Jones spoke before he had a chance to. "Did you see who just came in?"

"Yes. Did you get a look at the cup?"

"Got it all on tape. Could you tell the difference?"

Seth kept his voice low. "The cardboard sleeve is at least three times as thick as normal. She was telling the truth."

"The lab ought to be able to enlarge the pictures. But man, we gotta get our hands on one of those sleeves."

"What if she brought one in so the lab could measure it, photograph it and test it for traces of the drug?"

"Won't work. According to her story, the manager of each store keeps a running log of pickups, including dates and times. And the head pimp Maurice Gaspard checks each prostitute in each day, again with times. It's better than a chain of evidence."

A shadow blocked the afternoon sun shining into the shop. Seth glanced up at Jerome Senegal.

"I see," he said. "Then we'll have to make other arrangements. I'll speak with you later." Seth severed the connection. He set the cell phone back down on the table, resisting the urge to adjust its position for the camera angle. Even if it weren't at the best angle, it would still pick up their conversation.

Meeting Senegal's eye, he rose and held out his hand. "Mr. Senegal. Nice to see you."

"Lewis, isn't it?" Senegal grinned. "I guarantee I'm not likely to forget that name. Mind if I sit?" He indicated the other chair at Seth's small table.

"Sure." Seth sat back down.

The man with Senegal remained standing.

"Get me a café au lait. Want a refill, Lewis?"

Seth shook his head and watched with interest as the bulky man in the tailored suit marched to the counter and placed Senegal's order. *Bodyguard.*

"So, Lewis," Senegal said a few seconds later, accepting the steaming cup from the bodyguard. He sipped the fragrant chicory coffee and steamed milk mixture. He shook his head. "I surely don't like the name Lewis." His eyes were vicious as a blackbird's— sharp, intelligent, not missing a thing.

Seth set his cup down carefully, aware that every move he made, every word he said, was under intense scrutiny. If Senegal managed to unearth the final thread of memory that connected Seth to his father, Confidential's case could be lost.

"I apologize for my name, *monsieur.* Should I leave in order to save you from further offense?" He spoke carefully, affecting the slight continental accent and adding to it an attitude of boredom. Drawing on the rigid control of his military training, he concentrated on distancing himself as much as possible from New Orleans, from Robert Lewis, from everything connected to his former life. He had to *be* the wealthy financier Senegal thought he was if he wanted the mob leader's trust.

Senegal waved away Seth's response. "*Non.* Not at all." But his gaze still measured Seth, and his expression was thoughtful. "You say you're not from around here?"

Seth had expected the question. Still, his heart rate sped up. Confidential's entire case could depend on how well Seth handled the next few minutes. He realized he was feeling the same thrill of danger, the same satisfaction he'd felt during successful field ops. He felt useful. It was a tremendous boost to his ego. He'd spent too many months in a sludge of self-pity.

He leaned back and loosened his tie a bit more and sighed, as if he were relaxing after a hard day's work. "I said I'd lived in a lot of places."

An expression of intense anger darkened Senegal's expression, quickly covered with a toothy grin.

Adrienne's pale lovely face rose in Seth's mind, so frightened and worried, probably because of the man sitting across from him. Since he'd met his princess, Seth's priorities had changed. Accomplishing Confidential's goal would free her from the Cajun mob and remove the sadness and fear from her eyes. That alone would give him greater satisfaction than anything he'd done in Special Forces. A small voice that sounded a lot like Jones's whispered in his mind. *If she's innocent.*

"You don't impress me, *mon ami*," Senegal said. "You try to act the big shot, *non?* But you just a horny kid, worming your way into the designer panties of the rich Widow DeBlanc. You don't want to tell me where you from, that's fine with me. But tell me this. Just how much influence you really got with Crescent City Transports?"

Seth bristled at Senegal's comment about Adrienne, but he kept his expression bland. Senegal was playing right into Confidential's hands. Burke had instructed Seth to get this deal. He'd even given Seth the name of a contact at the transport company to refer Senegal to.

"Jerome Senegal doesn't conduct his own business affairs, not at the delivery level. He'll have a lieutenant to work out the specifics," Burke had told Seth. "You'll need to do the same. You're too big a fish to be making your own deals."

Seth wasn't about to make it easy for Senegal. He'd never gain the mob boss's trust if he didn't have his respect. And a man as ruthless as Senegal respected ruthlessness.

Seth set down his coffee cup and pushed back from the table. "Well, Mr. Senegal, I'd think a man in your position would already know the answer to that question. So, if you'll excuse me, this 'horny kid' needs to make a few transatlantic calls. Money never sleeps, as I'm sure you know."

He stood and picked up his cell phone. *"Bonjour, monsieur,"* he said, inclining his head. "Call me when you decide you *really* want to do business." Seth started for the door, his shoulders corded with tension. He'd just turned his back on the enemy, something he'd been taught never to do. He keyed random numbers into his phone with one hand.

"Wait, *mon frère*," Senegal called. "What's your hurry?"

Seth paused and turned, casually holding the phone so the camera caught Senegal. He raised a brow. Senegal's Cajun accent had become heavier, his face looked more deeply lined. Had Seth gotten to him?

Senegal's bodyguard took two steps toward Seth, but Seth glared at the heavyweight at the same time as Senegal held up a hand. "Please. Sit."

Seth's thumb hovered over a number key as if the call he'd been about to make were a matter of international concern, then he closed the phone and sighed, glancing at his Rolex Oyster. "A few minutes should not matter." He sat, but didn't relax, exuding an attitude of barely reined in impatience.

Senegal smiled, his white teeth brilliant against his swarthy complexion. "Me, I have coffee beans to deliver. You have a trucking company. We are a perfect fit. Tony Arsenault handles deliveries to the various coffeehouses. He will be pleased to discuss terms with your people."

Seth let interest show in his face as he sat back in the chair and lay the phone on the table. "Now, you're talking business."

ADRIENNE HAD TO DRAG herself out of bed. She wasn't sleeping well. Every time she closed her eyes, she saw her mother. The sister's warning echoed in her ears whenever she tried to rest.

She spent the morning at a small Internet café, searching for nursing facilities in nearby states. She couldn't afford to go very far. She'd found three possibilities. One was in Mississippi, a tiny nursing home in a town so small it was hardly on the map. One was in Memphis, and advertised its commitment to resident safety. And the third was a government run facility. She wasn't sure her mother would qualify, but it wouldn't hurt to ask.

She called Jolie, who'd guaranteed she could scratch up about twenty thousand.

"You realize I may never be able to repay you," she'd said to her friend.

Jolie's voice had held concern and compassion. "Repay me for what? I'm repaying you. I wouldn't have The Cater Caper if it weren't for you."

Now Adrienne stood in front of the large marble-topped chest that dominated the decor of her dining room. It was the only piece of furniture that was truly hers. It had belonged to her grandmother and had sat in the lobby of The Caldwell Hotel all her life. She caressed the cold marble. Once she'd hoped to give it to her own daughter.

She opened the top drawer and felt inside it. Toward the back was a lever, which she tripped. It was a secret lock for the bottom drawer, which appeared to the casual observer to be part of the base. She crouched and pulled it open, staring at the piles of cash. She knew exactly how much was in there. One hundred and forty-two thousand, three hundred dollars. It wasn't much, but add to it the twenty thousand or so from Jolie, and hopefully it would be enough to get her mother and herself to safety.

She'd bought new luggage yesterday. The middle-sized piece was just the right size to hold the cash. Somehow the purchase of the luggage made her decision seem starkly real.

What she was considering seemed impossible. She shuddered. The mob was ruthless. She had heard Marc talk about people who'd wanted out. Some of them had disappeared. Some had changed their minds. Some had ended up dead. There was no one she could turn to for help. She'd already endangered Jolie, her only true friend, by involving her. As soon as Jolie got her the money, Adrienne would sever all ties with her.

Then she really would be alone. Everyone she knew was potentially connected to the mob. Even Seth.

When she'd met him, she'd dared to believe he was different. In the short time she'd known him, she'd begun to fantasize that he could help her escape. She'd come so close to confiding in him, so close to asking for his help. But if he would lie to her about his ties to New Orleans, then how could she trust him?

Her eyes filled with tears that spilled over onto her cheeks. She brushed at them impatiently. She didn't have time for self-pity. There would be time enough for crying when she and her mother were safe.

Now she had to prepare.

She retrieved the mid-sized suitcase from the hall closet and put the cash inside. The stack of bills looked pitifully small inside the leather bag. She closed the case and put it back into the closet, then locked the empty bottom drawer just as someone knocked on her patio door.

Her pulse leapt. Was it Seth? She cursed her fickle heart.

But it wasn't Seth. It was Tony.

Her only reaction to the sight of his tall, menacing figure through the screen door was a contraction of her already tight muscles and a queasiness under her diaphragm. She rubbed her neck. She was stretched like a rubber band. Any more pressure and the band would break.

She opened the door, hoping to discourage him from coming inside by standing with her hand on the knob, but he stepped up onto the first step, towering over her, advancing until she backed away. He entered her kitchen.

"What do you want?" she asked bluntly.

"I understand your mother is doing much better."

His oily voice slithered down her spine like a slick, cold snake. She shuddered in revulsion, surprised that she still had room for any emotion inside her.

"What do you mean?" This wasn't his usual threatening message, couched in the form of a polite inquiry into her mother's health. He appeared positively cheerful.

He smiled, the scar on the side of his face giving his leathery countenance the distorted look of a Halloween mask.

Tony "The Knife" Arsenault was only happy when he was torturing someone. Had he hurt her mother?

A deep, primal fear radiated through her, washing all the strength from her limbs. She pressed her palms down on the cool granite surface of her kitchen counter, trying not to collapse.

"What have you done?" Her voice broke. "Is my mother all right?"

"Of course, *chère*. Your mother is fine. You have pleased Jerome, and as for me, I am very impressed. I was certain you could be *très* persuasive if you set your mind to it."

"What are you talking about?"

Tony flexed his fingers like a gunfighter about to draw his gun. The image of him holding the machete he was rumored to be so fond of rose in Adrienne's mind. She swayed as the blood rushed downward away from her head, making her feel lightheaded.

"It pleases me to report that your boyfriend has made a deal with us to deliver coffee beans."

The words hit Adrienne like a blow. She'd been expecting something like this, but she'd hoped she was wrong.

"So?" she said, forcing herself to sound unconcerned. "He's a businessman. I'm sure he makes deals every day." She was nowhere near as confident as she sounded. The way Tony's voice wrapped around the word *deal* made her feel physically ill.

Seth had made a deal with the mob. He had sided with the enemy.

"Of course. So, *chère,* as long as Seth Lewis continues to 'deal' with us in this particular way, you may assure the nuns at St. Cecilia's that your mother will not have any more unwelcome visitors."

Her blood felt like ice water running through her veins. "What particular way?"

Tony stepped around the counter. Adrienne took a step backward, but he stopped her with an iron grip on her arm.

"You're hurting me," she grated through clenched teeth.

"I know." He leaned down until his awful voice and hot breath assaulted her ear. "We have a nice setup for coffee deliveries with Crescent City Transports, thanks to your lover. You keep him occupied a little longer, *ma petite*. Then Jerome, he says you can be free."

She gaped at him, certain she'd heard wrong. "Free—? Did—did you say free?"

"You remember that, *chère,* the next time you think about running away."

Adrienne's heart pounded in her chest. "I don't know what you're talking about."

Tony twisted her arm slightly, just enough to send a pain shooting up through her shoulder. "You think you can make a move without us knowing about it? You think nobody will notice when you buy a set of luggage because you pay cash? Where were you planning to go, *chère?*"

She closed her eyes, unable to stop the helpless tears that slipped down her cheeks. She stood rigid as a stone until Tony finally let go of her arm.

He laughed. "You take care of your mother and play with your boyfriend. But remember, Jerome, he controls everything, including you."

He touched the side of her face with that hand that had killed people. She jerked away, glaring at him through her tears.

His dark eyes glittered with sadistic triumph. "Here is a tip about your boyfriend. Do you know that Jerome's first wife ran off with their gardener seventeen years ago? Do you know that the gardener's name was Lewis?"

Stunned, Adrienne fought to keep her surprise from showing. *Lewis.* She remembered Seth's questions about Jerome's house, and how tense he'd been when he first saw it. It made sense now. He'd have been around eleven or twelve at that time. He knew the house. He'd probably helped his father, Senegal's gardener.

"Jerome believes Lewis, the big shot, is nothing more than the gardener's son. It is your job to assure that he will stick around until we find out for certain."

So you can kill him, Adrienne thought dismally.

Chapter Seven

Adrienne faced an impossible choice—Seth's life or her mother's. She couldn't abandon her mother, but neither could she lead Seth into Jerome's deadly trap.

As the day waned, she stepped out the kitchen door, too tense to stay cooped up inside. In the shaded courtyard, the sunset gave a rosy glow to the tiny waterfall that bubbled into a stone pool filled with golden koi.

Water lilies and philodendrons spilled over the rocky edges. A canopy shaded the wrought-iron table and chairs, and protected numerous other potted plants that lent the tiny fenced area the feel of a lush tropical hideaway.

She sat on the side of the stone koi pond, trailing her fingers in the water, enticing the koi to the surface to investigate. Their mouths tickled as they tasted her fingertips and determined that she wasn't food.

Usually, playing with the fish soothed her, but today, she watched the fish with a growing unease.

She was trapped in her world as surely as the koi were trapped in theirs. She'd heard that the little golden fish grew as big as their environment would let them, but that if they were kept in a tiny place, they would remain tiny, tied forever to their boundaries.

Adrienne felt the same way. Small, helpless, tied to this house and the men who controlled her.

Agitated, she picked up the tin of fish food and shook it over the water. Two fish, one with a black tail and one with a stripe, made a beeline for the floating food, nipping at each other. As they fought, vying for the best position, a third fish, smaller and solid gold, zipped around them and while they were distracted, snapped up the morsels of food.

The two larger fish approached the little gold one. She hovered in the water for an instant, between the two, then flipped her tail and swam toward the striped fish.

"Good girl," Adrienne whispered. "Using them to take care of yourself."

The actions of the fish gave her pause. The little fish had hung back, biding her time, as the two larger black and gold fish sparred. She ended up siding with the larger, more protective fish.

But even with the protection of the striped fish, the little gold koi was still trapped. Every victory, even the smallest, had its price.

Tony had promised her freedom. But was the price too high? Was she willing to put Seth's life on the line to protect herself and her mother?

Seth could take care of himself—her mother couldn't, the logical side of her brain reminded her.

But the illogical side, the side that couldn't wait to see him, that needed the protective comfort of his strong arms around her, was just as persuasive. She couldn't let the mob ambush him. She had no doubt Jerome was capable of killing Seth just to placate his wounded ego.

And what if Tony was lying? He lied as easily as he breathed when it suited him. Would Jerome ever really let her go?

She paced back and forth in front of the koi pond, her thoughts in turmoil, her belly in knots.

What about Seth's motives?

She had truly believed he understood her, that he knew her deepest desires. She'd wanted so badly for him to be just what he seemed, an honest man, a tender lover, a compassionate friend.

But in her world, nothing was ever as good as it seemed. There was a dirty underbelly to everything. Her husband and her father had taught her that.

It appeared that Seth had a dirty underbelly, too. He'd used her. The one man in all the world to whom she'd dared give her trust. He'd played her, wooed her, seduced her, for the sole purpose of getting close to the mob.

She'd allowed him into her bed and into her heart, and that decision had plunged her more deeply into the same unbearable life she longed so desperately to escape. This time, she didn't have the excuse of innocence.

She'd let herself be taken in by Seth's enigmatic smile and the attraction that sparked like electricity between them. By his changeable eyes that could shine with soft green tenderness or glint like sun-shot gold passion.

She looked back at the fish, and saw the little gold one swimming alone, while the larger two chased and nipped at each other. No matter what the other fish did, the little one was alone.

Rubbing her neck, Adrienne took a deep breath. She was alone, too, alone and scared and uncertain who to trust.

No, that wasn't exactly true. She knew in her heart that Seth was the better man.

And because of that, he deserved to know that Jerome had figured out who he was. She picked up the portable phone off the table and dialed his cell phone, but he didn't answer.

"Dammit!" she muttered. Where was he? Her muscles were coiled like springs and her throat hurt from holding back frustrated tears. She only had so much strength left. She needed to use it wisely.

"Dammit, dammit, dammit!" she cried and whirled and slung the phone as hard as she could.

"Whoa!"

In one clean motion, Seth made a pretense of ducking and snagged the phone in the air as he walked around the edge of her house and approached the courtyard. "Why the tantrum, princess? Won't anybody deliver pheasant under glass this early?"

His amused voice and his pleasant smile scratched her sensitive nerves like cat's claws.

"Do you have to call me that?" She stomped up the steps into the kitchen, slamming the door.

It didn't slam. Instead, Seth stopped it with his hands, and followed Adrienne inside.

"What's the matter?"

She dashed away hot tears and took a long breath. She'd wanted to see Seth and she'd gotten her wish. Here he was.

She wanted to be angry with him, to hate him for using her. But seeing him standing there, crisp and cool in a white polo shirt and khaki pants, his handsome face marred by a bewildered frown, she renewed her resolve. She couldn't stand by and say nothing while he was in danger.

"Think for a minute. I'm sure you'll figure it out."

"You talked to Arsenault." He stepped toward her, but she held up her hand.

"Of course. You don't think he would waste a minute letting me know that you'd closed the deal, do you?"

"What is it with that guy anyhow? What kind of hold does he have over you?"

Adrienne shook her head. "What difference does that make now? You're in business with him."

"It makes a lot of difference to me. I'd like to break him apart with my bare hands. He's not fit to be in the same room with you."

She swallowed. He sounded like the man she'd thought he was. If only she could be certain. "Yet you used me to get in with him?"

"Give me a chance to explain."

Adrienne smiled as her stomach churned. "You don't have to explain. It's just business, right?" She spread her hands.

He peered at her, a strange softness in his penetrating gaze. It was as if he could see right through to the heart of her. As if he knew she was fighting with all her might to be strong. She yearned to give him all her trust, all her secrets, all her love.

"Right. Just business. Are you okay?"

Adrienne's smile felt pasted on. A lump grew in her throat. What had she expected? That he'd rush in here and tell her the whole truth? That he'd have some wild explanation that would make him the hero she'd hoped he was?

How foolish of her.

"Are you sure you're all right? You look sad." He stepped toward her, his fingers gentle as he lifted her chin and bent to kiss her.

"Don't, Seth. Please." She pushed against his hands. "I need to tell you something."

"Okay. You want to go in the living room and sit? You're pale. Better yet, let's go upstairs."

She held up a hand. "Seth, wait. Jerome knows about your father."

Adrienne's words stopped Seth in his tracks. Her face was damp with tears and ravaged with worry, her hands clasped together tightly. He'd been preparing himself for the possibility that Senegal would figure out who he was. But he hadn't expected to hear it from her.

"How do you know this?" His brain whirled. The only way she could know was if Arsenault had told her. Why would he tell her that, unless she was involved in their plan? Even as the thought surfaced, he denied it. There had to be another reason. Adrienne wiped her cheeks with her palms. Her hands trembled. Seth took them in his and held them to his chest.

"Princess, it's okay. You know I would never hurt you. You can tell me anything."

"Let's do go upstairs. It's getting dark outside and someone might be watching through all these windows." A shiver wracked her body.

Seth pulled her to him and kissed her forehead, then guided her up the staircase to her bedroom. He stood, his shoulder propped against the doorway, his arms crossed, as she drew the bedroom curtains. "I hate being downstairs at night. Those thin curtains don't hide anything." She shrugged self-consciously. "People driving by on the street can see everything."

She paced back and forth. He'd never seen her so agitated.

"I don't know why you came to the charity auction," she said. "But if you were looking to hook up with the Cajun mob, you were successful. Jerome is the head, and Tony is his right-hand man. I think Tony has killed people." She hugged herself and turned to face him.

"Jerome got suspicious of your name and has apparently been looking into your background. He knows that your father was his gardener, the man who ran away with his wife." She smiled wryly. "I had a feeling you were a native of New Orleans and not just visiting."

She stood there, alone in the middle of the room. It broke Seth's heart to see her so calm, accepting that he'd lied to her. She'd been lied to all her life. He didn't like being lumped in with the people who had made her unable to trust. But he knew that, for a while at least, that's exactly where he was. He hated that.

"Guilty as charged. But Adrienne, I really am Seth Lewis. I didn't lie about that."

Her eyes sparkled with unshed tears.

"And I will tell you the truth. I promise. But I can't just yet."

She swallowed and nodded. "I really didn't expect you to."

"Why do you think Jerome sent Arsenault to tell you about my father?" Senegal wouldn't have tipped his hand unless he thought he could gain something from it. Seth was convinced they had used Adrienne to send him a message. He might be dealing with them on coffee deliveries, but Senegal didn't trust him.

She lifted her chin, her eyes sapphire-dark with hurt and caution. Her gaze slipped past him and he had the feeling she was looking inward. "Because they are counting on me to keep you occupied until Jerome decides what he wants to do."

Her words sucker-punched him. He almost doubled over from the shock.

Senegal had instructed her to sleep with him? No. Not for a minute did he believe their attraction had been anything but real. The few feet between them yawned like a bottomless chasm. The truth was, they had both used each other.

"You have to get away. He'll kill you." Her voice was tight, choked with tears.

Her concern was like another blow to his solar plexus. "Don't worry about me, princess. I can take care of myself."

Her gaze met his as her hand massaged her graceful neck. She nodded.

The yearning to cross that chasm, to take her in his arms, was unbearable. But she didn't trust him much right now, and he couldn't blame her.

"What about you, Adrienne? Why do those two snakes have such a hold on you?"

She released a quivering sigh. "After my husband died, they sort of adopted me."

I'll bet they did. Seth recognized the sharp tinge of bitterness he'd heard before in her voice.

"It's your mother, isn't it? They're using her as a threat to keep you in line. To get you to do things like host charity galas to hide secret meetings, or to keep suspicious businessmen entertained while they check them out?"

She jerked as if she'd been punched, and the rest of the color drained from her face.

"I've never done anything like this—" She swayed. "You have to believe me…"

In one stride, Seth caught her. He lifted her gently and laid her down on the bed, sitting beside her.

"I know, princess. I shouldn't have said that." He brushed her hair off her forehead. "I'm here. I swear you won't have to worry about those bastards much longer. He leaned over and kissed her forehead. "I swear."

Her blue eyes shimmered in the dim light. "You lied to me."

He stretched out beside her and pulled her into his arms, resting his cheek against the top of her head, breathing in the fresh floral scent of her hair. He had hurt her so badly, and she hadn't deserved it. His heart beat painfully as he looked at himself from her perspective. "Please believe me. I've hated this deception. I never wanted to lie to you."

"Tell me the truth now."

Seth controlled his breathing with an effort. He used sheer willpower to keep his heartbeat steady. Tell her the truth about his real mission? About Confidential? He couldn't do that. It would put her in even more danger. But God knew he didn't want to lie to her any more.

"I grew up in New Orleans. In the Ninth Ward in a tiny shotgun house. There was never enough money. My three younger sisters got the only other bedroom, so I slept on the screened porch, right under my parents' bedroom window. I heard everything. It didn't take long to figure out why they always fought. My father serviced more than just the wealthy wives' gardens." He squeezed his eyes shut against the memories. "After he abandoned us, I dropped out of school and went to work. Then my mom got sick and died, and it was up to me to take care of my sisters."

Adrienne splayed her hand over the muscles of his chest, and turned her head up to kiss the underside of his chin.

"So I did what I had to do. I joined the army. Planned to make a career out of it. Did real well until—" He stopped. He was close to telling too much.

"I've been a lot of places, seen a lot of things. But I've never seen anything like you." His voice almost broke.

He never would again, either. This petite, lovely young woman had come very close to doing the one thing he'd sworn no woman would ever do.

He'd vowed when his father left that no woman would ever have that kind of hold on him. He'd sworn when his mother died that he'd never spend his life pin-ing for anyone he couldn't have. But he hadn't known his princess then.

"So that knee injury? It wasn't a motorcycle accident in some exotic locale?"

He shook his head.

"You were wounded in action."

"Hey, princess. It's no big deal."

"Seth, I'm sorry about your father and your mother. About your knee." She hesitated. "Your sisters live here, too?"

He nodded and lifted her chin with a gentle nudge of his finger. He'd said all he could say. He needed to stop her before her questions spilled over into areas he wasn't willing to talk about.

He kissed her, softly at first, giving her a chance to stop him if she wanted to. He prayed she wouldn't want to.

Adrienne closed her eyes as Seth's firm gentle lips nibbled at hers. She wanted to resist. She tried. She had many more questions, like why he'd shown up at her house that day, why he'd been so determined to cut a deal with Jerome. But his kisses took her breath away.

"I've missed you these past few days," he whispered.

Adrienne looked up at him, this man to whom she'd given her trust. His face couldn't lie.

He wrapped his arms around her and cradled her head against his chest. She slid her fingers across his chest, skimming them teasingly over his nipples.

He drew in a swift breath and she felt his desire stir, grow, against her.

"I've missed you, too. Can you stay?" She closed her eyes, and pressed her nose against the soft cotton of his shirt. "Please? I haven't been able to sleep. I need you to stay."

"I'll be right here as long as you need me," he murmured against her lips. *If only he could promise her that wasn't a lie.*

SOMEWHERE CHIMES WERE ringing. Adrienne hoped the melody was part of her dream. Seth's lovemaking had transported her, just like always. In his arms she was the person she wanted to be. She felt free, strong, brave enough to stand against any foe. She felt like a superhero. With Seth by her side there was nothing she couldn't do.

But that was just a dream, and the persistent ringing was pulling her back to reality. She resisted, not wanting to open her eyes and face a world where she was a pawn in a game she didn't even understand. Where no matter what she did, someone would be hurt. Despite Seth's midnight promises, she knew he couldn't keep her safe. His own life was in danger. And now that she'd told him about Jerome's plans, her life and the life of her mother were forfeit, too.

She had to escape—soon. And she had to do it alone.

Fully awake now, with familiar apprehension burning in her stomach, she opened her eyes. Behind the annoying ringing, she heard water running. Seth was in the shower.

Sighing and pushing her hair out of her face, she crawled across the bed. It must be his cell phone. He kept it with him all the time, even in bed.

His pants were draped across a chair. She dug the phone out of his pocket, but it was too late. It had stopped ringing. When she looked at it, a message was displayed from someone named Jones.

Congratulations. Seduction of wealthy widow a success. Bug yielded mucho intel. Call in.

She stared at the display, disbelief and deep pain twisting in her gut, making her nauseous.

Grabbing her robe, she leaped out of bed and ran for the door, just as Seth emerged from the shower, a towel draped precariously around his lean hips.

"Hey, princess. What's your hurry?"

She slammed the bedroom door and flew down the stairs. In the kitchen, she put her hands over her mouth, trying to calm her panicked breathing and the nausea that threatened to overtake her. She grabbed a bottle of water from the refrigerator and took a couple of swallows.

Seduction was a success.

The cold words echoed around her. How could she have been so stupid as to believe Seth's sad little story from last night?

He was working for someone else. Maybe Jones. It made so much sense. But why? She swayed, and held on to the granite counter to steady herself. After another swallow of water, she held the bottle to her temple. The coolness helped.

Seth showed up almost immediately, his pants on and partially buttoned, his polo shirt bunched in one fist. "Adrienne, I'm sorry. You shouldn't have seen that message."

"No kidding," she choked.

"I can explain."

Her vision was misty with tears, making him looked haloed with light. His skin shimmered gold in the morning sun, droplets of water shining like diamonds on his chest and in his damp hair. A shadow of stubble darkened his cheeks and chin. He was so handsome that her throat constricted from the sheer beauty of him.

Adrienne straightened, refusing to give in to his plea. "Explain? Explain what? You've told me nothing but lies. You're obviously working for someone. Is it Jones?"

Seth saw fear and the pain of betrayal in her dark blue eyes. "Adrienne, you have to trust me."

Her head jerked. "Trust you? What could you possibly say now that would make me think I can trust you?"

Seth reached out, but she backed away. "You know me better than anyone ever has. You know I'd die before I'd allow anyone to hurt you."

"And yet you 'seduced the wealthy widow' for *someone's* benefit."

Seth winced at the sad censure in her sparkling blue eyes. God, he wished he could tell her the whole truth. He could prove to her that he was trustworthy if he could tell her how hard he was working to extricate her from the Cajun mob. But all he could do was make promises he prayed he could keep.

He watched her draw strength and determination from inside herself.

"Do you know what that tells me? It tells me I don't know you at all," she said quietly.

Her words were like daggers to his heart. "Yes, you do. You know the deepest parts of me. Just like I know you."

She shook her head desperately, but Seth knew he was right. "We have something. Something precious. There are things I can't tell you. But I swear on my life, I'll protect you."

He would never shirk his assignment, but he would give his life to protect her if it came to that.

"Was anything you told me last night true?" She clutched the bottle of water against her breast.

"It was all true. You know everything about me that matters. You know that I can't look at you without nearly losing control. You know that I could spend an eternity just kissing you. You know what all that beautiful blond hair does to me."

"That's just sex."

"Is it?" He reached out again, this time brushing her cheek with his fingers. "Is that all it is to you?"

Her eyes filled with tears. "I trusted you."

He touched the corner of her eye and she blinked. A little tear slipped down her cheek.

"You weren't wrong, princess. I swear. You can trust me."

"Prove it."

He watched her carefully as he lifted her hand and pressed a kiss into her palm. "Just tell me how," he murmured.

Adrienne tasted bitterness in the back of her throat. He still thought he could seduce her into believing him.

"Tell me who you're working for."

A look of caution shadowed his face as he dropped his gaze.

"You can't—or won't."

He lifted his head. "Knowing who I'm working for would make you vulnerable."

"Vulnerable?" She laughed shakily. "How could I be any more vulnerable? They can get to my mother. They've proven that." She shook her head in helpless wonder. "They know I'll do anything to keep her safe." She stopped. *Anything.*

She straightened. "Now if you could help me move my mother to a guaranteed safe place, where no one can touch her, then I might believe you."

Seth's eyebrows raised and a look crossed his face that Adrienne hadn't seen before. It was a combination of understanding, fury, and steely control, with a dash of irony. After a few seconds, he nodded.

"I can get your mother to safety, but you've got to

promise me something, too. You have to do exactly what I tell you to do."

Adrienne propped her fists on her hips. "Is this the part where I'm supposed to trust you?"

He nodded. "This is exactly the part where you're supposed to trust me. I'm going to make sure you never have to be afraid again."

"How can you promise that?"

"I can't tell you that—yet. I can tell you this much. I'm not in bed with the mob, no matter how it looks. I'm on the other side. I'm one of the good guys." He bent to kiss her but she held up her hand.

"Don't," she said. "Please don't touch me. You don't have to seduce me again. We have a deal."

Seth cursed under his breath. "Princess, there are things you don't understand. But right now, we can't give any indication that our relationship has changed. I promise I won't touch you in private if that's what you want, but we have to act like lovers in public."

"Act like lovers." Her back stiffened. She lifted her head, a brave sad smile on her face that ripped Seth's heart into shreds. "Sure. If you can do it, so can I."

Seth told her he'd get her the specific information about moving her mother and warned her not to mention anything to anyone, not even the director of the nursing home, until he called her back.

Adrienne watched him leave, pushing his fingers through his hair as if he were trying to control his thoughts as much as smooth his sleep-tousled hair. Anguish tore her apart as he disappeared from sight.

She looked at the digital display of the stove's clock. It was getting late. She'd have to hurry if she hoped to get to the nursing home in time for her appointment with Sister Ignatius. She'd made the appointment to appeal to the sister to allow her mother to stay.

Seth's reassurances had done little to assuage her concern. Tony's words still ate at her. *As long as Seth continues to "deal" with us in this particular way, you can assure the nuns at that nursing home that your mother will not have any more unwelcome visitors.*

It was a double threat, warning her that her mother's safety depended on Seth's loyalty to his new business partners.

Now she was stuck in the middle, with the Cajun mob on one side, threatening her as they had since her husband had died. On the other side was Seth and whoever he was working for, promising her she could trust him with her mother's life, and her own. She didn't dare trust either side.

The only thing she was certain of was that she could not continue to live like this. One way or another, she would break free of the Cajun mob.

THE MORNING SUN was high enough to creep into the alleys and intensify the smell of the garbage. Lily Harrison knew she was courting danger by grabbing a few more minutes of sleep, but she was so tired, and sleeping helped her forget how hungry and lonely and scared she was.

A shadow blocked the sun. She looked up with a start. A man loomed over her. She'd been dreaming about her dad, dreaming he'd called in the entire CIA to save her. At first she thought the shadowed figure was him.

"Daddy?" she croaked, but the man stepped forward, into the light. It wasn't her dad.

Damn. She scrambled up, ignoring the cramps in her empty stomach.

"Get away from me." She sidled away from the menacing figure, preparing to run toward the other end of the alley.

"It's okay, kid. I'm a cop. Why don't you come with me back to the station and we'll call your parents."

His words made her eyes fill with tears. There was nothing Lily wanted more than to see her dad. But she'd made so many mistakes lately. She had to be careful.

"I—I need to see your badge please."

The man laughed. "My badge? I heard you were a handful."

"What? You *heard?* Who are you?" Lily backed away as the man's smile turned into a threatening scowl. She turned and ran into a human wall.

She looked up into a dark menacing face with gleaming white teeth. They'd found her.

Lily screamed.

Chapter Eight

"What the hell were you doing, sending a text message like that?" Seth turned on the shorter man as soon as the door swung closed on the secret offices of New Orleans Confidential.

"Whoa, Seth. Hold on a minute. What's the big problem?"

"Anyone could have seen that message."

Jones stared at Seth. "On *your* phone? The one that stays in your pocket twenty-four hours a day?" He stopped and then laughed. "Your hot little widow got hold of your phone, didn't she? I guess your phone wasn't in your pants. Or you weren't."

Seth clenched his fists. "That's none of your damn business. You almost blew my cover. Now she knows I lied to her."

Jones rolled his eyes. "Oh man, you got it bad. Well, get this. What goes around comes around. You'd better come down off that cloud and get it through your head that she's up to her pretty little neck in the drug dealing and prostitution. Why else would she still be so chummy with them?"

Seth took a long, calming breath. He was wasting time and energy. Jones had made up his mind a long time ago about Adrienne. Plus, Conrad Burke would be here any second. Seth didn't want Burke seeing two of his Confidential agents arguing.

"You said it yourself, Jones, when you were talking about the prostitute. If Adrienne were to act any differently, they'd kill her."

Jones's eyes widened. "You really believe she's totally innocent, don't you? Well, you're a majority of one, my friend."

"One's enough. I'm right."

The door on the opposite side of the room slid open and Conrad Burke and Tanner Harrison came in. Harrison looked even worse than he had two days ago.

"Did Jones fill you in, Seth?" Burke asked as he sat down at the conference table.

As the others sat, Seth glanced at Jones, who sent him an exasperated look. Seth had laid into Jones before the ex-P.I. had managed to say a word. "Not completely. We got interrupted."

Burke clasped his hands in front of him on the table. "Okay. The bug you planted in his study gives us a good basis on which to build a case for the mob being the suppliers of Category Five. In another conversation, Senegal says something that is garbled, but sounds like 'Gonzalez,' which is the name of the local leader of a band of South American insurgents who are trying to overtake the democratic government of Nilia. We'll be following up on that."

Burke nodded at Seth. "Also, good job on arranging that delivery deal with Senegal. At this very moment, McMullin is picking up a shipment of coffee beans for delivery to the Cajun Perk warehouse. That truck will make a brief detour to our lab here. With any luck, our on-site chemists can isolate the raw drug within a few minutes and have the truck on its way. Then we'll have proof that the drug is being brought into the country concealed in the bags of coffee."

"What if the chemists can't isolate the drug in that short a time?" Jones asked.

"Then we'll work out a plan to substitute a bag of coffee, or 'misplace' one, to give them time. Once we can figure out how it's imported and what the refining process is, we'll have enough information to begin to search out where the mob's refinery is."

Seth listened to Burke explain the specifics and felt satisfaction warring with apprehension in his gut. Everything was coming together. At this rate, it wouldn't be long before Confidential could call in the police and shut down the drug ring. And he was proud to be a part of that. He was grateful to Burke for giving him a second chance to do some good.

It would make everything so much easier if he could believe Adrienne was involved with the drugs. But he knew she wasn't like that. The deal she'd made with him this morning to protect her mother proved that.

She was innocent and good and brave. The mob had a hold over Adrienne—her mother. And she was protecting her mother the only way she could. Her only sin was bad judgment in men. He grimaced. Including him.

"Seth?"

Burke's whiskey-smooth voice pulled Seth out of his thoughts.

"Yes, sir. Sorry, sir."

"You need to hear this. Our prostitute has managed to slip one of our agents a special sleeve containing three packets of refined Category Five. That confirms Cajun Perk as the drug distribution center. Now we can connect Cajun Perk to Jerome Senegal and the mob." Burke shot Seth a warning look. "Through Adrienne DeBlanc. She's the sole owner of Cajun Perk."

"Right. She owns the coffeehouses." Seth took a deep breath. "But she has nothing to do with the drugs. She told me herself that she was advised to invest in Cajun Perk. My guess is Senegal arranged it or used threats to force her to do it." Seth clenched his fists. "The mob is using her as a scapegoat."

Seth's words hung in the air.

Jones coughed quietly.

"If that's what they're doing, it's working." Burke's voice was still smooth, but Seth heard the underlying censure and knew it was directed at him. He took a deep breath and focused on his job, like he'd been taught during his Special Forces training.

"Yes, sir," he said crisply.

Burke held his gaze for a beat, then nodded slightly. "Now, although we don't yet have the location of the drug lab, we can't afford to continue to let the refined drug stay on the streets. It's killing people. You probably read in the paper this morning of the unexpected death of the chairman of the board of the Hartfield Corporation."

"He died from Category Five?" Jones asked, his eyes wide as quarters. "The newspaper said it was heart failure. My wife is a friend of his daughter. They went to high school together."

"The result was heart failure. But it was caused by the drug. So we're gearing up, Tanner." Burke nodded at his companion.

Harrison's hot gaze took in the men around the table. "Surveillance has borne out that all Cajun Perk locations are frequented by young prostitutes." Harrison's voice was hoarse with determination, as if this was a personal mission. "This backs up the statement from our informant that she can go into any Cajun Perk and obtain a drug-filled sleeve. We can't afford to wait any longer. We're planning a simultaneous raid on all Cajun Perks."

Harrison's words ripped through Seth like a knife through rotten cloth.

A raid. A raid that would result in his princess being arrested, possibly even indicted. The vision of Adrienne's blue eyes condemning him rose before Seth's inner vision. The idea that rough hands would handcuff her and force her into a police car and then into a jail cell burned in his gut like acid.

He forced himself to clear his head. His job was to bring down the drug ring. He couldn't afford to let personal feelings get in the way.

But personal feelings were one thing; a promise was another. He'd promised to protect her mother. He'd prove to Adrienne that at least in that sense he could be trusted.

Harrison continued. "I will organize and coordinate the simultaneous raids."

"He's the expert, from his days with the CIA," Burke added. "Jones, you'll be teamed with Mason Bartley, and you and the other teams will remain in constant contact with each other and with Tanner. Tanner will be working from here, so he can keep an eye on all the operations at once through the monitors and the radio equipment. You take your orders from him on this. Seth, because you're known to Senegal, you won't be involved in the raids." Burke sat up. "One last thing. Tanner's daughter, Lily Harrison, is missing. She's seventeen, blond hair, blue eyes, five feet three inches. We have evidence that she was in the bordello."

"Conrad." When Harrison spoke, Seth glanced at him. His lips were compressed tightly and white at the corners. His eyes looked haunted. "My daughter is not Confidential's primary concern, but I'd appreciate a heads- up if anyone sees a teenager who fits her description."

Seth studied the ex-CIA agent. So that's what his problem was. He was worried about his child. Seth knew he'd be out of his mind if one of his sisters was out on the streets.

Harrison met Seth's gaze. "And if anyone is worried that I won't be concentrating one hundred percent on this job, they should say so now."

Seth didn't blink. "No worries here, sir."

"No problem," Jones added.

Burke stood. "That's everything for now. We'll be in contact several times a day. Stay alert. The raids could go down at any moment."

Seth and the other men stood, preparing to leave.

"Seth, could you hang around a minute?"

"Yes, sir," Seth said. Was he about to be fired? He stood stiffly. He'd almost screwed up his life when he'd come back from overseas, bitter about losing his career in Special Forces. Confidential and Conrad Burke had given him a second chance. Had he screwed this up, too?

Jones sent him a nod as he closed the door on his way out. Seth didn't feel reassured.

He lifted his chin as he waited for Burke to speak. His feelings for Adrienne DeBlanc had nothing to do with his ability to do his job.

"Seth, I need to know if you're okay with this."

He swallowed. "Yes, sir," he snapped.

"Now listen, son. You're not in the army anymore, and I'm not a drill sergeant. I'm your boss, but I'm also a married man, with two babies. I can see what's happening between you and Mrs. DeBlanc. I need to know from you, how serious is it?"

Seth hesitated, and knew immediately from the look in Burke's eyes that Burke had his answer.

Seth opened his mouth to deny that his feelings for Adrienne were serious, but he couldn't bring himself to say it.

"Sir, my personal feelings don't enter into this." That was the best he could do.

"That's bull, son. Of course they do. You're human. If you care about someone, personal feelings always enter in. Now if you don't mind, stop standing there at attention. I'm going to sit down."

Seth relaxed. When Burke nodded toward a chair, Seth sat down gratefully.

"You were twelve when your father deserted your family, right?"

Seth stared at Burke in surprise. When Burke had hired him, there had been very little talk about Seth's personal life. Burke had seemed totally focused on Seth's military background and his experience with weapons and explosives.

"That's right."

"So you became the man of the family. You took care of your mother and your sisters."

Seth didn't respond.

"Then after your mother died, you looked at your options, and joined the army to assure yourself of a good, steady job. You put your sisters through school."

"Sir, I fail to see how—"

"Son, you're one of the most determined and focused men I've ever met. I can see why you went into Special Forces, and why they chose you. Tactical warfare, munitions and explosives—those jobs take a special type of soldier, one who can follow orders *and* think for himself. You have those qualities. When you go after something, you go after it with every fiber of your being."

Seth thought about Burke's words. "I guess you could say that. I try to do what's right."

Burke nodded. "And that's why I hired you. I'm depending on you. You've shown me what you're made of. You've carried out every part of your assignment, going far beyond what I had expected. You believe Adrienne DeBlanc is innocent."

Burke's statement demanded the truth, and Seth gave it to him. "Yes, sir. I do."

"Then I believe she is, too. Have you been able to verify the extent of Tony Arsenault's involvement?"

Making a fist, Seth pounded it once, twice, on the chair arm. "No, sir. The most I've been able to get from Adrienne is an admission that he does some work for Senegal. I'll get him, though."

"What about Mrs. DeBlanc? Will she testify against Senegal and Arsenault?"

Seth sat there as images of Adrienne flashed through his brain. Her wince of pain as Tony squeezed her arm hard enough to leave bruises on her creamy skin. Her caution when he first met her. Her frightened eyes and the determined lift to her chin as she cut a deal with him to protect her mother, even though she still wasn't one hundred percent sure she could trust him.

"Sir, the mob is threatening her with her mother's safety as well as her own. Her mother has had a stroke and is in a nursing home. If she could be free of the threat to her mother—"

"What's your plan?"

Seth swallowed. "She's desperate to protect her mother. She'll do what I say. When I give her the word, she'll notify the nursing home that an ambulance will be arriving to have her mother moved. Mrs. Caldwell is paralyzed from a stroke, but she's not on life support. I'd need two Confidential agents and an ambulance to move her, and guards twenty-four/seven wherever we put her."

Burke's brows went up. "You don't ask for much, do you?"

Seth paused before answering. He had nothing to lose, and Confidential had everything to gain.

"Sir, if we can assure her that her mother is safe, I believe she'll testify to everything she knows."

Burke nodded and picked up his cell phone. He spoke briefly, outlining the plan Seth had just given him. "Is there a safe house available? Right. Twenty-four-hour nursing care, physician on call." He looked at Seth. "Which nursing home?"

"St. Cecilia's."

"When can you arrange for permission to move her?"

"Anytime. All I have to do is call Adrienne."

Burke gave final instructions to the person on the other end of the phone, then hung up.

"Call her now."

Seth pulled out his cell phone. When Adrienne answered she sounded distracted.

"Can you talk?" he asked.

"Yes. I was just on my way out to visit my mother."

"Good. Notify the nursing home that she's being moved."

"Oh my God. When?"

"When?" Seth raised his brows at Burke.

"An hour."

"Right now. You stay there. I'll pick you up in fifteen minutes."

"Oh, Seth." Adrienne's voice sounded quivery. "Where? Where are you taking her?"

Seth glanced at Burke. "I can't tell you, princess. You have to trust me."

"I have to know! Please Seth. I can't let her out of my sight."

"I promise I'll take you to see your mother as soon as it's safe. This is what you asked me to do," he said gruffly. "Now you have to trust me to do it."

She hesitated and he knew what was going through her mind. Was he really one of the good guys?

"Adrienne?"

"Okay—" she choked.

"I'll be right there."

With a frown, Seth turned off his cell phone. It seemed he was destined to make Adrienne unhappy. He stood, suppressing an urge to salute Burke. "Thank you, sir."

Burke leaned back in his chair. "How long is it going to take before Senegal figures out who you really are?"

Burke's words left Seth speechless. He swallowed. "Sir?"

Burke shot him an ironic look. "Don't be coy, Lewis. It doesn't go with your military background."

Seth realized he was standing at attention, but he couldn't relax. "Yes, sir. I apologize, sir. I wasn't trying to keep anything from you. But until I saw Senegal's house, I had no idea—"

Burke held up a hand. "That it was Senegal's wife your father ran off with? Of course you didn't. But I did. Do you think I'd hire you without a thorough background check?"

"Then why did you send me in there? He might have recognized me. Might still. It could compromise the investigation."

"We never intended to hide our activities from Senegal. Just our identity. He's a smart man, but an arrogant one. Right now, his concentration is divided. He's working hard to keep a handle on both his drug trade and his prostitution ring. He knows someone is behind the bordello raid and several other minor hitches in his plans. We're goading him, keeping him off balance. And if he happens to be distracted by your name and takes the trouble to start thoroughly investigating your background, that will work in our favor."

"So Adrienne isn't the only scapegoat." Seth wasn't being ironic, just factual.

"I have absolutely no doubt you can handle yourself against Senegal, if it comes to that. We've been trying to decide the best time to raid the coffeehouses. I'd rather wait until we have proof of where the mob is getting the drugs, but right now the D.A. is getting jumpy. Wealthy prominent citizens are being victimized. He wants the operation shut down before anyone else dies. And so do I. You've heard me talk about Wiley Longbottom. He's a very good friend of mine, and he almost died because of that drug. I want it off the streets, now."

Seth nodded. He'd signed on to play his part. "If Senegal asks again, should I admit I'm Robert Lewis's son?"

Burke stood and came around his desk to stand in front of Seth. "I'd let him go on worrying. If he asks point-blank, don't lie. Just be prepared." He gave Seth a measuring look.

"I don't suppose it will be a surprise to you that your father is dead?"

Seth jerked. He'd always suspected it, but now he realized he'd never given up hope. "Senegal?"

"Nothing was ever proven. Robert Lewis and Senegal's first wife died in a single-car accident. Her car ran off one of the bridges on Lake Pontchartrain. They drowned. The names were never released to the press."

His mother must have known. Even if the names weren't released, the police would have contacted her. She'd never said a word. Seth compressed his lips together, pushing away unwanted sadness and the old familiar ache of abandonment. He thought about his younger sisters. They were probably better off not knowing, at least for now. "Thank you, sir," he said.

"Seth. About Adrienne DeBlanc. You know she has to be picked up, don't you?"

Seth closed his eyes, imagining her being led away in handcuffs, her chin high, her small form stiff and proud. "Yes, sir."

"I'd like to put her into protective custody, but that would raise red flags with Senegal. She'll have to be arraigned and indicted. As sole owner of Cajun Perk, she's right in the middle of this mess."

"Will she be able to post bond?"

Burke shook his head. "I seriously doubt it. That depends on whether her judge is in Senegal's pocket. He'll do his best to get to her. We'll do our best to protect her."

"Sir, I can protect her."

"You have other responsibilities. Stay focused, son."

"Yes, sir." Seth paused. "Will you have a lawyer for her? I don't want her to have to depend on one of Senegal's people."

"There will be an attorney waiting for her. His name is Brad Guilford. He's a Confidential agent. He'll make sure she's traumatized as little as possible."

"I need to be able to see her, sir."

Burke nodded. "I'll have Guilford arrange it. But Seth, it could be dangerous for her and for us if you mention Confidential."

"Don't worry. I won't say anything that will put Confidential in jeopardy."

As Seth turned to leave, Burke's hand squeezed his shoulder briefly. The gesture sent a fleeting memory skittering through Seth's brain. His father, back before Seth had known about the other women, clapping him on the shoulder when he brought home a good report card or won a ball game.

Coming from Burke, the simple touch meant as much to Seth as his Purple Heart or his Silver Star. His throat tightened with emotion, and he couldn't meet Burke's gaze.

"It'll work out, son. You're a good man."

Seth nodded. He was afraid to speak, afraid all the emotion churning inside of him would come rushing out if he opened his mouth.

Grief for the father he'd lost so many years ago, shame that he'd not come clean with Conrad Burke and, most of all, concern about Adrienne. He'd lied to her. He'd promised her he would protect her. He couldn't.

But he'd make sure her mother was safe, if it was the last thing he ever did.

Chapter Nine

Seth picked up Adrienne, and took careful precautions to ensure they weren't being followed. They arrived just ahead of the ambulance. Adrienne got out of the car and rushed inside.

Seth was slower. He carefully surveyed the grounds of St. Cecilia's for anything unusual. The grounds looked serene and peaceful, the iron gates lending an air of elegance as well as security. He saw why Adrienne had felt her mother would be safe here.

His heart ached with compassion for her. She'd done everything she could to protect her mother from the powerful Cajun mob.

The banked coals of his fury at what Arsenault and Senegal had done and were doing to her threatened to catch and burst into flame. She deserved to be safe, to know her mother was safe.

As the ambulance pulled in, Seth saw Alex McMullin at the wheel, he acknowledged him with a look, but kept his distance. For anyone who might be watching, Seth was here with Adrienne, not associated with those involved in transporting her mother to another facility.

Seth followed Adrienne inside as the EMTs opened the back of the ambulance and unloaded a gurney.

Adrienne was nowhere in sight. Just as Seth was

telling the receptionist to check with Sister Ignatius to verify that he had permission to see Kathryn Caldwell, he heard Adrienne's voice. She and a tiny, thin-lipped nun came down the hall.

"Seth. This is Sister Ignatius, the director of St. Cecilia's. Sister, this is Seth Lewis."

Seth turned to the lady and sketched a small bow. "Sister. I believe Mr. Burke let you know we were on our way."

The nun nodded. "Mr. Lewis. It is highly unorthodox to move a resident without first conferring with administration at her destination, and confirming transfer."

Seth nodded his head in agreement. "I deeply apologize for the irregular nature of this transfer, Sister. But I trust you were satisfied with the veracity of the request?"

The nun's eyes lit with a trace of amusement. "The chief of police and a member of the governor's staff called, yes."

Seth felt Adrienne's surprise. "The chief of—"

He touched the small of her back. "We'd better get going, Adrienne."

She recovered and held out her hand to the tiny woman. "Sister, I cannot thank you enough for the wonderful care your staff has given to my mother. I never meant to disrupt your facility."

"My dear, your primary concern is for your mother. I understand that."

The two EMTs passed them with Mrs. Caldwell on a gurney. Adrienne stopped them with a gesture. "One moment, please." She bent until her mouth was near her mother's. "Mother, these people are going to take you to a place where you'll be safe. I'll see you soon, okay?"

A tear fell from Adrienne's eye. Seth watched it

make a small wet circle on the sheet covering Mrs. Caldwell.

"Come on, princess," he said softly. "We can't linger."

She smoothed her mother's hair, then stepped back and allowed the EMTs to roll Mrs. Caldwell out the door and into the waiting ambulance.

Seth put his arm around Adrienne as the ambulance doors closed. Her entire body was quaking with a fine tremor.

"The chief of police and the governor's staff?" she whispered.

He nodded.

"So are you with the police?"

He tightened his embrace reassuringly. "Remember what I said? I'm one of the good guys. I thought you were going to trust me."

"I'm trusting you with the life of my mother. Are you certain this is the best thing?"

"She'll be in a safe house. No one can get to her."

Adrienne pulled away. "I hope you're right." Her liquid blue eyes questioned him. "Why can't I know where they're taking her? How can you know Tony won't find her?"

"He won't." Seth heard the steel that rang in his voice, and so did Adrienne, because she glanced up at him, frowning.

"Be careful, Seth. You don't know what Tony is capable of."

Seth looked at the long-sleeved silk blouse Adrienne wore to hide the healing bruises from Arsenault's hands. Cold determination settled on him. "I know what *I'm* capable of."

Adrienne shivered.

Seth pulled her closer and kissed the top of her head.

"Don't worry. You and your mother are in the hands of professionals."

He hoped she couldn't hear the doubt that he tried to keep out of his voice. He wanted to tell her about the raids, warn her that she would be arrested. But he'd given Burke his word.

Besides, no one knew when the raids would go down, and he couldn't take the chance that Arsenault or another of Senegal's goons might force her to talk. Too many lives were at stake.

"Come on, princess, let's go."

Adrienne's attention was on the ambulance that was disappearing down the winding drive. "How long do I have to wait before I can see her?"

Seth put his hands on her shoulders. "Listen to me. If I had my way, you'd be going with your mother and you'd stay hidden away with her until all this is over."

"All what?"

"I can't tell you that. You need to be on guard, ready for anything. You need to be brave."

Her blue eyes turned wary and she retreated. He felt the tightening of her muscles, saw the infinitesimal withdrawal in her expression. He squeezed her shoulders reassuringly, wishing he could explain everything.

How long would she be able to sustain her faith in him if he refused to tell her the truth? He hoped her trust wouldn't falter.

He knew Burke was right. Adrienne was too vulnerable. She could be broken.

"Why won't you at least tell me who you're working for?"

He looked at her steadily, openly, hoping she would understand the gravity of his words. "Because if you don't know, then no one can make you tell."

FIVE DAYS LATER, Tanner Harrison pulled off the simultaneous raids on the seven Cajun Perk coffeehouse franchises in the metropolitan New Orleans area without a hitch.

Burke and Harrison coordinated the raids through Police Chief Henri Courville, so the police had uniformed officers, CSI and detectives available at each coffeehouse. The raids were designed to do several things— expose the coffeehouses, thereby destroying their usefulness as distribution points for the drug, haul in their employees for questioning, gather any evidence that might hold a clue to the location of the refining lab and, most importantly, round up the on-hand supply of the drug and get it off the streets before more innocent people died.

Seth stayed at headquarters with Tanner Harrison. It chafed him that he couldn't participate in the raids, but Burke was right. He couldn't afford to be recognized.

Harrison definitely had the raids coordinated. The briefing room's plasma monitors were connected to cameras on Crescent City Transports delivery trucks parked across the street from each Cajun Perk coffeehouse.

The trucks were put into place at 6 a.m. Seth was assigned to watch the monitors, and that's what he'd been doing for the past four and a half hours. The prostitute had told them most of the drug exchanges took place in the late morning, right before the busy lunchtime.

He stretched and groaned, and glanced over at Harrison, who had been talking into a headset to the agents in the trucks, checking and rechecking their instructions. His gray eyes darted back and forth, from one monitor to the next.

Seth looked at his watch. Almost time. "Sir, I just

want to say I'm sorry about your daughter. I haven't seen anyone this morning that fits her description. But I'll be glad to help in any way I can."

Harrison shot him a glance and a quick nod as he checked his own watch and repositioned his headset. "Lewis, you've got an open line to Chief Courville, to call for extra backup if needed."

"Yes, sir."

Harrison spoke into the microphone of his headset. "Okay, people, we're on countdown. Pick up everybody then get out of the way, so the police and CSI can do their jobs. We'll sort out the innocents later."

DISTRICT ATTORNEY SEBASTION PRIMEAUX learned of the raids from the chief of police in plenty of time to warn Senegal, but he chose not to. Instead, he scheduled an appearance at a discount store opening in his wife's hometown in south central Louisiana. He didn't want to be anywhere near New Orleans when the raids went down.

As he sat in the back of his limousine drinking whiskey and looking out over the bayou country where he'd grown up, he thought about the cardboard sleeve hidden in Adrienne DeBlanc's wedding album. His careful planning and instinct for survival was about to pay off. The evidence was sure to surface when Mrs. DeBlanc was arrested, especially since he'd arranged for an anonymous tip that the police might find drugs in Adrienne De-Blanc's house. Because of him, her indictment was assured.

Senegal would be pleased, and Primeaux would never have to worry about those pictures with the underage prostitutes. Primeaux wiped his forehead with a handkerchief. It was too bad he wouldn't be able to hit

Senegal up for another hefty campaign contribution. But it would be detrimental to his career to associate with Senegal now.

ADRIENNE FELT lost. Her mother was safe, according to Seth, but Adrienne hated the uncertainty of not knowing where she was. It heightened her feeling of helplessness.

At least when she'd been working on her secret plan, saving and hiding money away so she and her mother could disappear, she'd felt as if she were working toward a goal.

She hated being at the mercy of other people. First her father, then the mob and now Seth, and whoever he was working for. There was nothing she could do but wait.

She hefted the suitcase full of cash out of the closet and dragged it over to the marble-topped chest. Releasing the lever, she opened the secret bottom drawer and knelt to transfer the cash back into hiding.

She hadn't missed the warning in Seth's words at St. Cecilia's. He was working for someone, possibly the police, who was trying to take down the Cajun mob. Her entire body began to quiver at the thought. She hoped they could, but her experience with her husband and Tony and Jerome told her that some powerful and influential people in New Orleans were in the mob's pocket.

She hoped Seth and his mysterious avengers knew what they were doing.

As soon as all this was over, she would take her mother and get as far away as she could. Some place where Jerome and Tony couldn't find her. Maybe whomever Seth was working for could help.

As she placed the last stack of bills into the drawer,

a familiar knock sounded on her front door. *Seth.* She could see his silhouette outlined through the beveled glass. A tension she'd barely noticed dissolved from her shoulders and neck. Maybe he was here to take her to see her mother. Rising, she pushed the drawer closed with her foot and went to the door.

As soon as she turned the lock, Seth slipped inside and closed the door behind him. He looked cool and handsome in a casual blue jacket cut perfectly for his athletic body, tailored tan pants and a white shirt.

Adrienne couldn't help the flutter of her heart or the stirrings deep inside her. Just his presence made her feel hopeful, even though a frown marred his even features.

"Seth? Is everything okay? It's not Mother, is it?"

He shook his head and placed a hand on her shoulder. "Adrienne, we don't have much time. You've got to listen carefully."

A police siren sounded in the distance. Seth lifted his head and listened for a second. His expression turned hard.

Trepidation spread through Adrienne. He was on guard, almost predatory, as if he expected an ambush from behind. His fingers were curled, his body perfectly balanced. This was a different side of him, the military side. She'd never seen it before.

"There are raids going on all over the city."

"Raids?"

He held up a hand to quiet her and his fingers tightened on her arm. "Remember I said you were going to have to be brave? The police are going to arrest you. Be cooperative, but don't answer any questions until I get you a lawyer."

Alarm reverberated through her. "Arrest? I don't understand."

He touched her cheek. "I know you don't. I wanted

to get here sooner but I couldn't. Just remember, don't talk. I'll get you a lawyer who can help you. Do not use Senegal's lawyer."

Oh God. A sliver of alarm embedded itself into Adrienne's stomach like a stiletto. Had the mob found out she'd moved her mother out of their reach? "Is Jerome doing this? Why would they arrest me?"

"They're going to accuse you of dealing in illegal drugs."

"Drugs? Me?"

A car pulled up out front and cut its engine. "I can't explain it all now. Just remember what I told you." With his hand still on her shoulder, Seth opened the front door and guided her out onto the porch.

Two uniformed officers were getting out of a patrol car just as another car pulled up behind them.

Adrienne reached for Seth's hand. She needed to feel his strength.

"Hold it right there," one of the uniforms said as a man and a woman in street clothes approached.

"What is this about—?"

"Just do what they say," Seth whispered as the woman held out a leather-clad badge.

"Please stand still, ma'am."

Adrienne's scalp tightened and her skin felt hot as adrenaline pumped through her veins. "Seth?"

"Step away from the lady, sir, and come down here."

Seth backed up two steps, his arms held out slightly from his body as he descended the steps.

Adrienne wanted to follow him.

"Don't move, ma'am." The woman tucked the tail of her blazer behind a holstered gun.

Adrienne stared at it, hardly comprehending that this woman was here to take *her* into custody.

"I'm Detective Sharon Freeman. Are you Adrienne DeBlanc?"

"Yes. What is this?"

"Ma'am, step down off the porch. Keep your hands away from your sides at all times."

She looked at Seth, who nodded fractionally. She stepped down onto the sidewalk.

"That's far enough, ma'am."

Fear knotting her stomach, Adrienne glanced at Seth, but his attention was on the detective. His gaze flickered briefly but didn't meet hers.

The policemen's faces were carefully blank, but excitement gleamed in their eyes. Seth still didn't look at her.

"Do you know who I am?" Adrienne asked the woman.

Detective Freeman shot her a grim smile. "Oh, yes, ma'am. We certainly do." Her words dripped with sarcasm.

Embarrassment heated Adrienne's face. "I didn't mean—I just think you have the wrong person."

She felt Seth's disapproval. He'd told her not to talk.

The detective gestured toward the taller of the two officers.

He stepped up to Adrienne, pulling a pair of handcuffs from his belt. "Mrs. DeBlanc, we're placing you under arrest for trafficking in illegal substances. Please turn around and put your hands behind your back."

"Trafficking?" Seth was right. How had he known?

She looked at Detective Freeman, but the woman's menacing stance and her cold green eyes offered no further explanation as the officer informed her of her right to remain silent, her right to an attorney and so on.

As the cold metal closed around her wrists, a cold dread settled around Adrienne's heart. Seth had told her he was one of the good guys. He'd gotten her mother to safety. But how had he known about the arrest?

She looked at him, standing near the detectives. Whose side was he really on?

Detective Freeman jerked her thumb toward the policeman. "Put her in the car. Then search the house."

"What are you looking for?" Adrienne's wrists were already hurting from the pressure of the cuffs. "If I knew, perhaps—"

Freeman laughed. "Perhaps you could save us the trouble of searching? That'd be nice. We're looking for drugs, Mrs. DeBlanc. Evidence linking you to a drug and prostitution ring that's been operating in the New Orleans area." She nodded at the officer. "Pat her down."

"She doesn't have a weapon." Seth's voice commanded attention, but to Adrienne, it sounded like the promise of a guardian angel. He was trying to protect her.

Tears of desperation turned to tears of relief as he finally looked at her. There was a look in his changeable eyes that she hadn't seen before. He stood like a marble statue, determined, unyielding, like a military officer. But what made her heart ache was what wasn't there. The tender look he'd always reserved for her was gone. His jaw appeared sculpted from marble. His gaze was cool, professional.

He looked away as the officer ran his hands over her body, and she thought she saw a shadow cloud his eyes.

"I assume you have a warrant?" he asked the detective.

Detective Freeman rounded on him after her sharp eyes ensured that Adrienne was unarmed. "Of course. Duly signed by Judge Duvall."

Judge Duvall. Adrienne had met Arthur Duvall several times, at Jerome's house. Her heart sank to her toes. She had been set up. She shot a desperate glance at Seth, but his expression was guarded. He turned his attention back to Detective Freeman.

The officer took Adrienne's arm and guided her toward the police car. His grip caused her wrist to pull against the sharp metal of the cuffs but she bit her lip, determined not to complain or even wince.

He opened the rear door and pushed her inside. As the door closed, fresh tears welled up and spilled from Adrienne's eyes. Through the dirty car window, she saw Seth glance toward her but she couldn't read his face. She prayed that somehow he could work a miracle and get her released.

She shifted, trying to release the pressure on her cuffed hands as the detective's words echoed in her head.

Trafficking in illegal substances. If the police had information that she was involved with drugs, then she was certain their search warrant would turn up the evidence to prove it. She knew how the Cajun mob worked.

She was going to prison.

"Seth Lewis, I presume?" the detective demanded.

Seth tore his gaze away from the unbearable sight of his princess being handcuffed and shoved into a police car. His jaw was so tight it ached. Trying to mask the fury he knew burned in his gaze, he assessed the detective.

"That's right."

"I was told you'd be here." The detective's voice was tinged with a faint disgust. She obviously wasn't happy about it. "I don't know who this company is you work for, Mr. Lewis, but I'd appreciate it if you'd let me do my job."

"No problem. I'm here to help."

Freeman looked him up and down, then glanced at the patrol car where Adrienne was being held. "Right." She adjusted her blazer back over her holster and crossed her arms. "If you don't mind, I'd like to see some ID."

Seth pulled his wallet out of his back pocket. "I'm undercover. The ID supports my undercover persona."

Freeman nodded, checked his wallet quickly, then handed it back to him.

"You got a weapon?"

"Small Sig Sauer, right ankle."

"All right. Let's go." Freeman called to her men. "Bert, stay with Mrs. DeBlanc."

One uniformed officer and the other detective preceded Seth and Detective Freeman into the house. As he stepped through the door, Seth glanced at Adrienne's pale face shining from the dark interior of the patrol car.

The three officers systematically tore her house apart. Seth folded his arms and leaned against the wall, watching. Freeman kept her eye on him. She didn't like his presence, didn't quite trust him.

He approved. She was a good cop. He wouldn't trust a private undercover agent from a mysterious organization either, if he were in her shoes.

He followed Freeman into the study, remembering Senegal and District Attorney Primeaux ducking in there for a secret meeting.

The detective donned gloves and began her search. She opened and emptied each drawer in the desk, examining certain documents closely before discarding them.

"You're good at your job," he commented.

Freeman glanced up at him and turned her back on the desk. She started pulling books out of the bookcase. "I do my best, even when I'm given orders from the top to allow a P.I. to hang around."

"I'm not a P.I. And we're on the same side."

"Hmph. You expect me to believe you're hoping we find incriminating evidence here?"

"I'm not *hoping* anything. I want the same thing you do. To get the drug off the street."

Detective Freeman turned around and put a silver box on the desk. "What have we here? Looks like the happy couple's wedding album."

Seth couldn't read the engraving on the front of the silver album, but he had no doubt that Freeman was correct.

Just as she was about to open the box, there was a shout from the living room.

"Freeman, get out here!"

Detective Freeman picked up a silver box and gestured to Seth. "After you, Mr. Lewis."

Seth preceded her out of the study.

"What is it, Sam?" she asked her fellow detective.

"I wanted you to see this before I touched it." Sam was crouched in front of the huge marble-topped chest in Adrienne's dining room.

"See what?" Freeman sat on her heels to take a look.

Seth stood a few feet back, watching. Even from his vantage point, he could see what Sam was so excited about. Apparently the base of the chest held a secret drawer. The drawer was cracked. Seth could imagine that if it were closed properly, it would appear to be just a part of the base. No one would know it was there. But it hadn't been closed. Something had stuck in a corner. It had the distinctive color and pattern of a dollar bill.

"Did you get a picture?"

Sam nodded, holding up the instant camera.

"Okay then, open it," Freeman commanded. Sam did.

Seth's heart sank as Freeman whistled and Sam whooped.

"Damn that's a lot of cash," Sam exclaimed.

"Yeah." Freeman looked at Seth.

He wiped his face of all expression.

"Do you know what Mrs. DeBlanc was planning to do with all this?"

"No."

"It looks like enough to make a quick and easy getaway."

Seth wanted to protest, but he kept his mouth shut. He was certain he knew what the cash was for. It was Adrienne's attempt to break away from the mob. She had probably been saving it for years, planning to take her mother and disappear.

It hurt his heart to think of her secreting away money little by little, hoping that one day she could afford to buy safety for herself and her mother.

Freeman frowned at him, then turned back to Sam. "Bag it, and tag the chest as evidence." She laid the silver box she carried down on the dining room table. "Now let's see the happy couple's wedding pictures."

She opened the box and flipped through the photographs, stopping with a sound of pure pleasure. "So. Our Mrs. DeBlanc hid a truckload of cash, and now look what we have here." She held up an object.

Seth's whole body tightened in shock when he recognized what Detective Freeman was holding. He wasn't surprised, but he was worried. He had to prove the mob had set up Adrienne to take the fall for their drug-trafficking operation.

Detective Freeman smiled at him. "Good work, Lewis. Looks like we've got our evidence. Hey, Sam, take a look. It's a cup sleeve from Cajun Perk. See these bulges here, and here, and back here?" She pointed.

"This sleeve contains packets of Category Five."

JEROME SENEGAL SAT in his study, worrying a Cuban cigar and waiting for Arsenault to call. He glanced at his cell phone every few seconds. Tony better not have gotten himself picked up.

A discreet knock on the heavy wooden door made him jump.

"What?"

The door opened and his personal bodyguard looked in. "Sorry, boss. Your wife wants to know if you're having dinner with them."

"No. Tell her to take the kids upstairs like I told her to, and stay there. You call Remy. See what the word is on the street."

The cell phone on his desk rang. "Go!"

Senegal snatched up the phone and peered at the caller ID. He let out a whoosh of breath and pressed the answer button.

"Tony. Where are you?"

"Metairie. They hit every Cajun Perk at the same exact moment."

"Who did? Who'd you see?" Senegal demanded.

"Police, and some plainclothes guys who looked like FBI or DEA."

"Courville's got to be behind this. Nobody knows who tipped 'em off?"

"Must have been one of those *putains* from the bordello raid," Tony scoffed. "That's all I can figure. Who do you think the plainclothes muscle is, eh? DEA?"

"No. Primeaux would have let me know."

Senegal heard Tony snort.

"Primeaux. I'd believe a *putain* before I'd believe him. Where's he at, anyhow?"

"He ran. He's lower than a gator's belly and yellow

as a gator's eye, but he'll be back. How many got picked up?" Senegal asked.

"Hard to say. I have been listening to the police scanners. I think they rounded up about thirty distributors and whores."

"The drug lab?"

"The lab, it is safe," Tony assured his boss. "Nobody even came near it."

"What about DeBlanc?"

"They arrested her at her house," Tony replied. "Her boyfriend Lewis was with her, but they left him behind. He headed back to Crescent City Transports."

"Probably arranging for a lawyer for her. Get one of ours in there. Send Favre. We can't afford to have her talking. Make sure he reminds her who she takes her orders from."

"Boss, they found something in her house. My contact says it's a cup sleeve with drugs in it. Did you plant it?"

"Hell, no!" Senegal cursed again. "You know I've never touched one of those things." He paced, chewing on the unlit cigar. How were the police managing to stay one step ahead of him? He'd never had this kind of trouble before. It had all started with that bordello raid.

"Primeaux must have done it. That slime ball D.A. He thinks he can protect himself from me. He probably did it the night of that charity thing. He stayed behind in DeBlanc's study. Well, all the better to pin the Cajun Perk operation on her."

"I surely don't like Primeaux. He's going to turn on us, *c'est vrai.*"

"I don't pay you to worry about him. I've got him right where I want him. You get Favre inside with our little Mrs. DeBlanc. She's the wild card. If she decides to start talking about what she's seen, she could ruin everything. Get Favre to let you see her. Then you can pull her chain, remind her of her mother's delicate condition."

"Maudit!" That's what I was on my way to tell you. Her mother has disappeared. I found out right before the raids went down."

"Quoi d'autre? What else is going to happen?" Jerome cursed fluently in Cajun French. "How does a paralyzed woman disappear? When did this happen?"

"A couple of days ago. The nurse's aide we planted said an ambulance rolled up to the door, Adrienne appeared with Lewis by her side and her mother was gone within ten minutes."

"Lewis. I'm sick of hearing about Lewis. He's involved with this somehow. I want him taken care of. *Non.* Wait. On second thought, bring him to me. I want to have a talk with him first. And find Adrienne De-Blanc's mother. If we can't find her, we must get to Adrienne and eliminate her."

Chapter Ten

Adrienne was photographed and fingerprinted. Her clothes were taken away, except for her underwear, and she was forced to endure the pain and humiliation of a strip search.

Then she was given an ill-fitting orange jumpsuit and placed in a holding cell with several other women. The cell was gray and dark, with a dirty, stainless steel toilet in one corner.

She asked to be allowed to call her lawyer, but no one paid any attention to her.

She sat on the edge of a grimy bunk and tried not to look the other women in the eye. The three women she was housed with were rough-looking. Two were older, with the worn tired faces of over-the-hill prostitutes. The third couldn't have been more than about eighteen. She had a ring in her nose and one in her lip, and her hair was coal-black and shaved on the sides and back. Her eyes were lined with black. She complained constantly about not being able to smoke.

Adrienne felt nauseated, probably because of the smells. The cell smelled of urine, unwashed bodies and a sour odor, like vomit. She sat with her arms crossed and her eyes closed, jumping whenever one of the women ventured toward her. She had no idea how long she'd sat there before a female officer came and got her.

When Adrienne stood, she swayed, the edges of her vision darkening. "I'm sorry. I'm not feeling well."

One of the hard-edged prisoners laughed harshly. "Didja hear that? Miss Hoity-Toity is 'not feeling well.' Well, I'm 'not feeling well,' too, guard. Can I get a beer?" She and the other older woman laughed.

Adrienne's head swam and acrid saliva filled her mouth. She reached out to steady herself. "I'm going to—"

"Oh, hell," the guard said. "Out of the way, you two." The woman grabbed Adrienne by the back of her orange overalls and hoisted her bodily toward the toilet.

Adrienne fell to her knees just in time.

The other women groaned and shrieked.

"Ugh!"

"Eww!"

"Get us outta here, guard. That's nasty!"

But as soon as Adrienne's stomach stopped heaving, the guard pulled her upright. Adrienne coughed and for lack of any other choice, wiped her mouth on the sleeve of her jumpsuit.

"Come on, honey, your lawyer's here."

"My lawyer?" Adrienne croaked, still nauseated, although her stomach had stopped heaving. She prayed it was the lawyer Seth had promised her. Maybe she could finally find out what was happening to her.

The guard shrugged and pushed her ahead of her. The walk to the interrogation room was difficult, because Adrienne's head was swimming and her vision was still black around the edges.

The guard sat her down in a hard, straight-back chair.

"There you go, honey," the woman said, not unkindly. "You want something to drink?"

Adrienne nodded gratefully. "Water, please?"

The guard nodded and left.

Adrienne pillowed her head in her arms and closed her eyes. She felt a little less sick that way. What was the matter with her? She was never sick. It was probably nerves. She felt like crying, too, and she couldn't stop her hands from shaking.

The door opened. Adrienne looked up, her dry mouth craving the water, but it wasn't the guard. It was Detective Freeman and her partner.

"Mrs. DeBlanc, I hope you don't mind if we ask you a few questions."

Adrienne shook her head and licked her dry lips. "I thought my lawyer was here."

"We're just wondering how Category Five ended up in your wedding album."

Adrienne stared at the woman, trying to make sense of her words. Nausea still pressed at the back of her throat and her mouth was dry. "What's Category Five? I don't understand."

"Come on, Mrs. DeBlanc. The drug was hidden in the silver wedding album in your husband's study. The money was hidden in that chest. You had a nice little setup going. I know you owned the Cajun Perks, but you didn't run the whole business, did you?"

The drug. The money. Cajun Perk. Adrienne swallowed against the bitter nausea that tickled the back of her throat. She had been set up by the best. The mob couldn't be beaten. They'd made her the scapegoat for their drug operation.

"You found drugs in my house." She didn't even bother trying to make it a question.

"You must have been working with someone. Come on, tell us. It could go lighter for you if you identified the source of the drugs."

Adrienne sat up straight. She wiped her eyes and pushed her fingers through her hair. "I'm not saying anything else until my lawyer arrives. I was told he was here."

The door opened and a medium-sized blond man in a light tan suit came in.

"I'm Brad Guilford, Mrs. DeBlanc. Your lawyer. Mr. Lewis sent me." He offered his hand.

Adrienne shook it briefly, embarrassed that the mention of Seth's name caused grateful tears to spring to her eyes. She blinked.

"Mrs. DeBlanc and I need to talk, Detectives."

The detectives looked at each other, and Freeman crossed her arms.

"Privately."

With exaggerated sighs, they stood and left the room without another word.

Adrienne was confused and scared. The police had found drugs in her house. She pushed the wooden chair back and stood, pacing back and forth in the small room. She still didn't know whom to trust.

"How do I know you really were sent by Seth?" she demanded, her voice hoarse from her bout of vomiting.

Guilford turned around in his chair. "Come and sit, Mrs. DeBlanc, so we can talk." He nodded his head toward the mirror on the opposite wall. She looked at it, understanding that the detectives were probably behind it watching their every move.

She perched on the edge of the chair opposite Guilford. "Can they hear us?"

Guilford faced the mirror. "Turn off the microphones." He turned toward her, his back to the mirror. "Seth said to tell you that your mother is safe. She's being guarded by the good guys."

Adrienne let out a breath she hadn't even realized she

was holding. "Thank God," she said. Relief stung her eyes. "Where is Seth? Is he connected with the police?"

Guilford shook his head. "There are some things I can't tell you, Mrs. DeBlanc."

"Then tell me this," she said. "Can you get me out of here?"

"I'm afraid not. You need to understand that this may be a long process."

"But I don't have any knowledge about drugs. If drugs were found in my house, then someone put them there."

"Who?"

She considered his question. It didn't surprise her that someone had planted falsely incriminating evidence in her house. It could have been Tony. It could have been Jerome, the night of the charity auction when he'd used Marc's study to talk with District Attorney Primeaux.

Jerome had set her up. It was just his good luck that not only had the police found the drug, they'd found her stash of money. Drugs plus money equaled guilty. She shuddered.

"I want to talk to Seth. Where is he?"

"You need to listen to me, Mrs. DeBlanc. Refusing to cooperate could get you locked up for a very long time."

The familiar fear inside of her grew. She nodded. "I know."

"What about the money?"

She swallowed, wishing for the water the guard had promised her. "The money is mine. I was trying to save enough to get away."

Guilford sent her a questioning look.

"It's a long story."

The attorney smiled kindly. "I'm paid by the hour."

The thought of telling anyone about the Cajun mob, explaining how Jerome Senegal had ruled her life with threats and the intimidating presence of Tony Arsenault terrified her. But she couldn't see any other way to break free of the Cajun mob.

She needed to see Seth. The only times in her life she'd ever felt truly safe were with Seth. Nausea rose in the back of her throat. "Could you please find me some water?" she whispered, rubbing her temples. "And call Seth?"

Guilford stood. "Of course. I need to check in anyway. I'll be back in a few minutes and we can talk about what's going to happen next."

He left the room. Feeling light-headed, Adrienne pillowed her head in her arms. But that didn't help.

Acrid saliva filled her mouth. Desperately, she looked around for a trash can, but there wasn't one. She moaned and cupped her hands over her mouth. But since she hadn't eaten, all she did was heave. She coughed and wiped perspiration off her face, just as the guard entered the room bringing a paper cup filled with water.

"Oh, thank you," Adrienne said, sitting down again and sipping carefully. The water soothed her throat and eased the nausea.

The guard dug into her pocket and handed Adrienne a crumpled tissue. "You coming down with something?" she asked, peering closely at Adrienne's face.

Adrienne shook her head. "I never get sick. It must be all this." She made a vague gesture.

The other woman made a noncommittal sound. "You been feeling nauseated for a few days?"

Adrienne started to shake her head automatically, but paused. She'd felt queasy a couple of times before today. "I've been under a lot of stress lately."

The guard nodded sagely. "When was your last period?"

"My last—" Adrienne gasped as the woman's meaning sunk in.

"Honey, you sure you ain't pregnant?"

SETH PACED WHILE the lawyer gave Burke the high points of his conversation with Adrienne and her arraignment.

"She's wants to see Seth," Guilford said. "She won't tell me anything that we can take to court."

"She's scared," Seth said. "Let me see her. I'll convince her to talk to me."

Guilford shook his head. "Well, you'd better hurry. They're planning to move her to St. Gabriel to await trial. The mob almost certainly has contacts on the inside."

Seth hurried.

He was led into a room with a glass wall dividing a table and phones on either side. He'd barely sat down when a door on the other side of the wall opened and Adrienne came in.

She paused when she saw him, her dark blue eyes huge in her pale face. She looked thin and small in the ill-fitting orange jumpsuit. Her hair was pulled back with a rubber band. At least they didn't have her in shackles.

He swallowed hard against an unfamiliar tightening in his throat as the guard led her to the chair opposite him. She sat and the guard backed off a few steps.

Her lips moved, forming his name. Her expression begged him for reassurance.

He couldn't help it; he reached for her, knowing his hand would encounter the glass barrier. He splayed his fingers against the glass and picked up the phone.

For an instant, Adrienne didn't move. Then her eyes sparkled with tears and she put her small hand on the glass opposite his. A single tear spilled slowly down her cheek as she picked up the telephone handset.

"Hey, princess," Seth said. "Your mother is safe."

Her face nearly crumbled. More tears followed that first one. "Thank you," she murmured almost too low for him to hear.

"How're you doing?"

"I'm—okay." She lifted her chin.

He knew she wasn't okay. She looked small and frightened and sick. His fingers on the glass curled into a fist. If he could smash the barrier and swoop her up and away like some swashbuckling hero of legend, he would. But this wasn't a fairy tale and he wasn't a hero. He was just a man with a promise to keep.

"Adrienne, you've got to talk to the police. We can't get you out of here unless you can give us proof that someone set you up."

She took her hand off the glass and wiped her cheeks. "We? Seth, who do you work for? I'm so scared. I don't know who to trust."

"You can trust me. I'm working with the police. I swear to you, princess, with your help we're going to get Senegal."

Her knuckles whitened around the telephone receiver and her face grew even paler. She reached out toward the glass, then stopped herself.

"Hey, what's going on? Are you sick? You look like you're going to faint."

She licked her lips and Seth's gaze followed her tongue as his body tightened with familiar, aching desire. Even through glass, he thought wryly.

"Seth, there's something—" She paused.

His pulse sped up. "What is it? Give me something

I can work with to get you out of here. You've got to tell what you know."

A shadow crossed her face, gone so quickly he wasn't sure if he'd imagined it. Then she nodded. "I had no idea that Cajun Perk was being used to distribute drugs."

"How did you end up as the owner?"

She looked at him and Seth saw her decision etched on her beautiful, wan face. She'd decided to trust him. He didn't know what had made the difference, but he was light-headed with relief.

"Tony. He brought me the papers and made me sign them."

"Arsenault?" The name lit a fire in Seth's chest. "Tell me."

"Since Marc died, Tony has handled my money." Her eyes never left his face and she squeezed the telephone receiver as if she were squeezing his hand. He could feel her fear and her courage through the phone line.

"He monitors every purchase. He tells me what investments to make. He came to my house with a folder and had me sign a stack of forms."

"Did you read them?"

She nodded. "I tried to, as much as I could. But Tony was in a hurry, and he can be persuasive."

Seth grimaced as he remembered the bruises on her arms.

"I know the franchise was Cajun Perk, and mine was the only name on the contract. Tony signed as witness, but not with his own name."

"Did you see what name he signed?"

"No, but it wasn't Arsenault. It was much shorter."

"Where are those papers?"

"In Marc's safe-deposit box. I have a key. It's in my jewelry box, on a silver chain. Tony has the other key."

This was exactly what they needed. Tony held the second key to Adrienne's safe-deposit box. And his fingerprints would be all over the box and the contract. "We just might be able to put Tony away and prove your innocence with this. How do I get into your house?"

"One of the rocks in the koi pool is fake. There's a house key inside it."

"Does Arsenault know that?"

She shook her head. "Nobody does. Jolie gave me the fake rock several years ago, after I locked myself out one day."

"Good. Now listen to me, princess. Guilford will come back and talk to you about your trial. Tell him what you told me. Make an official statement."

He touched the window again. "Adrienne, you may be taken to St. Gabriel."

"The women's prison?" Adrienne swayed. She grabbed the phone with both hands. "Can't you get me out of here?"

"As soon as I can. But in the meantime, you've got to be brave. I'll come back to see you soon, okay?"

She nodded hesitantly.

"Don't give up on me, princess. I've got a lot of things I want to show you."

"Seth? There's something else."

Out of the corner of his eye, he saw the guard glance at his watch and start toward Adrienne. "Hurry. The guard is coming." He put his mouth close to the phone.

"Seth, I—"

The guard touched her shoulder. She froze. He leaned over and said something to her. Reluctantly, she hung up the phone. As she stood the guard gripped her arm.

Don't hurt her! Seth wanted to rip the phone out of

the wall, crash through the glass and take the guard down. But as much satisfaction as that would give him, he knew it wouldn't help Adrienne.

At the door, she twisted back to look at him. He kissed his fingers and touched the glass. His last glimpse of her was her white, frightened face and her hand reaching out toward him as if to catch his kiss.

SETH LEFT the police station and drove directly to the Garden District. He parked around the corner from Adrienne's house and started off down the sidewalk as if he were out for an afternoon stroll. But he stayed alert and ready, in case he needed to reach for his weapon.

Adrienne's house was cordoned off with police tape. Seth jumped it and went around to the patio. He ran his hand over the rocks stacked in and around the koi pool, until he found one that wasn't a rock just under the surface of the water. It felt like fiberglass, and there was an almost invisible seam around the middle of it. He twisted it open, revealing a key.

Sure enough, the key fit the kitchen door. Quickly he slipped inside. The house was a mess. The police had turned everything upside down and left it that way.

Seth winced as he entered Adrienne's room. Her mattress was pulled off the bed, and all the bedclothes and curtains were piled in the middle of the floor. All her dresser drawers were overturned.

The floor was littered with dainty bits of colorful satin. They made him think of her lying atop him dressed only in lacy scraps of royal blue.

He wiped his face and looked around. Her jewelry box was half-open on the dresser. He remembered noticing how small it was. He'd figured most of her jewelry was locked up, because the little teak box couldn't have held more than a few items.

He was right. There wasn't much in it. An antique amethyst pin, the diamond tennis bracelet he'd seen her wear before, a few pairs of earrings and several gold and silver chains. He spotted the key and picked it up, untangling the silver chain attached to it. As he did, something colorful caught his eye. It was the worthless bead bracelet he'd given her at T-Jean's Crawfish Shack.

Carefully, Seth picked up the little string of beads, sliding it over three fingers. He stared at it until his vision became hazy.

He'd never had a close relationship with a woman. He hadn't had time. As soon as he'd graduated from high school, he'd joined the army, and military life didn't encourage settling down.

Bull. Who was he kidding? He'd never had a relationship because he'd never wanted one. What if he ended up being like his father? What if the woman he fell in love with died, like his mother had? He'd never allowed himself to think about the future. Instead, he'd devoted himself to caring for his sisters.

No wonder he'd been so lost when the army had sent him home. He hadn't known what to do with himself.

He touched the beads with his thumb and smiled. It was the luckiest day of his life when Conrad Burke saw his accidental foiling of a bank robbery—had it only been a couple of months ago?

His princess had sure turned the tables on him. He'd planned on seducing her. Instead, she had captivated him with her beauty and sexiness and her vulnerability and courage.

He started to put the beads back into the box. Instead, feeling a little bit silly, he slid the elastic band over his left wrist and headed for the door.

Somehow, wearing the bracelet made him feel closer to her.

SETH ENTERED the secret offices of New Orleans Confidential and turned the safe-deposit box key over to Burke, with the information Adrienne had given him about Cajun Perk. If they were lucky enough to lift a print from either the box or the contract, they could prove Arsenault's involvement with Cajun Perk and therefore with the drugs. They still needed something concrete that linked Arsenault to the mob, though.

"How about I find Arsenault and tail him," Seth suggested. "He's up to his neck in all this. We just need to catch him in the act."

Burke didn't disagree. He studied Seth for a moment, then spoke. "Take Jones with you. If Arsenault is involved as deeply as you think, then maybe he can lead you to their lab. When we find out where they're refining the drug, then with any luck we can cement the case against Senegal, not to mention shut down the operation."

Jones rounded on Seth. "I hope you've got your priorities straight, Lewis."

Seth faced Jones. "You're welcome to request another assignment, Jones, if you don't want to work with me."

Burke stood. "That's enough. Jones, I believe Seth is right about Arsenault. Are you willing to give him backup or do I need to assign someone else?"

Jones's pleasant face turned red. "I'll do my part, sir." He nodded at Seth. "I've got your back."

"Good." Burke sat back down. "Now let's go. Every minute counts. Keep in contact. We've got readiness teams around the clock. Once you find the lab, notify me immediately."

Seth left the Mercedes parked in the Crescent City Transports parking lot and took the streetcar to his home where he lived with his three sisters. There, he dressed in a pair of jeans and a faded black T-shirt and picked up his ancient Mustang. He and Jones worked out a plan. Jones parked a banged-up truck owned by Confidential and lettered as a painter's truck a couple of houses down from Senegal's ostentatious mansion.

Seth parked his Mustang on Prytania Street across from the St. Louis Cemetery, ready to pick up the tail if Jones gave him the word.

They weren't in place two hours before Jones called Seth.

"Arsenault just drove into Senegal's driveway. I almost missed him. He's driving a different car."

Seth's pulse hammered. "Yeah, he does that. Be careful. He's liable to leave in a different vehicle, too. Senegal's got a stable of cars in that garage on the second lot."

"That whole building is a garage? Damn."

Seth slouched behind the wheel of the Mustang as he waited. Even with the windows down it was hot as hell. Not much of a breeze in August in New Orleans.

Waiting gave him plenty of time to think. Today was Adrienne's arraignment hearing. He drummed his fingers impatiently on the steering wheel and glanced at his watch.

She'd be coming into the courtroom about now with Brad Guilford. Had they put her in shackles? He slammed his palm against the wheel as his brain fed him an image of her delicate wrists and ankles weighed down with iron.

The idea of her there, alone, maybe even looking out over the roomful of people searching for him was unbearable. He wiped his face, sat there for a couple more minutes, then opened the Mustang's creaky driver's door and got out. His muscles cramped from inactivity and tension.

After checking his cell phone to be sure it was on,

he stuck it in his pocket and walked along the sidewalk, as if he were interested in the aboveground vaults and crypts that were so typical of New Orleans.

In his mind, he played out Adrienne's arraignment. Her Not Guilty plea, the judge's request for a bail recommendation, the prosecution's argument that the discovery of the drug and the large amount of cash proved that Adrienne was a flight risk. She had refused to allow Guilford to mention her mother, so Seth was certain the judge would refuse her bail.

That meant she would almost certainly be sent to St. Gabriel, considering the overcrowded conditions of the municipal jails.

Seth's hands curled into fists. He wanted to pound something—or someone—so badly. He thought about taking out his frustrations on one of the trees that grew along the cemetery's fence, but that would just bloody his knuckles and attract attention.

He turned on his heel and started back toward his car. His cell phone rang. He jumped.

"Yeah?"

"Seth, it's Guilford. The arraignment went as expected. Ms. DeBlanc will be transferred to St. Gabriel tomorrow."

"Can I see her?"

"Doubtful." Guilford paused. "She's here now."

Seth thought about Jones, and whether he might be trying to reach him. *Just a few seconds.* "Put her on."

"Seth?"

She sounded like she'd been crying. "Hey, princess. How're you holding up?" He heard the difference in his own voice, how it softened when he spoke to her. Man, he had it bad.

"I'm okay," she said tremulously. "My mother?"

"I talked to the nurse assigned to your mother.

She's doing okay. She's eating a little bit, and she's less agitated."

"Thank you."

Seth heard the unshed tears in her voice, and the fear.

"Seth, will I see you before they take me to St. Gabriel's?"

"I don't know. I'm tailing Arsenault. He doesn't know it but he's going to lead me to the drug lab."

She gasped. "Seth, please don't underestimate him. He's a monster."

"I know exactly what he is. Don't worry about me. You just be careful. Anyone around you could be connected to Senegal."

He heard voices in the background.

"I have to go. Seth, I—"

Seth gripped the cell phone tightly. Her hesitant voice sent shards of pain through his heart. "I know, princess. Me, too. You be brave, okay? I'll see you soon."

"Lewis?" Guilford was back on the line.

Seth looked at his watch. "I'm almost out of time. Listen, man, thanks."

"No problem."

Seth clicked off the phone and climbed back into the Mustang. She was losing hope. He could hear it in her voice, and it nearly undid him. She'd been so brave, giving a statement to the police about Arsenault and Senegal. She'd provided a lot of information about the two of them and their dealings with various city officials, even as high up as District Attorney Primeaux. But without evidence, it was her word against theirs.

He had to find that evidence, so he could prove that she had no knowledge or involvement in the drugs or the prostitution. He had to get her out of there.

There was no doubt in his mind that Senegal had

people on the inside. Every moment she stayed in there, her life was in danger.

He keyed in Jones's number, surveying the area around him, including the cemetery.

"Jones. Anything?"

"I was just calling you. A black Town Car's coming your way."

"I see it now. Is it Arsenault?" Seth slouched down in his seat again, pulling his New Orleans Saints baseball cap down to shadow his face.

"I think so."

"Got him. I'm on him. You follow me. I'm leaving the line open."

Seth rose up in his seat and lifted the cap enough to catch a glimpse of the driver's profile through the darkened windows. He'd recognize that beak of a nose anywhere. It was Arsenault.

With the thrill of the chase hammering in his blood, Seth cranked the Mustang and pulled out to follow Arsenault.

"Heading east on Prytania," he said for Jones's benefit. "Whoa." Arsenault put the brakes on. For an instant, Seth was afraid Arsenault had made him, but the Town Car turned right.

"What is it?" Jones's voice was sharp.

"We're turning right onto Washington."

"Gotcha. I see you."

"That was a short trip. Wonder what the deal is?"

"Do we know where Arsenault lives?"

"Nope. He must live under a different name. Okay, here we go again, turning right on Annunciation."

"He's going to spot you in that red Mustang. I'll take over for a minute. If he stops I'll drive past."

Seth pulled over and in a moment, Jones's truck passed him. "Give me every move he makes, Jones."

"He's stopping at an old house. Damn." Jones whistled, the sound shrill and distorted through the cell phone.

"What?"

"This place looks abandoned. It's fenced, and all overgrown with shrubs and vines, but a gate in the fence opened automatically, and Arsenault just drove right in."

"Drive back around and park behind me. I'm going to take a look."

"You wait there. We need to call Burke."

"I will, as soon as I've gotten a look at whatever's in there."

"Lewis."

"Trust me on this, Jones. All I want to do is take a look at the house."

Seth looked in the rearview mirror as Jones's truck pulled up behind him. He cut the cell phone connection, got out of his car and walked back to the truck.

Jones was frowning. "This is what I was afraid of. You're going off half-cocked because you've got a personal beef with Arsenault."

"Give me some credit, Jones," Seth growled. "You think I'd risk blowing this whole operation because of something personal?"

Jones looked him straight in the eye. "Yes."

"Funny you didn't mention this when Burke asked you. Can I depend on you or not? Because I can do this alone."

Jones stuck his jaw out pugnaciously, but his eyes assessed Seth. "I keep my word. I've got your back. I just hope you don't get us both killed."

Seth leaned on the window frame. "I've got experience in stealth operations. I can get in there and see what's going on inside that abandoned house. And I can do it alone. But I'd rather know you're backing me."

Jones nodded. "Like I said, I keep my word. But, we don't have probable cause."

Seth looked down at the ground, then back up at Jones. "What about that anonymous tip?"

Jones frowned. "What anonymous—oh." His face relaxed into a grin. "Oh, *that* anonymous tip. The one I'll get if you see anything interesting."

Seth smiled and nodded.

"Let's switch to mobile transmitters and cut the cell phones. That way there's no way we can be placed here or have our calls traced." Jones handed Seth a small box.

"Good idea." Seth cut the power on his phone and accepted the mobile transmitter from Jones. A specially designed earpiece with microphone allowed them to hear each other.

Seth sent Jones a small salute and walked to the end of the street, then turned the corner. He started down Jackson Street.

"Which house?" he muttered.

"Third on the right."

Seth spotted the fence covered with wild, overgrown vines. It stood out next to its neatly maintained neighbors. Upon a quick inspection, Seth discovered that there was a sunken break in the sidewalk right in front of the gate. With luck and a few scrapes, he should be able to crawl through.

But what would he find on the other side? It wasn't impossible that he would come up staring into the barrel of a gun.

A vision of Adrienne in shackles rose in his mind. It would be worth it.

"I'm going under the gate."

"I'm calling Burke."

"No," Seth whispered. "What if Arsenault is at home

scrambling some eggs or watching a movie? We'll blow our chance and tip him off."

Jones was silent a moment. "Okay. But please give me something soon. The suspense is killing me."

Jones's complaint brought a smile to Seth's face as he glanced around the street, then crouched down to feel under the gate. The bottom of the gate was smooth. At least he wouldn't wind up caught on stray wire.

Aware that he was possibly crawling into a situation he might not come out of, Seth quickly dropped flat and shimmied under the gate, all senses alert.

He came out exposed, on a driveway. Quickly he rolled to his left, into a bank of tall grass, and then crawled behind a shrub.

"I'm in," he whispered. "I'm about twenty feet from the house." He glanced around. "Arsenault's car is pulled up behind a panel truck. The windows on the first floor are all boarded up. The second floor has drapes."

"Lewis! A truck is driving up."

Just as Jones spoke, Seth heard metal screech against metal. The gate was opening.

At the same time, Tony Arsenault opened the front door of the house and stepped outside, pulling the door closed behind him. He watched the gate swing open, and waited as the truck entered.

Seth crouched behind the bush, hoping its foliage was thick enough to hide him.

As the gate swung closed, Arsenault's gaze swept the overgrown lawn. He turned his head and stared right into Seth's eyes.

Seth froze, looking down so his eyes wouldn't glint. He could feel Arsenault's gaze pinning him like a laser sight on a rifle. The shrub he'd crawled behind was fairly thick and lush, and his jeans and T-shirt were faded to a nondescript color, but his Saints baseball cap was deep purple and the logo on the front was a bright gold.

He breathed slowly and shallowly, concentrating on not moving a muscle. Most people's eyes would scan right over him without noticing, as long as he didn't move. Special Forces operatives knew a lot about hiding in plain sight.

But Arsenault wasn't most people. If this was the location of the drug-refining lab, then the sadistic killer and everyone involved would be paranoid.

"Hold it!" Arsenault's voice rang out. "Who are you?"

Seth's heart rate tripled and he couldn't keep his muscles from contracting, doing their best to shrink away from the bullet he fully expected.

"Don't move a muscle. Where's the regular driver?"

Without fluttering a leaf on the bush, Seth let out a silent breath. He forced himself to relax his clenched fists as he observed the exchange between Arsenault and the new driver.

Arsenault was holding a gun on the man. "Remy!" he shouted.

The front door to the house slammed as Remy rushed outside.

"Yeah, Tony?" The red-haired thug went to stand by Arsenault.

They conferred quietly, while the pale driver waited, his hands glued to the steering wheel.

Apparently, whatever Remy told Arsenault satisfied him, because he nodded. Remy directed the driver to get out of the truck and start unloading the delivery. He kept his gun on the man the entire time.

The delivery consisted of boxes labeled AcmeChem Chemical Supply.

"Lewis?"

Jones's whisper came through Seth's headset. He didn't answer until the driver was done unloading the last box and he and Remy had walked back toward the front of the truck.

"Yeah."

"Damn!" Jones's breath whooshed out. "I was afraid they'd gotten you."

"Me, too, for a minute there," Seth whispered.

"What's happening?"

"Give me ten minutes and I'll have something for you. Meanwhile, stop the delivery truck as it comes out. That driver knows how to open the automatic gate. We'll need him."

The gate opened and the truck backed out as several boys who looked no more than sixteen or seventeen hurried out of the house and carried the boxes in through the front door. All Seth could see through the door was darkness.

The red-haired man Arsenault had called Remy took one last look around, then went inside and closed the door behind him.

Seth had to get a look inside that house. He studied the perimeter of the lot. Huge gnarled branches from a tree in the next yard hung over the roof of the carport.

He slid backwards under the gate and slipped into the neighbor's yard. No one was home. Within seconds, he had shinnied up the tree and crawled out onto one of the sturdy branches that extended over Arsenault's carport. There were heavy curtains on his second-story windows.

Using all the caution taught to him in Special Forces, he lowered himself silently onto the carport roof and crawled over to the roof of the house. The window nearest the carport was stuck, probably painted shut.

Seth took out his pocketknife and ran the blade between the window and the sill. Then he tried again to open it. It resisted, then gave, the sound of wood scraping wood deafening in the afternoon silence.

As soon as he had enough room, Seth rolled through the window and onto his feet, his gun drawn, ready to take out anyone who threatened him.

The room was empty.

Seth breathed an audible sigh of relief, knowing his luck wouldn't last. As soon as the thought crossed his mind, he heard voices outside the door. They were young voices, male voices, probably the boys he'd seen moving the chemical supplies.

Standing behind the door, he listened. The boys were speaking Spanish. Their voices faded and Seth heard footsteps descending a staircase.

After a couple of minutes, he moved to the other side of the door and eased it open. The stairs were directly in front of the door. There were two other rooms along the upstairs hall. Their doors were open, and Seth heard nothing. The upstairs seemed to be empty.

"Jones?" he said quietly into his headset.

"Yeah?" Jones sounded like he was stretched to the breaking point.

"I'm in. Just a few more minutes."

"Lewis, I'm calling for backup."

"Two minutes."

He heard Jones's frustrated sigh as he slipped out the door and over to the head of the stairs. Just as he did, Arsenault's voice floated up to him.

"*Oui*, Jerome. Double shifts for everyone. We just got a delivery of acetone. There will be enough in two days."

Seth heard a door open and close, and Arsenault's voice was cut off.

Enough in two days. Arsenault was talking about refined drug. Seth knew the lab had to be somewhere in
the house. He surveyed the downstairs, which was dark
except for a bright sliver of dusty light coming from
around a set of double doors beside the staircase.

He carefully slipped down the stairs and over to the
doors. Arsenault's muffled voice sounded from another
room, apparently still on the phone.

Seth knew he had no more than a minute or two, at
most. The neglected house had settled, leaving a half-
inch gap between the two doors. Seth put his eye to the
gap, almost coughing at the dust that hovered around the
door.

The sight before him started his heart to hammering.
Young men and teenage boys, dressed in nothing but
undershirts and undershorts and wearing surgical
masks, were working at a table. The entire room was
white, white paper on the floor, white cloths on the
table, white dust on the men's shoulders and floating in
the air.

Gotcha. A deep, satisfying relief cascaded like a re-
freshing shower over Seth. He took a deep breath and
had to fight to hold back a cough. His eyes watered, and
to his dismay, he began to react. He shifted uncomfort-
ably as his arousal pressed against his jeans. It was the
drug. He had to get out of there before he got distracted.

He spoke into the microphone of the mobile transmitter. "Jones, we got 'em. Tell Burke—"

A circle of cold steel pressed against his neck.

"Tell him goodbye."

Chapter Eleven

"Arsenault." Seth said the name for Jones's benefit. His heart pounded as he froze in place.

"Shut up." Tony Arsenault pressed the gun into Seth's neck. "Keep your hands where I can see them. This is a damn big gun and it'll blow your head right off. Although if I have time, perhaps I'll use my machete. It will be more satisfying, eh?"

With his left hand Arsenault jerked the transmitter out of Seth's ear and threw it down on the floor.

Seth didn't move a muscle, but he breathed an internal sigh of relief. He wasn't in immediate danger of dying. Arsenault wanted to talk to him, maybe even take him to Senegal.

He concentrated on keeping his heart from racing. In a minute, or an hour, Arsenault would make a mistake, and then Seth could make his move.

He kept his head up, using his peripheral vision to gauge Arsenault's movements, swallowing against the cold column of steel pressing into his throat.

Arsenault looked down and shifted his weight to one leg. He lifted his left foot to stomp on the transmitter. For that instant, he was off balance.

Seth brought his right hand up in a lightning-fast backwards chop, thumb stiff against his palm. At the same time he whirled, putting his entire weight behind the blow.

Arsenault overbalanced. The gun went off.

Seth's brain registered two things that he didn't have time to examine. A hot streak plowed across his skull, and something snapped in his hand.

Seth kneed Arsenault and went down on top of him. His primary concern was getting the gun and pinning Arsenault.

"Mon Dieu!" Arsenault screamed. "Remy!"

Seth jammed his knee onto the Cajun hit man's right forearm and punched him in the face with his right fist, sending excruciating pain through his thumb and wrist and up his shoulder. He grunted, and punched Arsenault again.

Blood gushed from Arsenault's nose. The blood was worth the pain in his hand.

He wrested the gun out of Arsenault's left hand, and braced against the heavier man's bucking efforts to free himself.

Seth blinked as a red haze clouded his vision.

As he pointed the gun at the man who had hurt Adrienne, he heard the doors crash, and sunlight poured into the house, shadowed by the silhouettes of men with guns.

"Lewis!"

It was Jones. He gestured to a man Seth had seen around the Crescent City Transports building. "Martinez, take this man into custody. His name is Antoine Arsenault. Read him his rights."

Martinez hauled Arsenault up by his collar.

Jones put a hand on Seth's shoulder. "It's okay, Lewis. Martinez has him. You can get up.

Seth tried to blink away the redness that clouded his vision, but he couldn't. He lifted his right hand, then decided that hurt too much, so he swiped his left hand across his eyes. It came away bloody.

"Cripes, Lewis. You're covered with blood. What happened to your head?"

"I think he shot me." Seth stood, his pulse pounding full throttle.

More men poured in the door, and Seth heard yelling and chairs scraping as Confidential agents took control of the drug lab.

"Tell 'em to wear masks. You don't want to be breathing that dust," Seth said as metallic drops of blood trickled down his face and into his mouth.

Jones gripped Seth's arm. "Come on, Lewis. They know what they're doing. I need to get you to the hospital."

"I'm fine." Seth pushed Jones away and turned toward the front door. "Where's Arsenault? I want to personally take him into custody."

"I think you made your point with Arsenault."

"Not enough." Seth blinked. The haze over his vision was turning darker. "Not enough for what he did to her."

Then to his utter and complete chagrin, Seth blacked out.

ADRIENNE SAT IN the steaming hot police transport bus, her hands and feet shackled, trying to steady herself against the seat as the ancient vehicle bounced over the road. There were two other women on the bus, sitting on the opposite side. They apparently knew each other, or were kindred spirits, because they started talking as soon as they were brought on and they hadn't stopped.

Adrienne felt sick, not only physically but emotionally. Seth had promised he'd come to see her, but the long hours had passed, and he hadn't shown up. She'd asked for telephone privileges, but she was refused. Now they were taking her to St. Gabriel's Women's Prison. She'd heard awful stories of overcrowded conditions, mistreatment, prison gangs.

How was she going to stand prison? How would she protect her baby? Despite Seth's reassurances and Guilford's calm, rational explanations, Adrienne was terrified. She put her hands on her stomach, thinking about the tiny, helpless life that grew there.

She and Seth had only known each other for a short time. Most of the time they'd been together they'd used condoms, but once or twice, like that night in the shower, they'd been careless.

She must have gotten pregnant the night of Senegal's daughter's engagement party. Seth had discovered the bruises on her arms. He'd been so tender, and yet so insatiable. They'd made love again and again through the night. She did the math. Her baby would be born in April. She looked down at her sore, shackled wrists.

Where would she be when her baby was born? Far away from New Orleans, caring for her mother? Some magical place where Seth loved her and wanted them to be a family? Or had his tenderness and caring all been an act? Would she be in prison?

She knew one place she would not be. No matter what happened, she would never go back to where she'd been, under the control of Jerome Senegal and his sadistic goons. She'd rather be in a real prison, locked up for her unwitting part in Senegal's illegal dealings, than shackled by the invisible bonds of fear and cowardice. She'd let others control her life for too long.

The bus bounced over a rough spot of road, and Adrienne felt the acrid bite of nausea in the back of her throat.

One of the women laughed loudly and spewed out a

string of filthy words, apparently describing her ex-boyfriend. Adrienne cringed.

"Hey, check out the socialite. My language bother you, Miss Priss?"

Adrienne sent an apprehensive glance toward the woman. "I apologize. I'm not feeling well."

"Well, then, we'll try to be discreet over here, honey. You stay over on that side of the bus, in the first-class section."

The second woman guffawed, then erupted into a fit of coughing.

Ignoring the women, and swallowing against the nausea, Adrienne cradled her flat belly and her mouth curved into a soft smile. She felt an enveloping warmth she'd never felt before. It took her a moment to realize what the feeling was.

It was love. She loved this baby that she and Seth had made. Seth. Strong, gentle, funny Seth. It wasn't just the baby her love encompassed. It was also the baby's father.

Her heart fluttered in her breast. She loved Seth. She was *in love* with Seth. He was the father of her child, and she wanted him to love their baby as much as she did.

A twinge of apprehension slipped like a splinter under her glow of happiness. Even though Seth had taken her mother to safety, even though he was working under the umbrella of the chief of police, he'd still used her.

He'd admitted it. But he'd sworn to her that he hated the deception, and everything he'd done had told her she was more to him than just an assignment.

But now the stakes were even higher for her. Their lovemaking had created a life. And Adrienne was determined to protect that life with her own if necessary.

But how would Seth react?

ADRIENNE AWOKE WITH a start as the bus jerked and swerved, throwing her against the window. She must have drifted off into an uneasy doze. She scrambled for a handhold, wrenching her wrists as the chains reached their limits.

The bus rolled to a stop, and the two women shouted. The guard yelled at them to shut up, and the driver cursed the car that had run them off the road.

"Everything's fine," the burly guard with thinning hair yelled, drawing his gun. "Now shut up and sit down!"

Something popped, glass shattered, and the guard tumbled forward as a pink spray spattered the seats in front of Adrienne. It took her a few seconds to realize the pop was a gunshot and the spatter was blood.

There were more pops. The windshield cracked, and the driver slumped over the steering wheel. Two men with white handkerchiefs over their noses and mouths boarded the bus. *They look like western outlaws,* Adrienne thought inanely.

The two women screamed as the larger man pointed a rifle at them and fired, the bullets jerking their bodies around like out-of-control marionettes until they crumpled.

Adrienne dove down behind the seat in front of her, crouching protectively over her belly. The sharp odor of blood and fear filled the air. She heard heavy footsteps walking toward her.

She tugged at the seat cushion, hoping she could use it as a shield, or a weapon, but it was fastened down. There was no escape.

She held the chain that shackled her wrists and ankles, wondering if she could swing it at their gun barrels.

A masked man stopped in front of her, his gun aimed at her head.

No! She didn't want to die. She wanted to live, to have her baby. She clanged her wrist shackles together, shielding her head.

Seth, I love you, she cried silently. *I always will.*

LILY HARRISON was in hell. When she'd run into the huge dark-faced man with the evil grin, she'd been sure her life was over. But instead of killing her, the dark man had clamped a beefy hand over her mouth and stuffed her into the back seat of a car. The other man had climbed in beside her and stuck a gun in her ribs.

They'd driven west, out of the city, on twisting, turning roads

"You can't do this to me. My father will hunt you down like dogs."

The fake cop laughed. "You gonna sic your Daddy on us, little girl?"

"For your information, my father was with the CIA."

"Hey, didja hear that? Her *father's* with the CIA."

The dark man looked in the mirror. His evil eyes assessed her. "What's your daddy's name?" he asked her in heavily accented English.

Lily lifted her head proudly. "Tanner Harrison."

"Gag her and blindfold her."

"No, don't—" The idea of being blindfolded and helpless around these two men whom she was sure worked for the killer she'd seen, scared Lily to death. She had no doubt they were taking her somewhere to kill her.

The fake cop stuffed a rag in her mouth and tied a handkerchief around her eyes.

Lily didn't remember much after that. She must have fainted or something. She'd woken up when the rain started. Soon after that, the car had swerved sharply and stopped.

Now she was tied to a straight chair that sat in the middle of a nearly empty room. The gag and blindfold were gone.

A dull ache in her belly reminded her that she hadn't eaten in a long time. Not only that, she needed to go to the bathroom, bad.

"Hey!" She tried to yell, but her voice was nothing more than a croak. "Hey!" she tried again.

A door opened, and Lily smelled something cooking. Something spicy.

"What the hell?" The fake cop stuck his head into the room. His face split into a gap-toothed grin. Not a nice grin. "So, you finally woke up, little Miss CIA?"

"You wait," she said. "My dad will find you."

"That's what we're hoping for."

Lily swallowed. "What do you mean?"

"I mean, when our boss found out your dad was CIA, he decided to keep you alive—for bait. I'll bet your dad would do just about anything to save his little girl."

That shows what you know. Her stomach turned over, making her feel nauseated. Tears ran down her cheeks. Her dad would probably be too busy to save her.

"My dad'll crush you," she said bravely.

"What the hell are you doing?" It was the dark man.

"Nothing." Fake Cop looked guilty.

"Put the damn gag back on her."

"No, wait." Lily licked her lips. "I think I'm going to throw up."

Dark man glared at her. "Gag her."

"No, please. I have to puke and my stomach is upset, too." She was serious. The idea of these two buggers hurting her dad increased the queasy feeling in her stomach. She belched, and hiccoughed.

"Damn. Take her to the john, but don't let her out of your sight."

Acrid saliva filled her mouth. "Hurry," she mumbled.

"I'm going outside to make a phone call. Take care of her."

She coughed and gagged as the dark man slammed out the door.

"Okay, okay." The fake cop hurriedly untied her feet. "Go! Quick. There's the bathroom."

Lily hurried into the bathroom, relieved that Fake Cop hadn't insisted on watching. After taking care of business, she splashed water on her face and looked in the mirror.

Seeing her wide, scared eyes and her dirty face, she burst into tears. For a few seconds, all she could do was lean over the sink, sobbing as water ran on her wrists.

Eventually, the nausea abated. The walls of the tiny room were thick wood, and a small window was directly above the toilet.

Lily looked at the closed door, then back at the window. Wiping her cheeks, she put the lid down on the toilet and stood on it. It was dark and rainy outside. Not daring to hope for success, she flushed the toilet and quickly pushed at the window. It opened.

"Hey in there." The fake cop's voice came through the closed door.

Lily took a deep breath and belched. "Just—a minute." She groaned and made what she hoped were convincing retching sounds.

"Okay, okay. Just hurry!"

Lily grabbed the top of the window and swung her legs through the opening. Her heart crashed against her chest like drumsticks against cymbals as she wriggled through and let go.

She hit the ground hard, burying all four inches of her stiletto heels into the soft wet dirt. As the rain soaked her, she fumbled with the buckles and stepped out of the sandals.

Pushing wet hair out of her eyes, she peered around her. The downpour was steady, throwing a blanket of soft noise over everything and providing a curtain to shield her from view.

She heard a muffled shout, a door slamming, a crash. Fake Cop knew she'd escaped.

Barefoot, cringing in terror, she ran into the darkness, tripping over roots, pushing at the vines and leaves that slapped at her face and arms.

A louder shout pierced the blackness, and a torch snapped on.

Desperate, Lily pushed through the underbrush that tangled around her feet like grasping fingers. The rain was fast turning the ground into sticky mud. Something moved near her and she heard a deep grunt. *Alligators.*

Shivering, her limbs wobbly and weak with fear, she shielded her face with her arms as she stumbled on.

Something jerked her backwards. She shrieked. Her heart stopped. She whipped around, kicking out instinctively, but it was just a branch. Her hair had caught on a branch.

Sick with relief, gasping for breath in the wet air, Lily almost collapsed. Tears and rain dripped down her face.

Two watery circles of light shone through the snarl of trees and vines, closer than she'd expected.

Sobbing, she ripped her hair free of the branch and forced herself to push on. She didn't want to die.

CONRAD BURKE did not want to face Seth. The kid had already been through enough for one day. As Burke strode into the emergency room, he tried to rehearse how he was going to tell him about Adrienne DeBlanc.

The unscheduled raid on the drug lab had come off almost without a hitch. Jones had called in the readiness team as soon as he heard Lewis say Arsenault's name.

The team was at the house within minutes, but minutes were too long when a cold-blooded killer held a gun to a Confidential agent's head.

Once again, Lewis had proven himself to be the man for the job. He'd used his lightning-fast reflexes and his hand-to-hand combat training to disarm Arsenault and take him down.

Burke took in the brightly lit emergency room with a glance. There were two private rooms guarded by uniformed police officers. In one was Lewis. The other held Arsenault.

"Burke." Phillip Jones emerged from one of the rooms and motioned to him.

"How's he doing?"

"Good. He's got a broken hand and a graze above his right ear that's still bleeding like a stuck pig, but he looks better than Arsenault. He was—enthusiastic about disarming him. Arsenault's got a broken nose and a black eye. And I believe he lost three teeth." Jones chuckled.

Burke nodded and went into the room.

Seth was sitting on the side of the bed, frowning at the bandage on his hand. When he saw Burke, he stood up.

"Sir, I'm sorry about this." He swayed.

"You'd better sit down until you're a little more steady on your feet."

"Yes, sir." Seth sat.

Burke assessed his newest agent. Even though he was only a few years older than Seth, his feelings for him were decidedly fatherly. He supposed it had a lot to do with Seth's background, which in some ways was similar to his own. Plus, since he'd become a father himself, he'd noticed those instincts growing stronger with each passing day.

"I hear you finally got your hands on Arsenault."

Seth ducked his head for an instant, then straightened and looked Burke in the eye. "Yes, sir."

"Good job."

"He got the drop on me while I was investigating the lab." Seth shook his head. "I apologize, sir. I never should have let my guard down."

Burke looked at the bandage above Seth's ear, which was stained with blood. "Looks to me like you handled the situation pretty well. Are they going to let you out of here tonight?"

Seth nodded. "As soon as the surgeon looks at the second set of X rays, he'll decide if I need surgery on my thumb. I don't think I do."

Burke took a deep breath and shifted to the balls of his feet. He hoped he could handle Lewis if he needed to, after he gave him the news about Adrienne.

As if reading Burke's mind, Seth said, "I need to get out of here. Do you know if they've transferred Adrienne to St. Gabriel yet?"

Burke nodded. "A bus left at four-thirty this afternoon." He put his hand on Seth's shoulder. "At 5:20 p.m. the bus was stopped."

Seth jerked and Burke tightened his grip. Seth's muscles bunched beneath his hand. Shock and alarm darkened his eyes.

"The guard and the driver were killed. One female prisoner was killed and one is in critical condition. Apparently, Adrienne DeBlanc was taken hostage."

Seth's face drained of color. "Apparently? They don't know?"

He tried to stand, but Burke locked his grip.

"Stay calm, son. She wasn't found at the scene, which is a good sign. It means she's probably still alive."

Seth stared at Burke, horror etched in the lines of his face. Burke steeled himself for a violent outburst. But Seth closed his eyes and took long, even breaths.

Burke watched in admiration as Seth got himself under control. It was obvious that the younger man was in love. He probably didn't know it yet, but Burke did. He'd seen it grow as Seth became more and more involved in Adrienne DeBlanc's life. Knowing from experience how love can turn a person's world inside out, Burke understood the strength Seth was exerting to stay quiet and still.

"We expect to be able to talk to the surviving prisoner by tomorrow. Meanwhile, you need to rest."

"Rest, hell!" Seth clenched his jaw and took another deep breath. "The mob has her. I've got to find her. She could be—"

Burke's hand clamped down on Seth's shoulder. He shook him slightly. "Listen to me, Lewis. You've got a job to do. The police want to question you about what you saw and heard inside the house before the raid went down. I have a team working with the police on finding Adrienne. Crime scene investigators are going over the bus now. We'll find her." He squeezed Seth's shoulder one more time for reassurance.

SETH WIPED HIS FACE with his good hand. Lord help him, his princess was in the hands of the Cajun mob. The thought of what they might do to her horrified him.

Guilt ripped through him with razor-sharpness. "I should have known Senegal would do this. I should have anticipated it."

"Come on, son, let's get you out of here. I'm going to have the doctor give you a sedative."

"No!" Seth could hardly breathe, he was exerting so much effort to keep from tearing up the place. Adrienne was missing, possibly injured. "Don't let them sedate me."

Burke's sharp brown eyes held his for a brief moment. Then he nodded and opened the door into the main triage area of the emergency room.

Seth held his bandaged hand next to his ribs as he walked out behind Burke. Jones was standing with another agent, Mason Bartley, who'd been in on the raid.

Bartley was speaking. "Hard to even imagine how much money an operation like that could rake in. Enough to be set for a lifetime, for sure. Sometimes it's hell being on the right side of the law." Bartley laughed.

"Yeah, well, I like it on this side," Jones replied. "Hey, Lewis, take a look." Jones inclined his head.

Seth turned. A dozen feet away, the police were leading Arsenault out of the other private treatment room. His hands were handcuffed behind him.

At the sight of the tall mobster who had caused Adrienne so much hurt, the anger Seth had held in check boiled over. He elbowed his way forward until he was face to face with the hit man. A massive bandage covered Arsenault's swollen nose and his right eye was bright red and swollen shut. Seth clenched Arsenault's shirt with his left hand.

"You're going to rot in jail, Arsenault. Tell us where Adrienne is. Maybe you can make a deal. What has Senegal done with her?"

Tony Arsenault recoiled. "Get this maniac away from me."

Seth smiled. "You know she had nothing to do with the drugs. Why don't you admit it? You're the one who set up her investment in Cajun Perk."

Arsenault stood up straight and looked Seth in the

eye. "Cajun Perk? What are you talking about? That was Mrs. DeBlanc's personal investment. I know nothing of drugs."

"You're a liar."

Arsenault looked around and shrugged. "Mrs. De-Blanc demanded to invest in the coffeehouses. I do not know what you are talking about."

"The bastard's lying," Seth grated. "What kind of scum are you, using an innocent woman as a scapegoat? That's why you had her abducted, so she couldn't testify against you."

Seth turned around, to find the uniformed policemen staring at their shoes. Burke's lips were pressed together, and Bartley and Jones exchanged an uncomfortable glance.

Phillip Jones spoke up. "I still say she had to know. I think you're blinded by love, Lewis."

Seth started to retort, but he knew it would do no good. He needed to use his energy to find Adrienne, so she could make her own statement against the mob.

He prayed to God he could get to her in time. There was only one reason her body hadn't been found with the other victims on the bus. Senegal had kidnapped her to make a statement.

He would kill her, Seth had no doubt. And her death would not be easy.

Chapter Twelve

Adrienne had never been so frightened in her life. She'd been blindfolded with a dirty rag and taken off the bus at gunpoint.

Then she'd been pushed roughly into the back of a van and the two men had climbed in after her.

She stiffened, clenching her fists, trying to get her feet under her, hindered by the shackles on her ankles. What were the killers planning to do with her? Why hadn't they shot her like they had the others?

Nausea pricked at the back of her throat. She was afraid she knew what their plans were.

When a heavy hand came down on her shoulder, she tried to scream, but the hand cuffed her on the chin.

"Shut up or I'll knock your pretty teeth out." A cell phone was pressed to the side of her head. "Somebody wants to talk to you."

Adrienne didn't speak.

"My dear, I'm sorry it had to be this way."

It was Senegal. Adrienne's whole body went taut with fury and fear. "You."

"You didn't do what Tony told you to. Didn't he demonstrate what the consequences of your disobedience would be?"

"He always does," she snapped.

"I need some information, Adrienne."

She didn't speak. She tried to push the phone away but a hand grabbed the chain between her wrists and jerked it.

She stifled a grunt of pain.

"Are you listening, Adrienne?"

"Yes," she grated.

"Who does Seth Lewis work for?"

She thought about Seth's words. *If you don't know, they can't make you tell.* She understood now what he'd meant. He'd known there was a possibility that Senegal would get to her.

"I thought he worked for you," she said.

"I'm disappointed in you. You were always so— malleable. You will regret if you do not tell me who is behind the raids."

"I don't know."

"*Dites moi!* You must tell me!"

"Jerome. I don't know who Seth is working for. All I can say is, I got screwed, too, just like you." She was shocked at her own words.

"Then it is too bad you were not better at pillow talk. You will die. No one turns on Jerome Senegal."

"Go to hell."

The man standing over her took the cell phone away from her ear and backed up. He was quiet for a moment, his silence striking fear in Adrienne's heart. How was Senegal planning to kill her?

The man said, "Yes, sir," and Adrienne heard a tiny beep as he turned off the phone.

Adrienne sent a prayer to heaven that her mother was safe, wherever Seth had taken her.

"Come on," the man said. "Let's go. We've got our orders."

The doors of the van slammed shut, and Adrienne was left alone.

She removed the blindfold, but it didn't make any difference. The inside of the van was dark as pitch and smelled like coffee and rotten fish. The odor, combined with Jerome's ominous words, made her queasy.

She curled up against the wall of the van and lay there as the men drove with what felt like dangerous speed. After the waves of nausea passed and her eyes had adapted to the dark, Adrienne searched the van's walls and floor for anything she could use as a weapon. But her captors had apparently thought of everything.

She found dirt and grit and some smelly shrimp shells. The only other item was a filthy blanket piled in one corner.

Gritting her teeth, determined not to be squeamish, Adrienne shook out the blanket, biting her lips to keep from shrieking as bugs scattered, but there was nothing under the blanket either.

She tried to slide her hands out of the shackles, but although the metal cuffs felt large and heavy, they were snug enough to prevent her from escaping. Her wrists were chafed and bruised by the time she gave up.

The van slowed, and Adrienne's heart pounded, but it only turned down what felt like an Interstate exit ramp and onto a bumpy road. It was another half hour before they came to a stop.

Adrienne steeled herself to die.

The door opened and sunlight poured in. Two menacing silhouettes immediately blocked the sun.

Adrienne opened her mouth to scream, hoping to attract attention, and dove at them, but her shackles weighed her down.

The silhouettes advanced. She swung at them with

her shackled hands. Panic sent adrenaline rushing through her system, giving her more strength than she thought she had.

The larger man grabbed her, putting his beefy hand over her mouth. She bit him. He yelped and backhanded her.

"Don't just stand there, grab her feet!" he shouted to the other man.

Adrienne kicked and tried to scream. Her lip stung. She tasted blood.

Good. She hoped her blood got all over them and all over the van. At least Seth would know what had happened to her.

Seth. He didn't even know about their baby. The baby she wanted with all her heart.

She fought with all her strength, but the two men easily overpowered her and pinned her down.

"Gimme that blanket!" The larger man covered her head with the filthy thing.

Adrienne couldn't breathe. She gasped and coughed, her throat and chest filling with dust and grime and who knew what else.

"Let me go!" she croaked, trying to scream, kicking as much as the shackles would let her. "Help!"

"I told you to shut up—"

A massive hand closed around her throat, pressing, cutting off her breath.

"No!" she mouthed.

Then everything went black.

ADRIENNE FELT a scrape along her left leg and heard cloth rip. Then her butt hit the floor—hard. Metal clanged against metal, reverberating inside her head like a discordant bell. She coughed and realized she was still wrapped in the smelly blanket, still shackled and still nauseated. Her eyes felt gritty, and she had dirt in her mouth and dust tickling her nostrils.

But nobody was holding her. She paused for a second, listening, but she didn't hear anything. Were her captors still there? She kicked out and pushed at the suffocating blanket, then rolled, hoping to get to her hands and knees.

The blanket was yanked off her. Her tortured lungs burned as she gulped huge breaths of air. Her throat hurt. She coughed.

The bigger man jerked her around until her bottom hit the floor again.

Eyes tearing, mouth too dry to swallow, Adrienne tossed her head, trying to shake her hair out of her face. She glared at the two men, blinking to clear her vision. She saw her captors' faces clearly for the first time.

Their bare faces glared back at her. They'd removed their masks. She recognized Marx, one of Jerome's bodyguards, by his distinctive flattened nose.

He didn't care if she recognized him. The significance of that made her want to cry. They were going to kill her. She'd never get the chance to identify him.

"You won't get away with this," she croaked. Her voice wasn't working.

"Shut up," the little guy said.

He was skinny with a pointed nose, dirty blond hair and a sparse mustache that stuck out like a weasel's whiskers. His mouth was a thin line, and his eyes were hardly more than slits.

Marx grabbed the chain between her wrist shackles and dragged her across the floor.

Wincing at the painful ache in her shoulders and wrists, Adrienne forced herself to look at their surroundings. She knew they were on a boat. She'd felt the lazy rocking ever since they'd first set foot on it. She'd been roughly handed down a narrow set of stairs and carried through a doorway or two before being dumped on the floor.

The room they were in was some kind of storage room. The walls were gray and pipes crisscrossed each other overhead and along the walls.

Marx dragged her toward the pipes. On the other side of the wall she could hear the rumbling of an idling engine, a big one. They were probably on a big paddle wheel or a ferry.

The little weaselly guy bent over and opened a duffel bag that Adrienne hadn't noticed before. He took out what looked like a thick black nylon life belt, strapped with duct tape. The tape secured an odd gray bulge to the material.

He held up the belt and came toward her.

There were wires hanging from the vest, and on one side was a black plastic box. In the dim light, Adrienne could see numbers on the box. It was a digital clock.

"Oh my God," Adrienne whispered. "A bomb."

"Smart girl," Weasel said.

"Shut up." Marx pushed her down onto the floor and buckled the vest around her waist.

She struggled and kicked hopelessly, while her brain told her there was no way out.

"Hold still. You're going to set the damn thing off." Marx grabbed the shackle chain and jerked her hands over her head. Her knees bent forcibly because of the chains.

Adrienne cried out at the pain in her wrists and ankles. "Good," she gasped. "I'll take you with me."

"Shut up."

"Marx." Weasel's voice was shaky. "Can she really set it off?" He took a step backward.

"Shut up and hand me that piece of cord."

Marx ran the cord through the chain at her wrists and tied it to a pipe directly over her head.

"Please don't do this," she begged them. "I'm pregnant. You're going to kill a helpless unborn child. I know you're not that coldhearted."

Weasel's brows raised and he looked at Marx. Adrienne felt a tiny surge of hope.

But Marx ignored her. He dropped to his haunches and reached for the black box at her waist. She tried to kick but the chains were drawn too tight. The best she could do was an ineffectual thrust with her knee.

"Marx, you know me. I brought you those lemon tarts."

Weasel giggled. "Lemon tarts?"

"Shut up!"

Adrienne held Marx's eye. "Why are you doing this?"

"Orders." Marx bent over, fooling with the clock.

"I mean why? Why now, after all this time? And why on a boat?"

"You got too close to Lewis. And Jerome knows Lewis is up to his neck in all the raids and stuff. He wants Lewis to suffer, so he's killing you."

It made sense, knowing Jerome. Seth's father stole Jerome's wife away. For a man like Jerome, having his wife run off with the lowly gardener was an embarrassment he'd never get over.

"I suppose knowing I'm pregnant will just be a bonus for him. Two for the price of one?" Her voice broke.

Marx ducked his head, a frown on his battered face. "Look Mrs. DeBlanc. I've got two kids myself. I don't get to see them much. My wife left me. But—I'm sorry about the baby."

Adrienne's breath caught in a sob. "Don't do it. Marx, please. Let me go. I can pay you. A lot. Name your price. Just don't murder my baby."

"You know Jerome. He'd kill me." Marx sounded truly regretful.

"Yeah," the weaselly guy said. "Besides, we get paid just fine."

Could she sway Marx if she kept him talking? "Why here? This is a boat, isn't it?"

"Senegal figures to make a statement. The police are having some kind of party here tonight." Marx pressed a couple of buttons on the clock. It was just like in the movies. Adrienne's pulse pounded in her strained wrists as she listened to the little beeps the box made as Marx set the timer.

"Marx," Weasel interjected. "We gotta get outta here. It's getting late."

"Marx, think of your wife, your children. What if someone were trying to kill them?"

Marx stood up, running colored wires up her arm and around her left wrist. Then he dropped them down behind her.

"I got my orders. It's four o'clock. The timer's set to go off in exactly four hours."

"What're you—gonna tell her the whole plan? Don't forget the gag." Weasel pulled two pieces of cloth out of his pocket.

Marx didn't look at Adrienne. "You do it."

"Open your mouth," Weasel ordered Adrienne.

She ignored him. "Marx. You're not a killer—"

"That shows what you know," Weasel snapped as he grabbed her hair and stuffed the cloth in her mouth. Before she could even take a breath or try to spit it out, he tied the second cloth like a gag, pushing the rag deeper into her mouth.

She gasped, trying to breathe. Marx took something out of his pocket and attached the wires to it, then he pressed it into the lump on the back of the belt.

"Don't move, Mrs. DeBlanc. There's a pressure sensor in the belt. If you try to get it off, it'll set off the blasting cap."

Weasel giggled. "Yeah. Then boom!"

Adrienne's heart pounded like a jackhammer as the two men disappeared, leaving her alone with her tiny unborn baby and a ticking bomb.

BACK AT CONFIDENTIAL headquarters, Seth paced while Burke, Harrison and Jones listened to Police Chief Courville's report on speakerphone.

"There was too much blood on the bus to say with any certainty that we've accounted for every person. So there's still a possibility that Adrienne DeBlanc's blood will be identified."

Seth shook his head. "If Senegal had killed her, he'd have left her at the scene. He likes dramatic gestures. Remember, he sponsored a citywide charity auction just to get a few minutes alone with D.A. Primeaux. And he hired one of the world's most famous magicians to make his daughter's new car appear in his backyard."

Burke sent Seth a glance. Seth clamped his jaw and continued pacing. All this rehashing of everything was useless. He needed something to go on. Senegal was planning to use Adrienne. Seth just had to figure out how.

"Arsenault has lawyered up, so we won't get much more out of him unless we plan to offer him a deal," Courville continued. "I'm waiting to hear from D.A. Primeaux about that. I'll have my chief of detectives, Andrew Monseur, available if you need anything, Conrad," Courville said, "but the annual Police Honors Dinner is tonight, on board *The Courtesan,* and many of my top management, as well as those being honored, will be there."

"Thanks, Chief," Burke said. "We appreciate the information." Courville hung up.

Jones looked at his watch. "Aw, hell. I forgot about the Police Honors Dinner. My wife is receiving an award. She'll kill me if I don't get home right now. It's nearly six o'clock now, and the boat is leaving shore by seven-thirty."

Seth stopped pacing. "Boat? *The Courtesan?* Where is it?" His brain raced. In Senegal's office that night, Senegal had griped about Chief Courville dogging his every move. He'd made a vague reference to paying the police chief back for his meddling.

What if Senegal was planning his grand gesture to coincide with the awards dinner?

Jones chuckled. "Why? You planning on crashing the party?"

"I might," Seth said fiercely.

"*The Courtesan* is a big-mother, paddle wheel boat," Jones commented. "Probably holds two hundred people."

Dread certainty settled over Seth like a blanket. He gingerly rubbed the bandage on his broken hand as his brain raced. "Two hundred of NOPD's top brass will be on a paddle wheel boat tonight? What if Senegal's plan is to get his revenge for the crackdown by killing two hundred of New Orleans finest?"

Bartley spoke up. "That would be way too risky. Senegal's not that stupid. What could he do with two hundred policemen around? You're not thinking straight."

Seth studied Bartley for an instant. He knew the older man was an ex-con, and he had a big mouth. But Burke had amassed a group of specialists who were the best Seth had ever seen. He couldn't believe Burke had misjudged Bartley.

"Bartley, are you just an 'aginner'—against everything?" Seth asked. "Or is there some reason every time something comes up about Senegal, all of a sudden you're the expert on what he would and wouldn't do?"

Bartley pushed his chair back from the table. "If you're suggesting something, Lewis, why don't you spit it out?"

Burke sat up and Bartley immediately sank back into his chair.

"Sorry, sir." Seth made himself relax. "Let me check out the boat."

"You still haven't rested, Lewis. I think you need to cool off for a few hours."

Seth shook his head. "I can't. I need to do this. It's a long shot, I know. I can't blame you if you think I'm going off half-cocked. But it's just the type of thing Senegal would do. I'll put in my resignation if you want."

Jones was studying his hands. At Seth's mention of resignation, he looked up. "Burke, I'd like to go with him."

Seth stared in surprise.

Jones sent him a sheepish glance. "I've worked with Lewis. He's had some odd ideas, but so far they've always turned out to be right. My wife will be on that boat. I can't afford to find out too late that Lewis was right again. I'll put in my resignation, too."

Burke's dark eyes flashed. "Nobody will be resigning. You two check out the boat. I'll inform Courville, but I know right now what he's going to say. This has to be a secret operation. Caterers and wait staff are obviously already on the boat, preparing for the dinner. And more will be arriving every minute between now and seven o'clock. We can't afford to panic two hundred people, or tip our hand, for what could be nothing."

Burke stood. "Lewis and Jones, go ahead. I'll have a readiness team on standby. They can be aboard in seconds if you need them. I'll alert Courville. The surveillance on Senegal stays in case this is a wild goose chase."

For an instant, Seth felt paralyzed by indecision. If his hunch was wrong, Adrienne would be hours closer to death and he would have wasted valuable time. If he was right, they had to move fast to have any chance of saving her. Her and two hundred other people.

"You two better get going."

"Yes, sir."

Seth and Jones left together. "Jones, I—"

"Hey, man. You're right too often for me to ignore your hunches. You've got a devious mind."

"I've seen what Senegal has done to Adrienne in the past. Now he's backed into a corner, and he's losing his power in this city. It's perfect opportunity, with this many powerful people in one place at one time. It's what I'd do."

Jones shook his head. "Like I said. Devious mind." He pointed toward his car. "Come on, I'll drive."

Chapter Thirteen

Jones called his wife to tell her he'd pick her up in plenty of time to get to the awards banquet.

Seth marveled at the difference in Jones's voice as he talked to his bride of a few months. His signature sarcasm and joking attitude were replaced by a gentle teasing wit and loving tone that strangely moved Seth.

So that was the sound of love.

Jones turned off his cell phone and pressed his lips tightly together, then sighed audibly.

"You're not going to pick her up," Seth said.

Jones shook his head and wiped his face. "Think she could tell I was lying? She'll be chewing tenpenny nails if she misses getting her award and you're wrong about the boat." Jones jabbed a finger in the air toward Seth. "And *you,* my friend, will have to face the wrath of Emily."

"I don't think I'm wrong."

Jones shot a sidelong glance at Seth. "I don't either."

Before Jones got his car parked, Seth was out and walking briskly toward the dock where *The Courtesan* waited, as striking as a picture postcard against the sunset-colored sky. Its four decks, with white painted railings and red trim that matched the red paddle wheel, looked as festive as a wedding cake. Steam rose from the small smokestacks at the stern, and the red wheel turned slowly.

Men in tuxes escorted ladies in evening dress around the decks. White-coated wait staff carried trays of champagne and hors d'oeuvres.

Uniformed policemen lined the bright white gangplank, lending an air of safety and prestige to the picture.

The boat held over two hundred people, and tonight most of those people were New Orleans' finest. Seth gave a low whistle.

"Yeah." Jones walked up in time to hear him. "The mayor, the D.A., Courville and every police captain in the city are expected to attend. Plus a whole host of other higher-ups in politics and the police force. In another half hour, this boat will be a floating time bomb."

Seth's heart hammered in his throat. "Time bomb." He raised his gaze, and Jones's face turned as white as Seth knew his own was. Bile churned in his stomach. Was Senegal capable of such wholesale slaughter?

Foolish question.

"If I'm right, neither Senegal nor any of his lieutenants will be here. And I'll bet you District Attorney Primeaux sent his regrets too."

"You really think Senegal would blow the whole boat up?"

"Confidential has made his life miserable and made him look like a dupe, and he hasn't been able to figure out who we are or how we're staying ahead of him. Yes, I think he'd blow the whole boat up."

"Damn, Lewis." Jones shuddered. "Thank God I caught Emily before she decided to drive over here alone."

Jones called Burke on his mobile transmitter, while Seth surveyed the area around the dock. Nothing overtly suspicious. No black-windowed cars parked a little too far away. No characters that looked like they didn't belong.

A dull thrum of apprehension beat in his temple like a steel drum. Adrienne was already on the boat. He knew it.

"Burke says Primeaux is out of town, and so is the mayor. He has no information on Senegal. But very few businessmen are invited. This is an internal police function. The deputy mayor is the keynote speaker, and Chief Courville is introducing him."

"Let's go." Seth checked his watch. "It's almost seven-thirty. They're about to leave the dock." He nodded toward the boat, where deck hands were casting off the massive lines that held it tethered to the dock. The engines were humming and the boat's whistle blew, warning of its impending departure.

They walked up the gangplank and stepped onto the boat. Jones spoke quietly to the uniformed officer who was checking invitations and IDs. The officer stiffened in surprise, then spoke into his shoulder mic. After a few seconds, he nodded.

"Let's go belowdecks. I want to find the engine room." Seth walked toward a set of stairs leading down.

Seth and Jones descended a second set of stairs. They were in the bowels of the boat. The engine's rumble surrounded them, becoming louder as the boat pulled away from the dock and gained speed.

"I worked on a casino boat for a summer," Jones yelled in Seth's ear. "The engine room is toward the stern—the back."

"You worked on the crew?"

"Uh, not exactly."

"What exactly?" Seth shouted.

"I sang in the show's chorus."

Seth growled. "I don't have time for this, Jones."

"Hey. I sneaked down to the boiler room with a dancer one night. Here." Jones pointed at a red door. "Engine room. But there's probably crew in there."

Seth opened the door and saw two burly men turning huge valves.

He gave them a mock salute with his bandaged hand. "Seen anything unusual?"

The men gave him the once-over. The bigger man shook his head. "Nope," he bellowed. "Everything's on time. We're pulling away now."

Seth nodded and backed out of the room.

Jones looked around. "It's an awfully big boat."

"A bomb in the engine room would do the most damage. But they have to make sure it can't possibly be found in time."

"What about Adrienne?"

Seth couldn't put words to the vision that rose in his mind at Jones's question. He shook his head grimly. "She's wherever the bomb is." His voice nearly cracked.

"Let's try the bilge."

The bilge. Under the engine room, under the decks. The lowest point of the boat. A perfect place to plant a bomb.

"Good!" A glance at his watch told Seth that they'd been on board almost ten minutes. It was twenty minutes until eight. Twenty minutes until the awards banquet started. Time was running out.

He leaned close to Jones's ear. "It's probably a hatch cut into the floor."

Nodding briskly, Jones took out a small, high-powered flashlight and began examining the floor for a seam that would indicate a hatch.

Seth's gaze roamed the small corridor. He pulled open a wooden door next to the engine room, but it was a storage room, nearly empty. No place to hide a person, not even one as petite as Adrienne.

"Lewis, I'm going to ask the engine room guys about the bilge. I'm getting the shakes. Not much interested in getting blown to pieces."

Something caught Seth's eye. Something bright.

"Jones. In here. I saw something."

Jones was right behind him with his flashlight. As the bright beam traversed the dull wooden walls, Seth's eyes followed it.

Then he saw it. A speck of orange.

"There!" He pointed at the bit of color. It was fabric, caught on a nail, with a few specks of blood staining it.

"It's her prison jumpsuit. She's here!"

Jones stepped up close to the nail and examined it. "Probably caught her leg or arm going by. That's where the blood came from." He flipped the light up and shone it along the wall.

Seth dragged his eyes away from the scrap of cloth. He wanted to grab it, to hold it, to make it give up its secrets about Adrienne's whereabouts, but he knew it was evidence. He couldn't touch it.

He sighted along the slant of light. "It's another door." He dove for it, palming his weapon before swinging it wide.

Jones's flashlight beam swept the room. Seth heard a whimpering cry behind him. He whirled.

There, tethered to a steel pipe on the wall adjacent to the engine room, was his princess. She was gagged with a dirty rag, and the chain between her shackled hands was wired to a steel beam. A black belt was fastened around her waist, and on that belt was a digital timer.

Seth's knees almost buckled. He'd seen similar devices in Iraq. It was a suicide bomb, a particularly sophisticated one. He'd defused several during his ten years in Special Forces. But this bomb was wired to the one person who meant more to him than anyone else in the world. For a brief agonizing moment, all he could do was stare.

Adrienne's blue eyes glittered wildly, her hair was a rat's nest of tangles, her cheeks and forehead were streaked with grime.

"Damn," Jones whispered. "We've got to stop the boat, get the bomb squad."

Seth knelt in front of Adrienne, whose wide eyes, full of relief and trust, stared up at him.

With his left hand he clumsily retrieved a knife from his pocket and cut her gag. He carefully removed the rag from her mouth.

She coughed and sobbed. "Seth—"

"Stay calm, princess, and be still." He touched her cheek and gave her a smile that he had to dredge up past the horror digging into his gut. He prayed that his fear wasn't etched on his face. "This belt doesn't go with your outfit. We're going to have to get rid of it."

Adrienne blinked and a tear rolled down her cheek. "You always think I'm overdressed," she whispered.

His heart swelled with pride at her brave little joke. He looked into her eyes and saw how close she was to panic.

"You hold on, Adrienne. Let me take a look at this thing."

While Jones speed-dialed Burke, Seth examined the wires attached to the black belt. He traced them carefully. They ran from her back, which was pressed against the wall, up and around the rope and her left wrist, then back down to a digital timer under her left arm. He gingerly ran his fingers around the back of the belt. He encountered a lump. Plastic explosive. The wires ran from there.

He knew exactly how much force a lump that size could exert. Enough to take out the engine room and kill and injure a lot of people.

Forcing himself to concentrate on the here and now, rather than past visions of bomb blasts, he looked at the changing numbers on the timer's display. He cursed.

"Jones. There's no time. We only have seven minutes. I've got to defuse the bomb."

"Burke conferenced in Police Chief Courville. There's a bomb expert on board. He's on his way down."

"Seth?" Adrienne croaked. "They told me not to move, or I'd set it off."

Hell. He'd hoped the bomb makers were amateurs. "I know, princess. There's probably a pressure sensor rigged to the timing device. It's going to be tricky." He took at her swollen, damp eyes, the streaks of dirt on her cheeks left by her tears, the red marks left by the gag. Lifting his hand, he wiped a tear away with his thumb and cradled her face in his palm. "You're the most beautiful thing I've ever laid eyes on." He forced a smile. "Even in orange."

Adrienne smiled sadly through her tears. "We don't have a chance, do we?"

Seth put his other hand on her face and gave her a quick kiss. "Listen to me. As long as there is time on that clock, I'm not giving up. Promise me you won't."

She shook her head. "I promise. I'm not—giving up."

He heard the doubt and fear in her voice. He wanted to grab her close and reassure her, but he didn't have time. He had a bomb to defuse and only about six minutes to do it.

Adrienne saw the uncertainty in Seth's strong, beloved face, and knew he expected to die here. His caress and his kiss had eased the excruciating pain in her shoulders for an instant, but now the strained muscles cramped.

"Stay still, Adrienne. I've got to examine the wires. Your job is to not move a muscle."

She froze as Seth bent his head to study the black box under her left arm. His dark hair curling slightly at his nape, his broad shoulders were directly in her line of sight. She drank in the beauty of his form and the strength that emanated from him like a scent.

This is what his son would look like. Seth's strength and integrity would be an intrinsic part of their child's personality.

Tears blurred her eyes and rolled down her cheeks. She'd spent hours alone with her thoughts. With the horrible knowledge that the bomb belt was strapped over the precious life she and Seth had created.

Seth straightened and slid the light up her body, following the wires up to her shoulders and farther, to where they wrapped around her wrist, and back down to the plastic explosive.

His face was harsh and grim in the dim glow from the flashlight.

Could she let him die without knowing about his child? Adrienne didn't know if it were crueler to tell him, knowing their baby would die with them.

Would giving him such a shocking emotional jolt jeopardize the lives that might be saved if he could defuse the bomb or contain the explosion? Or did he deserve to know, no matter what the outcome?

She watched him, and thought about his father abandoning him, leaving him to care for his mother and his sisters when he was too young to shoulder such responsibility. She thought about her own father, who had betrayed her and lied to her.

Seth deserved to know.

"Seth, there's something I have to tell you."

"Shh, Princess. No last-second regrets, okay?" He smiled down at her. "I don't have any."

Then a shadow crossed his face. "Well, maybe one." He ducked his head and shone the flashlight toward where her back rested against the wall.

Adrienne looked at the man who had shown her the difference between a bully and a real, honorable man. The man who had taught her that love was not fear and pain and the constant struggle to please. Love was pleasure and respect, a joining of equals.

"Seth, we made a baby."

He froze. "What did you say?" His voice was muffled, deadly quiet.

His head was down near her shoulder. He didn't sit up, he didn't look at her. He did not move a muscle.

Adrienne licked her dry, cracked lips. "I'm pregnant."

Seth sat back on his heels and stared at her, his tricolored eyes glinting like gems in the flashlight's glow.

"You just thought you'd mention this before we're both—excuse me, all three blown to bits?"

She winced at his cold tone and ducked her head to avoid his gaze.

"We have just over four minutes." He laughed, a harsh sound. "So the gardener's son made a baby with the rich socialite. That's ironic."

The agony in her arms and shoulders paled against the anguish in Adrienne's heart. His bitter words reflected all the pain that he had carried in his heart, all the resentment he'd felt toward her because in her he saw the same type of woman who had stolen his father.

"You're not your father, Seth. You—"

"When had you planned to tell me this?" he asked. "Or had you?"

"I just found out. Seth, please—"

The clattering of footsteps down the stairs startled Adrienne into silence.

"Lewis! Here's the bomb expert, Detective James Roy."

"What have we got here, son?"

Seth spoke without looking up. "Jones, can you hold the flashlight? I only have one good hand. It's a standard digital timer, sir. We have about three minutes. The wires are tangled around her wrist and down her back to a lump of plastique."

"Enough to take down the boat?"

"Yes, sir."

"No chance to remove the belt?"

" There's a pressure sensor on the inside of the belt. At least that's what they told her. But I can't access it."

"Right," Roy said. "Can't take a chance. So—"

Seth nodded.

Adrienne could hardly breathe. With every word the men spoke, the hopelessness of their situation became clearer. She sniffed quietly, trying to be brave, trying to stay calm.

"I'm sorry, Seth," she whispered, but he didn't seem to hear her.

He and Roy crouched beside her.

"We have to take the chance of moving her."

"Right. I have an idea." Seth looked at her as he talked. "I'll wrap my arms around her and lift her enough so you can get to the wires."

Roy glanced at her and at him, then nodded.

"Princess, don't move. I'm going to pick you up and turn you slightly and maintain pressure on the sensor.

You stay absolutely still. Let me do the moving. Once I have you turned enough, Roy will pull the wires between the plastique and the power source."

"And then?"

Seth's hazel eyes bored through hers, deep into her soul. "Then we'll see."

His carefully expressionless voice terrified her. Her numb hands wanted to touch him, to hold on to him as the fiery blast tore them apart.

"Seth, I love you."

He cradled her body against his, and lifted her slightly. Pain like she'd never felt in her life shrieked through her shoulders and arms. Her legs were completely asleep. Her neck felt so stiff it could break. Darkness clouded her vision.

Seth's muscles quivered against her and the staccato beat of his heart against her chest matched her own racing pulse.

"That's good," Roy said, his voice tight.

Seth froze, his arms tight around her and his breath fast and shallow against her ear.

"Jones, shine the light right here."

Adrienne saw the light quiver as nausea and pain engulfed her. She closed her eyes and took a long, sobbing breath.

"Fifty-six seconds, sir," Jones said in a shaking voice.

Seth whispered something in her ear. It was the last thing she remembered.

Chapter Fourteen

The newspaper headline read *Mysterious Bomber Foiled As Police Bigwigs Narrowly Escape Death.*

> *In a stunning press conference this morning, Police Chief Henri Courville revealed the reason for the excitement at the dock of the* Riverboat Courtesan *last night.*
>
> *Detective James Roy defused an explosive which could have killed two hundred members of the New Orleans Police Department, their spouses and several city dignitaries.*
>
> *The explosive, which sources tell us was rendered harmless with only seconds to spare, had been smuggled aboard the boat sometime during the afternoon by person or persons unknown.*
>
> *Witnesses say that until the boat was abruptly returned to shore prior to the Annual Policemen's Awards Banquet, they were unaware of any problem.*

Seth looked up from the paper. Adrienne, her face nearly as white as the lacy pillow cases beneath her head, was still asleep.

She looked like an angel, surrounded by white, her

head crowned by a pale golden halo of hair, her hands with their bandaged wrists folded serenely over her belly.

Her belly, where their child grew. Seth rubbed his eyes in weary chagrin. He hoped they weren't as puffy and red as they felt. He'd never cried in his life—well, not since he was twelve years old anyway. But he'd cried last night.

Cried and prayed.

From the instant he'd taken her into his arms, pressing her body tightly against his, expecting every second to be his last, he'd cried.

By some miracle, Roy had told him, the blasting cap was cleanly exposed and it was, in Roy's words, "a piece of cake" to separate the wires from the cap. The bomb makers had obviously not planned for a last-second rescue.

Once Roy had given the all clear, Seth had lifted his princess in his arms so Roy and Jones could remove the belt. When the timer buzzed at zero, they had all jumped, then laughed self-consciously.

Seth had walked off the boat and directly to an ambulance that was waiting at the dock. He'd brought Adrienne back to her house after the emergency room staff had given her a sedative and discharged her into his care. Burke had used his influence to make arrangements with the authorities for her to be released into Seth's custody instead of being carted back to jail.

He'd sat here all night, watching her, only leaving her once, when he'd heard the newspaper slap against the front door.

He wiped his eyes again and cleared his throat.

Adrienne stirred and opened her eyes.

"Seth," she whispered, then touched her throat. "I can't talk."

"Morning, princess." Seth watched her expression change as she remembered.

"Oh my God," she croaked, lifting her huge blue eyes to meet his gaze. "How did —"

"You get here?" Seth smiled tenderly. "I brought you home last night. I thought you'd be more comfortable in your own bed."

Adrienne's cheeks turned pink and she folded her hands over her belly. "The hospital? I don't remember. Is everyone all right? Is the baby?"

How typical of her, to think of others when she was the one who was strapped with enough explosive to blow her to bits. "Everyone's fine. You're fine. Though the doctor said you should have a complete physical and start taking some prenatal vitamins."

Adrienne sat up. "What about you? What happened to your hand? And your head?"

"A little encounter with Tony, but he got the worst of it."

Adrienne's face paled at the mention of Tony's name.

"He's in custody, princess. He will never come near you again."

"Seth—"

"Adrienne, wait a minute." He stood and walked over to the window. He was dangerously close to tears. He was getting tired of his sudden tendency toward crying. It wasn't fitting for a member of Special Forces. He'd spent his entire adult life staying away from emotional entanglements, only to end up more entangled than he'd ever dreamed of being.

Rubbing his eyes, he turned around.

"I've never been close to anyone, except my sisters. Never wanted to be. I saw firsthand how much it can hurt." He cleared his throat. How could he explain what her honesty, her trust, her innate goodness, had done for him? How could he make her understand that without her, his life would be empty. He'd go on, but it would just be an existence, not a life.

Adrienne got out of bed and came over to stand in front of him. She looked so small and vulnerable in the cotton hospital gown with her wrists and ankles bandaged where the shackles had chafed them.

"Seth, it's okay. I know how you feel about me, about who I am. I wish I could have been born differently. I was born with money. I am a rich widow who lives in the Garden District. I can't change where I've been. But I'm not like the woman who stole your father's love."

Seth cupped her face in his palms. "Don't you know I know that?" he said brokenly. "You are brave and honest and beautiful, and I treated you badly. I am so sorry I had to lie to you. I never meant to deceive you."

She put her hands over his. "You never treated me badly. You showed me more fun, more joy, than I've ever known. You treated me like a woman, like an equal." She looked up at him, her eyes dewy and soft. "And you gave me this." She pulled his hands down and placed them on her stomach.

"Seth? I hope you want this baby."

"Want—" Seth couldn't speak. The damn lump was back in his throat and his damn eyes were stinging. "Do you remember what I told you when we were defusing the bomb?"

For an instant, Adrienne's gaze clouded as she thought about those awful minutes. Then her eyes widened and tears welled in them. "You said, 'I love you, princess. We'll be together, wherever we are.'"

He swallowed. "I meant it."

Holding out his arms, he lifted her and carried her back to the bed. Then he knelt in front of her and pulled off the bead bracelet he'd slipped onto his wrist when he'd retrieved the safe-deposit box key. He rubbed the line the tight bracelet had cut into his flesh.

Then he took her left hand and slid the bracelet onto her ring finger, looping it around four times. Something wet fell on the back of his hand. He looked up to see tears flowing down Adrienne's face.

"Don't cry, princess," he whispered, wiping her tears away with his fingers. "I don't have a fancy ring to give you, but I offer you my heart. Will you marry me?"

"Oh, Seth. You have no idea. This is the most precious piece of jewelry I've ever been given. I love you so much." She held the ring to her lips for a moment. "But what about prison? Aren't I a fugitive?"

Seth shook his head. "I pulled some strings. As we speak the Confidential agency is taking care of clearing your name."

"The Confidential agency?"

"We have a lot to talk about, princess. But you never answered my question. Will you marry me? Will you live with me and let me be a father to our baby? I promise you'll never regret it."

"What about my money, and this house?"

"I think I can overlook that if you can forgive me for not telling you everything."

Adrienne put her fingers against his lips. "Like you said, I know everything about you that matters."

Seth kissed her fingers then took her hand and kissed the bead ring. "Is that a yes, princess?"

"Tell me something," Adrienne said, her pulse fluttering. "What was the one thing you would have regretted if we'd died on the boat?"

He met her gaze and a slow smile curved his lips. His beautiful gold-shot eyes glittered with dampness. "That I wouldn't have a lifetime to show you all those things I promised you we'd enjoy together."

Adrienne's heart soared. "In that case, I'll marry you on one condition. That you take me to the Café Du Monde right now. Our baby is craving beignets."

And the story concludes....
Next month don't miss the exhilarating final
installment of
NEW ORLEANS CONFIDENTIAL
A FATHER'S DUTY
By Joanna Wayne
Will leave you riveted!
Turn the page for a sneak peak...

Chapter One

August in New Orleans was like a nasty disease that clogged your lungs and made you sweat from every pore in your body. It was near midnight now and still there was no relief from the heat or the humidity, especially not here on the edge of the French Quarter where the stench of stale beer, fried seafood and someone's pot habit hung heavy in the air.

Tanner Harrison had loved the inner city and the French Quarter once. He'd fed on its boisterous revelry, couldn't get enough of the jazz, the food or the Big Easy attitude. That had been years ago. Now the area was like everything else in his life, a plague to be endured. But tonight desperation added a new element to his restless discontent. It rode his nerves like a hissing snake looking for somewhere to sink its fangs.

Lily. Sweet, innocent Lily. Climbing on to his lap and cuddling into his arms for a bedtime story. Skipping through Hyde Park on a summer's day, her tiny hand clutching his. Waving goodbye as he'd boarded plane after plane after plane, always turning at the last second so he didn't see the tears sliding down her cheek and she didn't see the back of his hand flick across his own wet eyes.

Only Lily was no longer living in London with her

mother. And his seventeen-year-old daughter was no longer innocent.

His daughter was here in New Orleans, last seen turning tricks for Maurice Gaspard. Tanner had seen it all in a lifetime of law enforcement, but nothing had ever made him physically ill the way thinking of Lily like this did.

He jerked to attention when he spotted a young woman running toward him, her high-heeled shoes bumping and scraping along the uneven sidewalk, her long blond hair flying behind her. Her skirt barely reached her thighs and her blouse was skintight, a bit of gauzy material that dipped low and revealed everything short of her nipples. He braced himself and studied her face as she came closer, looking for signs of the Lily he knew beneath the layers of makeup.

It wasn't Lily, but she wasn't much older than his teenage daughter, and she was running scared. Tanner reached out and grabbed her arm as she rushed past him. She clawed at him with long, fake fingernails that were painted a bright red.

"Let go of me."

"Right after we have a little talk."

She twisted to see behind her, then tried again to pry his hand from her arm. "I'm not working now, so get your rocks off with someone else."

"I'm looking for Lily Harrison."

"That's your problem."

"I just made it yours, too. She's my daughter." Tanner pulled out the picture of Lily, frayed and bent from being carried around in his sweaty pocket. He handed the photo to the woman, then tugged her under the streetlight so she could see the details. "This was taken six months ago. If you've seen her at all, I need to know where and when."

"I don't know nothin'. So let go of my arm."

But Tanner figured she did know. Like the rest of Gaspard's women, she was just too damned scared to talk. No one squealed on the sleazy, revengeful pimp.

"Who are you running from?" Tanner demanded.

"I'm not running. And if I was, it's none of your damn business." She threw in a few gutter words for emphasis.

"Look, man. I don't know your Lily, but there's a young blond girl in that courtyard back there, and she's hurt bad. If you want to do something, go help her, just leave me out of it. Please, leave me out of it."

Tanner took off running. He reached the courtyard in seconds. The victim was sprawled across the hot concrete, one leg dangling over a fountain that was dry and green with slime.

Tanner knelt beside her and brushed the long, blood-matted hair from her face, then felt the breath explode from his lungs in relief when he realized the half-dead woman wasn't his Lily.

He checked for a pulse. It was weak, but it was there. He grabbed his cell phone and called for an ambulance. The young woman opened her eyes and stared at him.

"Please. Don't hurt..."

"I'm not the one who attacked you. Just lie still. There's an ambulance on the way."

Tanner lifted the woman's head. "Who did this to you?"

"No one. I...fell."

"Like hell you did! Was it Gaspard?"

She shuddered and closed her eyes without answering.

He knelt beside her and monitored her pulse and labored breathing until the shrill cry of the sirens pierced the night.

Tanner put his mouth close to her ear one last time as he heard the footsteps of the paramedics approaching. "Do you know a girl named Lily Harrison? She's British."

The victim's eyes fluttered open as if she were trying to focus, then rolled back in her head before closing again.

"One word will do. I'm begging. Do you know where I can find Lily?"

There was no answer. Tanner moved out of the way as the paramedics loaded her onto the gurney. He had his doubts she'd live to see the hospital.

GEORGETTE DELACROIX jerked awake and set up straight in bed, then grabbed the ringing phone. "Hello."

"Mrs. Delacroix?"

"Yes?"

"This is Amos Keller."

It took her a second or two to place the name. "The ambulance driver?"

"Yes, ma'am. You asked me to call you if I picked up another beating victim who appeared to be a prostitute."

Her pulse quickened. "Yes. Did you?"

"Yes, ma'am. Picked her up in a courtyard on Chartres Street."

"How long ago was that?"

"A few minutes ago, but if you want to see her while she's still alive, you better hurry down here."

"I'll be right there. Thanks for the heads-up on this."

"Glad to help. Whoever did this deserves to be locked away."

Twenty minutes later, Georgette was rushing through the emergency ward, looking for someone to point her to the right room. It was always faster than dealing with the admitting nurse and her legalese and protocol.

"Code blue in Room twelve. Code blue in Room twelve."

Georgette dodged a nurse wielding a crash cart, then followed her to Room 12. A man in jeans and blue T-shirt stepped out of the room and Georgette slipped past him only to be ushered out of the small treatment room by a thin, middle-aged nurse with a no-nonsense expression.

"No visitors. Not now."

But the quick glimpse Georgette got of the activity in Room 12 was enough to know that they were fighting desperately to save the life of a young woman who'd obviously been beaten. The clothes thrown over a hook were a good indicator that the woman had been working the streets.

Georgette had no firm evidence to back up her suspicion that the skinny, weaselly-looking pimp with hair that looked like black wire dipped in axle grease was responsible for this, but odds were that he was. All she needed was one breathing, talking witness to help her take Maurice Gaspard to trial. Judging from the sounds coming from Room 12, she wasn't likely to get that witness tonight.

She studied the man slouched against the wall opposite her who'd come out from the victim's room when she'd walked up. A friend? Or one of Gaspard's flunkies sent to make sure the woman didn't talk?

Georgette sized him up quickly. Early to mid-forties. A couple of inches over the six-foot mark. Hard bodied. Thick, dark brown hair that could use cutting. A defiant stance.

"What happened to your friend?" she asked, nodding toward the closed door to Room 12.

"She's not my friend."

"So why are you here?"

"I stumbled on her in the French Quarter after someone had beaten the hell out of her. I called the ambulance."

"And then you followed it to the hospital?"

"Are you a cop?"

"No." She put out a hand. "I'm Georgette Delacroix, a prosecutor with the District Attorney's office."

"You're working a little after office hours, aren't you?"

"I was hoping to see the patient before she..."

"Before she dies. You can say the word. It's pretty obvious she's fighting for her life in there."

"I know, I sincerely hope she makes it."

"Yeah."

The door to Room 12 opened and the doctor appeared. "Is anyone here with the patient?"

Georgette stepped up.

"I'm sorry," the doctor said. "We did all we could, but we lost her."

"Were there bullet wounds?" Georgette asked.

"No. She'd been hit over the head with a blunt object and severely beaten. I'm sure the police will do a full investigation. We'll need someone to stick around and give them and the hospital some identifying information on the expired patient."

"I'm afraid I'm as in the dark about that as you are." Georgette introduced herself and looked around for the man who'd been standing there a few seconds earlier. He was halfway down the hall, hurrying to the exit. She excused herself and chased after him.

"I'd like to ask you a couple of questions," she said when she caught up with him.

"Ask away," he said, not slowing his pace.

"Did the victim say anything to you when you found her?"

"Yeah. She begged me not to hurt her. Evidently she was too out of it to realize I wasn't the guy who'd attacked her."

"Exactly where did you find the body?"

"In a courtyard on Chartres Street, river side, a couple of blocks off Esplanade."

"Do you live in that area?"

"No."

"Work there?"

"No. I was looking for someone. I found the victim instead."

"Did she mention her own name or anyone else's name?"

"No."

"Look, I don't know why you were down there that time of the night, and right now I don't really care. I'm not trying to prosecute you for soliciting or buying illegal drugs. I just need evidence to put the guy responsible for killing that young woman in jail."

"It doesn't matter how many questions come to mind. I've told you everything I know." He reached in his pocket and pulled out a business card. "But you can reach me at work if you want to waste your time. Crescent City Transports. The name and number's on the card."

She reached out her hand to take the card. His fingers brushed hers and she was hit by a jolt that all but sucked her breath away. She dropped her hand, and the card fluttered to the floor as images played in her mind with dizzying force.

A young blond woman, face bruised, her hands and feet tied, her eyes red and swollen. And scared—very, very scared.

"Are you okay?"

The voice cut through the images, and Georgette

forced herself to focus on the man standing in front of her. "What did you say?"

"You look as if you're about to pass out. Do you want me to get a doctor?"

"No, I'll be fine. I guess I've just overdone it a bit lately. Sometimes I forget to eat and my blood sugar level dips." That was a lie, but she'd used it before. It was far more believable than the truth.

"Can I give you a lift home?"

"No. I'll go to the snack area and get some juice from the vending machine. I'll be fine after that."

"If you're sure."

"I am."

She watched him walk away, still troubled by the force of the vision and the fact that it was somehow associated with the man who claimed to have just stumbled over a dying prostitute in a deserted courtyard....

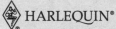

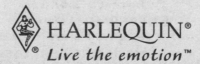

If you enjoyed what you just read,
then we've got an offer you can't resist!

Take 2 bestselling love stories FREE!

Plus get a FREE surprise gift!

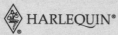
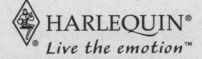

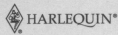

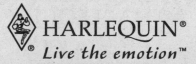